INTERNAL INVASION

Gean B. Atkinson

Also by Gean B. Atkinson

Pilots of My Soul

ISBN 1-930252-42-0

Copyright ©2001
Wyndham House Books
All Rights Reserved

This book is a work of fiction. Names, characters, places and incidents are the product of the author's imagination or are used fictitiously. Any resemblance to actual events, locales or persons, living or dead, is coincidental.

No part of this book may be reproduced or transmitted in any form or by any means, electronic or mechanical, including photocopying, recording, or by an information storage and retrieval system, without permission in writing from the publisher.
For information address: PageFree Publishing, Inc., 733 Howard Street, Otsego, Michigan 49078

Our nation—this generation—will lift a dark threat of violence from our people and our future.

We will rally the world to this cause by our efforts, by our courage. We will not tire, we will not falter and we will not fail.

—President George W. Bush
After the terrorist attack on the World Trade Center
September 2001

Dedicated to Kirby, Sterling and Amanda

Author's Note

When I began searching for a topic for this novel in the summer of 1999 I consulted several futurist publications to determine what might be of interest to the reading public when the work was completed in June of 2000.

Although the list spanned twenty or thirty topics it was clear to me that none of them would profoundly affect each of us, and our children, as the sinister growth of terrorism. And unfortunately, it looked as if it that brand of violence would still be active and destructive well into the 21st century.

At first I was hesitant to use that subject as my storyline. We in Oklahoma had experienced terrorism intimately in April of 1995 when the Alfred P. Murrah Federal Building was bombed by Timothy McVeigh and the issue was still a sensitive one. One only need visit the beautiful memorial in downtown Oklahoma City to experience the poignant feelings of grief that still reside within the community.

Finally, however, I adopted the subject, feeling it was a reality that we as a nation must address, sooner or later.

When terrorists attacked the World Trade Center on September 11, 2001 I was sickened that my forecast had been right. Another community —alas, the entire nation had been stripped of its tranquility and outraged at the hateful and intolerable act of mass murder of innocent Americans.

It is a curse that our children will have to deal with in the coming decades, as have citizens in Northern Ireland, England and Israel. But there is a difference here.

America and its allies can win this war against the cowards who kill and then hide behind a religion as a justification. But it will take patience. And support. And patience. The war is against a shadowy enemy who knows no borders, no rules and no honor.

With strong leaders who are unrelenting in their hunt for these purveyors of evil and a determined citizenry that will support those efforts, we can prevail. We must prevail.

God Bless America.

Gean B. Atkinson
October 2001

Acknowledgments

To Sally for enduring the dips and climbs of our always lightning speed life together.

To Don Kyte for making sure I didn't embarrass the FBI; To Brigadier General Dick Hefton USAF (Ret) and Dave Amis, Sr. (WMA '48) for guiding me through the complicated corridor of aerial combat.

To Melissa Burget, the smartest pharmacist I know, for much needed help on the chemistry necessary for *Zaner* vitamins. To Franci Hart and Dr. Reba Collins, both accomplished authors in their own rights, for the guidance and encouragement.

To Cleta Mitchell who pointed me in the right direction and then lit the fire; To Parviz "Ray" Dolatabadi and Faraj Samani who shared their intimate knowledge of the geography and languages.

And to my mother and father who gave me the gift of love that makes anything possible.

Chapter One

Somewhere in the western part of Afghanistan
September 2001

The rusted Mercedes truck ground slowly over the sandy, unpaved road. Without lights, the going was difficult but its occupants did not want to be spotted by the U.S. satellites that revolved overhead, mingling with the billions of stars, constantly taking photographs. The night had gotten colder and the creatures of the desert, spared briefly the day's blinding heat, scurried across the path of the struggling vehicle.

An Arab leaned from the bed and thrust his head into the cab of the old truck.

"How much longer will it take?" he asked. "We are hungry and cold."

"Not much farther, my brother. When we get there you will be told everything and made comfortable," the scruffy looking driver said.

They arrived at the obscure camp; several blacked-out camouflage tents hiding their inside light under tightly secured flaps, a few camels, and a 4-wheel drive Land Rover, and were promptly ushered into the largest canopy. The twelve men were served Turkish coffee, dates, bread and some meat and had no sooner begun to eat and drink when a tall Arab entered dressed in a long flowing cloak designed to ward off the cold of the night. With high cheekbones, narrow eyes, and wild, black beard he exuded an evil presence.

"Rise when the Reis (Ray-eez) enters," shouted the man who had been the driver just moments before. His announcement that the "Boss" was entering was a surprise.

The men quickly scrambled to their feet, their food dropping to the floor. The Reis motioned for them to sit on the Persian rug that had obviously served as flooring for many years. He quietly walked behind the men, his footsteps imperceptible, feeling their eyes follow him, and when he was confident he had their rapt attention, stopped directly in front and gazed down at them with his fists resting firmly on his waist.

"You have been brought here to serve Allah Almighty," he began softly. "It is his pleasure that you do so, for your task will strike at the heart of the Great Satan. It will shake the foundation of that enemy of Islam, of its whore-women and blasphemous men. Your task will bring the infidel United States to its knees in retribution for its sins against us and you hold in your hands, at this very moment, the sword of that revenge," he said his voice gaining volume and becoming more strident.

The men looked at their hands, which held only coffee, and wondered his meaning. The lamps flickered and for a moment, the scene resembled an old 1920 movie. With the aroma of incense in his nostrils, Ben Asam began to feel as if he had somehow been taken into a dream. He had begun his career as a chemist and was heralded in scientific circles and one with a bright future. But fate had a more violent prospect in store for him. He had been recruited into the mujahedin and had fought many battles for the Jihad.

Once a decidedly handsome man, the years of living the life of a desert fighter now gave him a coarse, hardened look. His body remained solid in its five foot-six frame and was more fitting for a younger man rather than its forty-year-old owner.

He expected to be a fighter tonight as always but this battlefield of intrigue was not as straightforward as he was used to.

"You have been chosen because you have proven you are willing to give your life to rid the world of the nation of the United States. Each of you has participated in operations against this devil nation. Now, you may do so again and you may even have the good fortune to die for Allah.

"We wage war against America because America has spear-headed the crusade against the Islamic nations, sending tens of thousand of its troops to the land of the two Holy Mosques. This is over and above its meddling in our affairs and our politics, and its support of the oppressive, corrupt and tyrannical regime that is in control.

"Here you will be given food and supplies for your journey. Tonight you will receive your briefing and tomorrow you will be sent to locations in America to begin your part of the plan. Your comrades in the mujahedin are eagerly awaiting your arrival.

"We must not wait long. The Satan and her Arab lackeys search for us. You will leave tomorrow." The Reis turned and started to leave the tent. He stopped when he saw Ben Asam and embraced him.

"I am happy you are here, my faithful one," he said to Ben. "This mission will need your strong leadership."

"I will serve you as always," Asam said. The Reis released him and left the tent.

A young Afghan, maybe 20, entered and turned up the lamps to allow his charts and posters to be seen and then delivered the briefing. Each aspect of the scheme had been thoroughly thought out and, although the hour was late and Asam was tired, he was impressed with the detail of the plan. It was diabolical, even brilliant.

Some of the small group would be dispatched to different parts of the world to execute stages of the plot that were literally years away. He, however, would be on the front lines and deliver the first strike. A strike from which the United States would not recover.

The final session was coming to an end when the briefer stopped abruptly and turned his head toward the tent's entrance.

"Quickly, get out and hide!" he yelled and grabbed his assault weapon as he dashed outside, throwing the tent flap open.

In seconds, Ben Asam heard the distinctive clack-clack of AK-47s and burps of Uzi's being fired, grenades exploding, and a quickly growing chorus of men yelling. He had heard these sounds before in combat and knew immediately they were under a fierce attack.

Suddenly, the fabric of the tent began shredding as a hail of bullets tore through the canvas walls, shattering tent poles and snuffing out lamps. The men seated just a moment before began to jump to their feet with eyes full of horror and fear only to be slammed to the ground by the automatic weapons fire that was piercing the tent.

In the dark, blood spattered against Asam's clothes as his comrades around him were riddled with bullets. He raced out of the tent, instinctively staying low, trying to adjust his eyes to the alternating dim light and bright flashes occurring all around. There was no place to hide and he had no weapon with which to defend himself.

The enemy had completely infiltrated the camp and appeared to be in total control. They were showing no mercy as they methodically killed the haphazard resistance the small band of unorganized and outnumbered terrorists could muster. He started to flee into the desert to escape the fighting when spouts of sand began to fly up in front of him. He glanced back to see an attacker dressed in black violently firing his weapon at him. Suddenly, the soldier's weapon jammed.

All of Ben Asam's twenty-year experience as a fighter in the Jihad, the holy war against America, told him in that split second what he must do. For only now would the attacker be vulnerable. Once the jackal cleared the jam he would continue to pursue Asam until he killed him.

Asam turned and rushed the gunman, throwing sand in an attempt to blind him. Surprised at the charge, the attacker fumbled the weapon. It was just enough time. Asam quickly had his arms around the man's neck. His arms were strong and bore the scars of hand-to-hand battles. They rolled in the sand, the pebbles sticking to his arms and neck. He pressed his radius bone against the man's windpipe until he blacked out, going limp in his arms. A quick, strong jerk insured the aggressor would not regain consciousness. Asam tore off the attacker's black hood to unveil the face of a middle-aged man who could have been an Arab.

He glanced around and saw the battle was winding down and that the Afghans were losing. Asam knew what consolidating a position meant. It would not be long before the invaders would be looking for, and executing, those left alive.

Asam grabbed a small prayer rug nearby. The camp was now obscured by a cloud of smoke that seemed to hang in the still desert air. He hoped it would give him the cover he needed to hide himself. He dug a shallow trench in the loose sand and, covering his face with the rug, crawled into it, pulling the dead attacker over him to obscure the hollow.

Asam lay deathly still and listened as the cacophony of sounds continued. The weight of the dead body was stifling. Slowly, the clatter of combat began to fade until the only trace of the battle was the acrid smell of cordite and the incessant hum of flies.

Asam was deathly still for what seemed like an hour until he was sure the battlefield had been deserted and then, carefully and slowly, tried to work himself to the surface for a quick appraisal. What he saw when he pushed away the limp corpse made his heart stop. The darkness was illuminated by burning tents and it was clear no one was left alive. The Arabs who had defended the training camp lay scattered on the sand like fallen leaves from a tree.

He rose and began to assess the damage, walking through the sand, checking the bodies to see if any were living. Many had multiple wounds but all had a head wound indicating the attackers had methodically delivered the coup de gras to each of them.

About the time he was ready to conclude that all were dead, he heard a moan and quickly went to the wounded man, the driver who had brought him in. He had a head injury, probably a horizontal butt stroke during the hand-to-hand fighting, and was bleeding from a nasty wound in the shoulder but he had somehow escaped execution.

"Is the Reis safe?" the soldier whispered, obviously in great pain.

Asam had not seen a body of the Reis in his search and felt confident enough to say, "Yes, he escaped. He's gone."

"Who were they?" Asam asked.

"Who knows?" the driver gasped. "They could be the CIA or the Saudis or even the Mossad."

"Saudis?" Asam said, incredulously. "But they are supposed to be part of our Arab brotherhood! Why would they attack us?"

"They have been humiliated by Osama bin Laden and his strikes against America. They are working with the Americans now to eliminate all liberation movements but they tell no one." It was obvious he was slipping into shock.

"We have to get you out of here," Asam said to no one.

"No, I can't make it. Leave me here," begged the driver.

"To be food for the scorpions and vipers? No, brother, I will not abandon you," Asam said, not having the foggiest idea how he would get out of the camp.

The enemy had already carried many of their dead and wounded from the field. They would be back soon to get the rest. He knew they couldn't afford to leave evidence.

"Can you walk?"

"I think so, but I'll need help," the driver answered, his eyes beginning to glaze over. Asam lifted the wounded man up and pulled his arm over his own shoulder.

"Listen, there's a way out," breathlessly whispered the driver. "There is a motorcycle hidden under the sand by the Reis' tent. Take me over and I will show you."

Asam carried the man to the appointed spot and began to dig with his hands. Quickly he felt something and pulled back a black tarp to find a new 4-wheel Yamaha ATV.

He freed the all terrain cycle and removed the protective bags on the motor, then, holding his breath, cranked the engine, thanking Allah that it responded immediately. He scavenged hats for both of them, as many canteens as he could find, an Uzi he strapped on his back and then put the driver on the 4-wheeler with a jacket and blanket to try to keep him out of shock.

In just a few hours the sun would be shooting stiletto beams of light over the horizon and Asam knew he didn't have much time. He mounted the cycle and pulled the man's arms around him.

"Hold on, brother, it's going to be a long ride," he said and then turned the cycle west toward Iran.

As the two left the camp, a wounded attacker raised himself up on his elbows to watch them pull away from the camp. He noted the direction and then reached inside his flak jacket and pulled out a small two-way radio. He uttered his last words and broadcast the direction that the men were headed and then collapsed face first into the sand.

Two Months Earlier

"This is our big chance, our only chance," Andrew Strong, his round face flush, whispered to his Executive Vice President, Laura Newcomb. They silently scanned the cavernous and barren-looking waiting room of Finklestein and Mark, Inc. as they waited for the signal to enter the office of the president. Metal desks, 30-year-old chairs, and outdated dog-eared magazines greeted them. Every desk in sight seemed to have stacks of papers piled one atop the other.

After a thorough review of the surroundings, they found themselves looking at each other with the question of "what have we gotten into" written all over their faces.

Located on a back street in Dallas' Southside, the entire facility looked like an undercover operation for some government spook agency. A four-story warehouse type building, no sign, no inviting entrance, just a dock with a metal door sans windows and a facade that welcomed longshoremen more than advertising experts. It had taken them forever to find it.

The dreariness of the outside architecture was replicated in the interior and oddly enough, there wasn't any literature about the company or their product. The receptionist area was presided over by a thin woman in her mid thirties with a cheap nameplate that said only "Megan." She looked so frail and threatened she reminded Strong of a baby bird.

If I weren't so damned desperate, I don't think this would be my choice of a prospect, Strong thought. Robust bellowing from the president's office interrupted his ruminations.

"Get those assholes in here and let's see if they're worth a shit," roared the voice as the red-faced secretary scurried out from behind her desk and went straight to Laura and Strong.

"Mr. Finklestein will see you now," she said through an embarrassed smile.

"Well, you must be Strong and you're Newcomb, right?" boomed Maurice Finklestein as he pulled his thin frame from behind the metal desk and came across the room to greet the pair. "I'll be go to hell, you look like you've got some sense. I didn't expect anything but hayseeds from Oklahoma."

"Well, we may have come in on a truck but we were driving," Strong shot back with a smile.

"Uh, huh, good point," said Finklestein, while trying to light a cigar.

Strong said happily, "I appreciate you seeing us, Mr. Finklestein. We came, as you know, to discuss your advertising needs. As I mentioned on the phone, we're very excited that you might be interested in our agency and think our shop would be a good match for you."

Strong was trying to size the guy up and he was surprised with a name like Finklestein he looked more like someone from a mosque than a synagogue. He was dark skinned with full black hair. Strong estimated he was in his early fifties and detected a stare that was as intimidating as any he had ever seen.

The steely-eyed Finklestein did not respond but only looked at the two as he spewed a long cloud of smelly smoke from his cigar. After a silence that only seemed like twenty minutes, he leaned forward on the desk and spoke directly to Strong and Laura.

"I guess you're wondering why I don't hire a Dallas advertising agency, aren't you?" he said, his gray eyes set deep in a narrow, oval face.

"It had crossed our minds," said Strong, not enjoying Finklestein's blunt manner.

"The sons of a bitches want too much. Contracts, retainers, all that shit and I've talked to a dozen of them. They all want *a seat at the table*! That's what they said, *a seat at the table*. My ass. I'm the client and I dictate what the objectives are. It really pissed me off.

"Then I figured a smaller town agency might be more flexible. I was getting ready to start looking in San Antonio when you called. That answer your question?" Finklestein asked rhetorically with raised eyebrows.

"I think so," Strong said. "I think, however, that you'll find our agency different. Let me tell you a little about us . . ."

"You don't need to tell me shit," Finklestein interrupted as he leaned back in his chair. "I've checked out your agency or I wouldn't even have let you in the door. You're small, at least by Dallas standards but you're one of the best creative shops in the region. But because you're in Oklahoma City nobody knows about you.

"You spent some time in the Marine Corps flying around and then came back home," he said pointing his cigar at Strong. "Worked for a couple of agencies and then started your own about five years ago.

Since you and your wife divorced, your whole life is tied up in the business. Am I right so far?"

"Uh, yes, I think so," said Strong in dismay, not sure if he should be outraged or flattered. It was a good sign the guy was serious enough to check him out but he had to admit it made him a little uncomfortable.

"And, if my information is correct, you can use the billings, yes?"

"Always," Strong confirmed.

"My budget is nearly five million a year. I manufacture and sell the most powerful vitamins available, anywhere" he said as the emptied a bottle of capsules on the table.

"They are damn miracles, and I want to sell more than any other bastard in the country. I want to dominate the market and within two years I want every man, woman, and child in this country to have taken at least one of my vitamins.

"I want two advertising campaigns a year and I want campaigns that will move product like no tomorrow. I started this business fifteen years ago and now I want out of it and the only way I can do that is sell it after having a few banner years. Do the first campaign right and I'll let you have the other one. Screw it up and you'll never see the inside this building again and I'll spend my days on the phone telling everyone I know what a rotten, incompetent agency you are.

"The first campaign needs to be on the streets in ninety days. Can you do it and achieve the objectives I've outlined?"

Strong was hit between the eyes. He wasn't ready. He had so many questions to ask and so much to tell about his creative philosophy and the talent he had assembled. This guy didn't care; he just wanted to know if they could do the job.

He was a bully, for sure, but one who was talking like he wanted to hire the agency. Strong wasn't sure how to proceed, but something told him he had better be bold or there would be no account. Maybe this was a test.

"Yeah, I can do it," Strong heard himself saying, "but you need to get out of the way."

Finklestein stared, but Strong was ready for him this time and looked him straight in the eye. He leaned forward in his chair and put his hands on Finklestein's desk.

"I'll give you the most powerful advertising campaign you've ever seen. It will ring your phones off the hook. It will empty your warehouse. It will make you a household word. It will have millions of people gulping your vitamins and believing their life is better because of them.

"But you *must* leave me alone to do my work. No interference. Agree to follow my recommendations. And five million won't begin to touch the kind of penetration you want, but we can talk about that later. Don't tinker with what I create and it'll make you more money than the gross national product of most third world countries," Strong finished and glanced at Laura who sat open-mouthed, not even trying to hide her shock.

My God, what have I done? Strong immediately thought, surprised at his words. My agency is on its ass. If I don't get this account I might as well close the doors tomorrow and here I am being John Wayne.

"Pretty goddamn cocky, aren't you?" Finklestein asked through narrowed eyes. "You want a *place at the table*, too?"

Strong was surprised Finklestein didn't throw them out. But maybe he was right. Maybe Finklestein appreciated this kind of bluntness. *Oh, well*, Strong thought as he silently took a big breath, *in for a penny, in for pound*, and launched into the next tirade.

"Not like you referred to. You set the objectives and parameters and we'll deliver, Mr. Finklestein. You're the boss but you're clearly looking for someone who can produce, and I'm that guy. I also know you'll run me or anybody else, out the door who tries to bullshit you. Ordinarily, I wouldn't be this blunt but somehow I get the impression you're not interested in the faint of heart and what you're asking won't be accomplished by a wimp," Strong said as he sat back in his chair and managed a smile while holding his breath. It was only his whole advertising agency at stake.

Chapter Two

FBI Headquarters
Washington, D.C.

"Do you have a sitrep?" asked Mike Phillips, the Director of Counter Terrorism.

"It's coming through now, sir," answered the communication specialist over the din of high-speed printers and VHF and UHF radios. "Looks like there was activity in camp 72. Infrared satellite photos show a bunch of them dead."

"Do we have any killer teams in the area?" asked Phillips, his hair falling into his thin but handsome face. He had a full head of brown hair but right at the front was a shock of white. Anyone who had ever met him never forgot him.

"Negative, sir."

"Then who the hell killed them? What about the CIA or the others?"

"No traffic saying they were conducting operations," the specialist replied quickly.

"Shit. I don't mind some of those terrorist bastards getting wasted. Fewer we have to track. I just want to know who's doing it," said Phillips as he stared at the bank of giant screens on the wall.

The phone next to Phillips lit up and rang sharply. He grabbed it, never taking his eyes from the data being displayed and barked,

"Phillips."

"Mike," the dignified voice said, "Nall here. I just received a call. Are we having some activity in Afghanistan?"

"I'm afraid so, Director. Looks like 30 or 35 KIAs. I think everyone was killed. It was that Osama bin Laden cell at camp 72 we were watching. We don't know yet who did it," said Phillips.

"What about the other bases?" the Director asked.

"Nothing. The one outside Jalalabad is quiet and so are the ones at Farmada and Darunta," Phillips answered.

There was silence on the other end of the phone. "I see. Let's visit, shall we?" said Nall and hung up without further conversation.

Phillips got up and walked through the ultra secret control center. The room was dark to minimize the eyestrain of those seated at the dozens of computer terminals and quiet to make radio transmissions intelligible. Overhead spotlights illuminated walkways and desks and it reminded Phillips of the bridge of a ship during night operations.

"I'll be in the Director's office. Interrupt me if something changes," Phillips told the specialist.

"Right, boss," he answered.

Phillips hesitated for another moment scanning the overhead screens then left the control center and walked directly to the Director's office past the secretary and knocked on the door.

"Come in," said Nall.

The heavyset Director of the FBI did not look up when Phillips entered the plush surroundings or when he issued the invitation, "Have a seat," and pointed to the circular conference table. He said nothing for several minutes and then got up from his large wooden desk, papers in his hands, and walked over to sit across from Phillips.

"Mike, I'm afraid we have a major threat. This is not the garden-variety terrorist we're dealing with. While this would normally be a CIA operation we have information that they're working on a devastating plan that will cost *literally* hundreds of thousands of American lives, thus it has a domestic relationship," Nall said, pushing his half glasses up on his nose. "There is no doubt this could be the worst terrorist attack yet seen, worldwide."

The Director took out his handkerchief and dabbed his lips as he stood up and began to walk and gesture. "We believe the incident in Afghanistan you just reported may have had direct connections with the attack we're concerned about.

"We had data that indicated the operatives were being massed for infiltration over here. That may have been a staging area for the terrorists programmed for the continental United States. I hope your analysis is correct and all were killed, but even then, there may be other staging areas. No idea at all who might have attacked the cell?"

"No, sir unless we have some vigilante group that we don't know about," Phillips said. His brow furrowed. He couldn't believe this. He forgot his normally respectful demeanor with his senior and blurted out, "Why didn't I know about this new threat? I've got the highest clearance issued. How can I operate the control center that is supposed to track all terrorist activities when I haven't been informed of something this horrific?"

"Because the President didn't clear you for 'need to know' until this morning," answered the florid faced Nall.

"The President?" Phillips asked incredulously.

"Exactly. It goes that high, it's that secret," said Nall, looking at Phillips, clearly disturbed.

A knock resounded through the heavy door. The Director responded by inviting the unseen guest in.

"Hello, Coy. Thank you for coming over," he said to the man who entered and resembled a young Ichabod Crane.

"Of course, sir," the man answered.

"Mike, this is Coy McWaters from the CIA. He's your counterpart over there, the Director of Counter-Terrorism."

The two men shook hands. "How are you Coy?" Phillips asked.

"Fine, Mike," responded McWaters.

"Excellent. You already know each other. I suppose we do have a small community, don't we?" the Director said.

McWaters moved to the head of the table.

"Coy has a critical briefing for you, thanks to your new clearance status. Please give him your close attention," Nall said.

"Of course, anything you hear is highly classified. For right now, it's to remain in this room."

Coy McWaters removed the articles from his briefcase and began.

"Mike, part of what I have to say may seem rudimentary to someone in your position and so I'm going to ask for your indulgence before I start. But I think you'll find that reviewing certain facts may place this in the correct perspective, at least it did for me.

"We both know that terrorism is the greatest threat to the security of our country for the twenty first century. Otherwise, obviously, you and I wouldn't have the jobs we have. But of all the scenarios we have examined, the one I'm going to present is the most devastating.

McWaters straightened his coat and continued.

"We, and I mean all of us in the counter-terrorism community, have been worried about an Anthrax attack on a subway that can kill 6000 people at once. We worry about explosions in crowded airports or a water supply being poisoned. We worry about this scenario and that scenario.

"About two months ago we got word from one of our few assets in the Mid-East that there was a plan in operation that would infiltrate terrorists into the U.S. whose plan was to kill a million, even two million, maybe more, Americans."

McWaters paused to let the impact of the numbers sink in.

Phillips was dumbstruck. He could think of nothing short of an atomic blast that could do that kind of damage. He had to summon all his self-discipline just to keep from shouting out questions.

"I don't have to tell you what kind of terror would grip this country with such a cataclysmic attack," McWaters continued. "Likewise, if any rumor of such an attack should hit the streets, there would be panic, hence the closely held secret status of the information.

"We want to bring pressure to bear to uncover and stop the plan but we have to limit our assets to only those with an absolute need to know. We cannot take a chance of it leaking.

"The problem is basically that we don't know how or when this attack is to take place. We think it will be within the next three or four months, but we aren't sure."

Phillips couldn't wait any longer and said, "My God, that hits just about the holiday season! Are you sure about this?

"We think this is bin Laden's doing. You and I both know bin Laden can finance himself. He doesn't have to have a hostile government bankroll him, and he absolutely refuses to compromise. We don't know yet how directly involved he is, but we feel certain it's one of his groups that will be executing the plan."

"But what kind of attack are you expecting? Only a huge explosion would do the kind of damage you're describing," Phillips asked nervously.

McWaters looked at the Director before continuing. Director Nall gave a slight nod.

"Unfortunately, no. Theoretically, a single ounce of BTX is sufficient to kill 60 million people. In fact, some data indicates one half ounce, properly dispersed, say in a reservoir, could kill every man, woman and child in North America."

"That's theoretical, Coy," Phillips argued. "People aren't going to all drink the water at the same time, if that's how it would be delivered. We all know that the water supply is not a highly vulnerable target . . . any of the extremely lethal biological agents aren't effectively transmitted by water and would be debilitated by the purification process.

"Besides, as soon as we had any indication of such an event, our emergency plans would sound the alarm and with proper action, we could render it harmless. No, it will have to be an explosive attack if they want to be sure of that much damage;"

Nall interrupted. "Perhaps you're right, Mike. Perhaps you're not. We can't take a chance. That's why I wanted you here, to bring you in on our strategy to eliminate this threat. If you're convinced it will be accomplished by explosives, then proceed with that track,"

"The program you're going to become involved in has two objectives of equal importance. First, of course, we must prevent this attack from occurring. It would shake the very foundations of our government.

"The call for retribution could easily upset the balance of power we have between the political left and the right. Demands for tightening of security, which comes at the cost of personal freedoms, would become overwhelming. The backlash would be swift and without thought.

"What backlash do you think would occur?" Phillips asked.

"I think a mob mentality would envelope the nation and we'd be launching attacks on anybody who even looks like a terrorist, people as well as nations. You were both in Desert Storm and you know how delicate that region is. I'm not interested in starting something that could end up in World War III.

"Secondly, I want bin Laden captured and brought to trial as an international terrorist, period. I want the bastard to die for what he's done to Americans and what he would like to do, in Africa, in Saudi, and God knows where else.

"But more importantly we must show the world that no one can commit reprehensible acts such as these and remain unpunished. President Reagan said it best, 'You can run but you can't hide,'" The Director said.

"Sir, how are we going to possibly stop a murder plot when we don't know who, when or where and then manage to capture bin Laden in three months or less? The CIA, the Mossad, Interpol have all been after him for years and have come up empty. How is the FBI, and maybe State, going to do what they haven't been able to do? Not to mention the fact that our charter is to deal with issues inside the country," Phillips said.

"Because, Mike, it won't be any of those groups. It will be *you*. You and six other handpicked professionals from our team, CIA, and the State Department. Of course, the entire resources of both departments will be yours; they simply won't know who you are and why they're jumping.

"All intelligence-gathering mechanisms in this government, including the NSA, will be funneled to you under the code name *Project Mighty Wall*. No one will know exactly who you are but they will all have strict orders to provide you everything they have and to follow any instructions you issue.

"You'll achieve what the bureaucracies have so far failed to do. And as regards the charter of our agency, you are being detached administratively from the FBI and attached a special black organization funded by unappropriated sources, again, *Mighty Wall*" Director Nall said with emphasis on "unappropriated" or secret funds.

"What kind of chain of command will run this?" Phillips questioned.

"You'll be in charge of the operation and McWaters, here, will be your deputy. You two are probably the country's preeminent authorities on terrorism. Now, I'd like for you to begin your planning and report back here tomorrow afternoon with some kind of proposal.

"I'm sorry, gentlemen, but I have another meeting with the President on this very subject. Until tomorrow, then," said the Director, having invisibly maneuvered himself by the double doors, prepared to open them to usher the two men out.

Just as the men rose to leave, the phone rang. Nall walked over, picked it up with a curt "Yes?" paused a moment, and held the phone out for Phillips.

Phillips did not expect a call here and looked around to be sure the Director didn't mean someone else. He took the phone knowing if it were for him it meant that there was a change, an important change, in the status of the situation in Afghanistan.

He listened and then placed his hand over the receiver and looking at the Director and McWaters said, "They picked up two signatures in a retrograde movement in the Afghanistan terrorist massacre. Two of them got away."

He turned to listen further and then said, "I'll be right there." He hung up the phone and as he walked toward the open door said, "They picked up a third signature. There's either another one escaping or somebody's after the first two."

It was hard to keep a straight course in the unstable and featureless sand. Huge dunes rose like titanic waves on a crystalline sea and they would clear the top only to find a drop off that made steering nearly impossible. Fortunately, the 4-wheeler had a compass and, coupled with Asam's inherent familiarity with the desert of his youth, the twosome progressed steadily. There were points where he had to get off the 4-wheeler and push it out of the ocean of sand. At those times he would have to unload his friend, manhandle the vehicle to more navigable terrain, and then reload his passenger and start all over again. It was exhausting.

Once started, with no other sounds in the desert, the roar of the engine was all consuming. It was impossible to hear anything else and yet in at least two instances, Asam thought he heard a strange whine, only to dismiss it as a reaction to the incessant noise of the engine.

Finally, the third time the whine emerged, Asam quickly stopped and turned off the 4-wheeler's engine, more to convince himself he wasn't hallucinating than to detect the sound. And sure enough, it was clear and high pitched. He held his breath so he could hear better. Perhaps he could determine from where the sound was coming.

It seemed to be behind him. No, to his left. No, it was in front of him. Asam clinched his fist. *It was circling him!* He looked to the sky but it's profound darkness made it hard to see anything. But he did see something. He tried to make it out and then it struck him. It was a drone. A drone! Just like the ones the Americans used during the Gulf War. A radio controlled plane used to track troop movements and one was tracking him. *It probably had infrared cameras so it could see him in the dark!*

He took his Uzi and tried to get a fix on the airplane. He began to fire in short bursts, leading it as he had been taught. Asam was frustrated after firing several rounds at an invisible target and cursed to no one in particular. Then he heard the silence. Perhaps he had hit it! He couldn't be sure but at least he couldn't hear it any longer. He stood silently, listening.

Satisfied the noise was gone he turned to remount the 4-wheeler and looked in horror at his front tire. It was flat. He examined it closely and could feel a hole through the wall. It had been pierced by a bullet, and in the last few minutes. He was not alone.

As he swung around with his weapon he couldn't see anyone. He didn't even feel the intruder's presence until he turned and saw a man crouched and leaping over the 4-wheeler, hitting him on the side and driving him into the sand.

Asam couldn't get his hand out from under him. The man had his arm encircling Asam's neck, tightening his grip and cutting off his breath. They rolled in the sand and still Asam could not get loose. The man's arms were the size of logs. His strength was more than Asam had ever experienced. Asam tried to reach for his knife but, again, he couldn't get his hand free.

Asam began to see black spots in his vision and realized he was passing out. Beads of sweat from the struggle were mixing with sand and burning his eyes. His lungs were straining to take in air. As muscular as Asam was, he could feel his power draining from him.

Suddenly, the man released his grip and lay deathly still on top of Asam. Asam mustered all his strength and tried to take advantage of the unexplained reprieve and wrestled from under the man. Gasping, he quickly turned over to prepare for another assault and saw the reason for the respite.

The man had a 6-inch dagger buried in his back.

Asam looked up and saw his passenger, still bleeding from his battle wounds, staggering and falling backwards. He had saved Asam's life.

Asam crawled over to him. "Hang on, brother," he said trying to catch his breath. "We'll get out of here. This bastard didn't fly out here. He had to have transportation. We'll use his."

"Who was he?" the man asked in short gasps.

"Probably one of those who attacked us at the camp. They may have spotted us when we escaped. I told you, they didn't want to leave anyone to tell tales. Don't worry. I doubt they would commit any more men to take care of us. We should be able to make it to safety without any more trouble," Asam said. He hoped he was right.

Asam struggled to his feet and began to walk away to find the man's vehicle. After about ten minutes and 100 meters, he found it, a 4-wheeler, just like his. He started it and drove it over to his friend. Once mounted, they again headed out into the endless desert.

Andrew Strong had to smile as he looked out his office window. Life was finally starting to get decent again. Six months ago he was an unhappy divorcee whose advertising agency, The Idea Group, was about to go belly up and today he was a much happier divorcee with a $5 million account on board.

Every day is a new day in this business, he thought. He still didn't understand why a Dallas company would choose an Oklahoma City advertising agency, but what the hell; it was not a decision he would second-guess.

Strong was not what women would consider good looking, that is until they talked to him. At 5 foot 9 and 135 pounds he appeared skinny. His receding hairline sat on a round face with a large but not unattractive, nose.

It was when his natural charm and humor, his sparkling eyes and warm smile that could melt the coldest personality, kicked in that caused his appearance to become more and more appealing. Friends and acquaintances all found themselves laughing and having a wonderful time not long after he entered a room. He had laughed his way into more good deals than most people ever saw. But that was social. The only time he brought his humor into play in the office was to diffuse a tense situation. Otherwise, he was all business

He swiveled his high-backed leather chair around to see Laura Newcomb, in all her splendor, standing in the door. He had hesitated to hire her, even with her top-notch credentials, simply because he was concerned about falling for such an incredibly beautiful woman. At 28, she was tall, 5'7" with a lithe, flowing body that had the fluid motion of a model when she walked. Her face was classic with a petite nose and smooth, flawless skin save for freckles that contributed to her youthful appearance. Her slightly crooked smile, which gave a hint of coquettishness, framed perfectly white and straight teeth.

But to Strong, her beauty, after a close working relationship, had become imperceptible. She had become more a figure he respected than one for which he lusted. She was smart as hell and he liked that.

"I'm getting the credit reports on Finklestein and Mark and you'll be happy to hear that every reference absolutely can't say enough about them. Pays in full before 30 days. That's what every one of them says," Laura said.

"That's wonderful. You don't look too happy, though. What's wrong?" asked Strong.

"Oh, nothing," she said as she ran her hand through her burnished blond hair. "I've just never seen these kinds of references. The vendors are almost secretive about their relationship. They only say it's a wonderful account, pays in full within ten days. And," she added with her eyebrows arched for emphasis, "they won't tell you how long they've been doing business.

"Of course, there are no credit limits. Who would dare have a credit limit for Finklestein and Mark? This is kind of suspicious," Laura said with a frustrated gesture.

"Come on, Laura, quit looking the gift horse in the mouth. We live most of our life worried that some client will default on their bills and leave us hanging out on a limb. Now, the only thing we have to fear has now been removed. Let's get about the business of creating the campaign," Strong said.

"Oh, alright, but they aren't listed in Dun and Bradstreet either. I just don't understand the references' attitudes, so protective of Finklestein and Mark."

"Listen, if they pay us within ten days, we'll protect them, too. That kind of cash flow can finance the expansion we're going to need to service the account," replied Strong flashing a warm smile.

"I know, Andrew, and I'm not trying to look for things, it's just all so easy. We walk in and get a $5 million account when we're worried about our next payroll and now we find the client is like Ft. Knox and doesn't even take 30 days to pay his bills," she said with a hint of disbelief.

Strong was becoming irritated. "You've said it and I'm aware of your concern. I'm not interested in hearing anything else unless you have some facts and not just conjecture," he said in his most businesslike tone.

Somewhere in the recesses of Strong's mind a little bell sounded. Newcomb was sharp and she was uneasy. It was not a good sign.

The conversation turned to other aspects of the account. Strong was in his element, organizing, making things move. It was the part of the business he loved. He could tell this Finklestein would be a bastard to work for but if they were successful, the rewards could move the agency to a totally new level.

"Laura, have creative ready to present to me in two weeks. I've got a great idea I want them to work on. We promote giving a year's supply of vitamins to a friend or loved one, you know, 'Give the gift of health' type thing. But we've got to get rolling on it if it's going to hit by the Christmas season. When is the research team going to be through?"

"Probably tomorrow. They spent three days in the Finklestein and Mark factory and are completing focus groups today," Laura said.

"Have media prepare the plan with the campaign beginning around Thanksgiving and going throughout the end of the year. We'll book it next week before all the Christmas television avails are gone," Strong said. "If we're going to present in October, then we'll need a spot market test done in September."

She could see the wheels turning in Strong's mind. "I'll see to it," said Laura, immediately leaving to go to the media department.

Strong worked on several aspects of the account's management and then got up to walk to the storage room to retrieve a new writing pad.

"Mr. Strong, call the operator," the intercom blasted.

Strong went to the nearest wall phone and punched the "0" and waited for the receptionist.

"Oh, Mr. Strong, we couldn't find you. Mr. Finklestein called. He didn't leave a number, said you had it," the receptionist reported.

I guess he thinks I ought to remember his number just because he's a $5 million account, Strong thought and then as an aside, *and he's right.* He reached for the dog-eared Dallas telephone book on the shelf and looked to the *F's*, only to find the company not listed. *What the hell,* he thought, and then noticed the book was an old one, 1998. *But still, didn't Finklestein say he had been in business for fifteen years? He would need to ask about that.* He went back to his desk and pulled out Finklestein's business card and dialed the number.

The phone rang and was promptly answered and, as soon as he identified himself, he was put directly through to Finklestein. "Hello, Strong. Your folks have been swarming around here so much we can hardly get any work done. I hope they're almost through," said Finklestein.

"As a matter of fact, they are. We're finishing focus groups and I think we're going to have some knocked out creative ideas for you pretty quickly," Strong answered.

"Good. Excellent. Tell me, who is your best person on operations, you know, systems, procedures that kind of thing?" It was a question that Strong had never been asked and certainly never expected.

"Well, I don't know that we have such a person. If I had to identify someone then it would be Laura . . . Newcomb. You met her on our first call."

"Oh, yeah, I remember. I'd like some of her time. I want our operations running smoothly when this hot dog campaign of yours breaks and I'd rather use your people to look at them, if I can, to not have to retrain another consultant. Besides, as much time as you've spent here, there shouldn't be much of a learning curve," Finklestein said.

"Of course, Laura would be perfect for that," Strong responded.

"Well, then send her down tomorrow. She can leave on the red eye and be here by 8 o'clock," Finklestein said and then abruptly hung up the phone.

Strong had never heard of a client asking for the operations person. That was very strange, especially considering that Finklestein and Mark was three or four times the size of The Idea Group. *Well, an hour sold is an hour sold,* he thought. *I'll send the janitor down there if they'll pay his hourly rate.*

Chapter Three

Iran's eastern border

Morning shafts of a desert sun were shooting down the unpaved streets as Asam pulled the 4-wheel motorcycle into the small village on the edge of the Iranian border.

People began to look out of their houses and eventually, a group formed and approached him. They came from each corner and were obviously simple, frightened people.

"Who are you? What do you want?" they asked looking at the rarely seen vehicle and the wounded man hanging on to Asam's waist with his head resting against his back.

"My friend is hurt," Asam said, motioning to the driver as he held him up. "He must have help and I must be in Mashhad by sundown. Will you take him and care for him until I return? I'll pay you well when I get back."

They looked at each other and then at Asam's dirty and disheveled appearance. There was a murmur among them. They did not miss the Uzi strapped on his back. Clearly, they were afraid of offending this violent man but no one spoke up.

"This man has been wounded by bandits. He cannot go with me any further. Surely, there is someone here who will follow Allah's teaching and help a fellow deliverer," Asam pleaded.

A tall villager slowly stepped forward and said, "Yes, we will take him but we cannot guarantee his life. He is hurt badly and we have no doctor here. We can offer him little."

"I understand. One of my friends or I will come for him in a few days. May Allah bless you," Asam said as he got off the motorcycle to help his friend into the arms of the tall man and watched as several villagers tried to help carry him. Asam remounted the 4-wheeler and cranked it back to life, then continued north toward the Iranian city of Mashhad, inhabited by the descendants of Genghis Khan.

It was late when Asam saw the glow from the lights of the community. He had wanted to arrive before dark but his progress was slower than he had hoped. He had to find his friend, Abdul Aziz. He had met him many years before and knew he was a man of the Jihad who could be trusted.

He stopped outside the town and turned the engine off to avoid causing people to look out their windows at the late night visitor. He pushed the 4-wheeler into the village and parked it in a deserted stable where it would not be seen. Asam then started out on foot to find his comrade at the last address he remembered for him.

He was filthy; his face covered with stubble, hair matted and with blood stains on his clothes. Trying to stay in the shadows to avoid directing attention to himself, he arrived at the apartment, a walk-up with chipped, peeling paint and a pungent smell of cooking.

Looking around first, he tapped on number six. There was no answer. Asam knocked harder a second time and was rewarded with a gruff, "Just a minute! Just a minute!"

The door opened and he found himself staring at his friend, who looked considerably older than he remembered.

"Ben?" said the bearded man in disbelief. "What has happened to you?"

"Don't ask Abdul. It can only cause you trouble. As you can tell, I need some help," said Asam.

"Of course, my friend, come in, come in," Abdul said as he pulled Asam from the hall, quickly shutting the door behind him and looking him up and down.

"You have some nasty injuries. Come in here," said Abdul and led him into the small bathroom, seating him on the toilet.

Abdul began to cut off Asam's tattered and soiled shirt and helped him remove it without tearing the skin from the wounds over his upper torso.

"Your body says you have been through quite a bit recently," Abdul muttered.

"Yes, that's true and I have more to endure," Asam said as he winced as the cloth was removed from his body.

"Abdul, I must get to the United States . . . Chicago, and I need to get there fast," said Asam, intermittently flinching with pain as the man continued to minister to him.

"I see. Well, there are a couple of different ways that can be accomplished. I have a few favors left in the government. If we can clean you up and make you look respectable, I think I can get you the papers you need and you can go like a businessman.

"The other option is to go aboard a private plane and dodge the radar until we can get you to the freighter out of the Persian Gulf as a deck hand. Not as fast, but less security checks," said Abdul as he carefully applied ointment to the other man's wounds. "Are you being pursued?" he asked.

"I don't think so, but then I didn't think the things that have happened to me would have occurred either. I have to get to Chicago now, regardless of the risk. If I fail, there is no one left to accomplish my mission. No one, and I mean no one, can know of my assignment," said Asam.

"Let me make some discrete inquiries. This government hates the U.S. but they would want to know why you are making the trip. However, there are several who can privately be of service. I will begin the wheels moving to provide you a new identity. Tonight, you rest," he said as he helped Asam to a sparse bedroom with a smelly mattress on the floor.

"Abdul, I have no money," Asam said as he carefully lay on the mattress. "I was supposed to be issued U.S. dollars but that became impossible. I will need money for this trip. Can you raise ten or twelve thousand in U.S. currency for me to take?" Asam said.

"I will try. Certainly, if we had more time I could, but with such a short notice, it will be more difficult. Now, sleep, and we'll talk about it in the morning," said the short man.

Abdul Aziz left the room, gently shutting the door. He walked over to the Uzi and placed it behind the refrigerator, carefully checking to insure there was no round in the chamber.

He picked up the phone and dialed a number and once it answered, whispered "fifteen minutes" and hung up.

He locked his apartment and walked down the creaky stairs to the darkened street and hailed a taxi. The beat-up cab took him to the heart of Mashhad and deposited him in Fedowsi Square. He walked slowly and cautiously, looking at his surroundings, each face and each person he passed to see if he could detect anything unusual. He sat by a statue of the poet Fedowsi and lit a foul smelling Turkish cigarette and watched as the smoke twisted itself into swirls as it hit the many currents of air in the square.

"What is so important that you require a meeting at eleven at night?" asked a decidedly Western voice behind him. Abdul did not turn around and kept his eyes straight ahead.

"I have a friend. I knew him in the old days. He is a fighter in the Jihad, and he is in need of help," the short, bearded man said.

"What kind of help? There are ways to help those people and you know them as well as I do. Why would you call me? You know the risk!" the man behind Abdul asked.

"Because this man is special and his needs are immediate. I don't know what his mission is but I'm sure it is of the highest priority. I'm certain it will strike the Great Satan in the heart, from within his own borders," said Abdul.

"What do you want?" the man replied.

"I need a passport, papers, and clothing and money, about $12,000 U.S. I want him on the first plane, in three days to Chicago as an international businessman. You must help. Believe me, this is important," Abdul said.

"Have him come to Shadid the Tailor's tomorrow at noon. We will make the arrangements then," said the man.

"He cannot do that. He is exhausted and suffering from some minor wounds. He will need to sleep for the next two or three days," said Abdul.

"Very well, estimate his sizes and come yourself," answered the man. "But you will owe me after this, Abdul."

"May Allah bless you, my friend," Abdul said as he turned to see the man had already disappeared.

It looked like any of the thousands of sandlot basketball courts across the country, where those who wish they were playing in the big leagues satisfy their desires by playing the game they love. But this team was different. The players were there for a much more dangerous game and almost all of them looked distinctly Middle Eastern. After a quick "for the public" pick-up game, they drifted off the court down the darkened alley and through a metal door into an apparently abandoned building.

Michael Phillips was the last to enter and secured the door behind him. He faced them and indicated for them to sit in the fold-up chairs already in the room.

"You all have had the same briefing I have and you know as much as I do. You know we've got to identify the terrorists, locate them and stop them. The kind of damage they are trying to inflict could be by explosive, or chemical/biological. We don't know. But it's most likely it will be by explosive. You each have the reports of suspects captured with bomb materials.

"They were either trying to get into the country or already here. It paints a pretty sordid picture of a group that is bringing in bombs piece by piece and that's hard to catch. If we've detected this many, you can imagine how many we've missed."

"If it is a bombing, where do you think it will happen?" asked one of the team members.

"Who said it's one bomb?" Phillips answered. "For all we know these assholes are planning to hit several places all at once, like the Viet Cong did at Tet in 1968. Wouldn't it be great if they managed to have them all go off at some events that were all televised? That would send the country into hysteria."

"New Years!" rang out from the group. The group turned to the person who had interrupted the briefing.

"Don't you get it?" asked the man. "Ever since they did the New Year's Eve celebration on the Millennium they have been televising New Year's eve events as they unfold around the world. They start with Australia and switch all over the world as the new year comes in."

Every eye was on the man.

"Jesus! Can you imagine what it would be like to have an explosion at every location? Twenty-four hours of revelers being blown to bits all over the world all on television. It would be devastating," said the bearded man.

It was a frightening thought and a dark silence settled on the room. Sensing the change in attitude, Phillips stood up from the corner of the desk and said in a strong voice, "Right now we don't know what the scenario will be but we have a plan to start learning, so let's begin by getting to know each other."

"Jennings!"

"Here" answered a trim young, man with a flat top.

"Mr. Jennings is an expert with a rifle. It's rumored he can put the eye out of a charging rhino at 500 yards," Phillips said. "Don't expect many charging rhinos but it will sure be nice to have that skill on board."

Jennings showed no emotion.

"Brill."

A hand went up from the middle-aged man with a white beard that had brought forth the disastrous New Year's Eve scenario; Phillips began to recite Brill's qualifications. "Mr. Brill is a gifted linguist and a communication expert. In a different time, he would have created languages instead of simply translating them."

"Sam Mays."

A dark- skinned, Mediterranean-looking man nodded.

"Sam is an artist. He can take the information you collect and recreate a face or faces that we can look for. He also has the dubious distinction of being a 3rd degree black belt and two-time winner of the National Tough Guy competition. If you don't like his art, he kills you."

The team gave a nervous laugh.

"Some of you may have recognized Carolyn Zudi. Carolyn is a former Miss Texas so you may have seen her in a variety of appearances. But more importantly she is a psychologist and something not many people know, a proven psychic. Be careful what you think around her."

There were a few more laughs and the group seemed to loosen up slightly.

"We think her skills may give us important insights into the people who are players in this menace," Phillips said.

The introductions continued with Phillips speaking without the aid of notes and demonstrating a complete knowledge of each team member. It was clear that each person came from a different government agency but his or her affiliations were never mentioned. After the last member was identified, Phillips stood with his arms out and began. "This will be our rally point for the U.S. Anytime we have to meet in secret we meet here. You need only say 'the home place.'

"We will be incommunicado from our families and friends for *at least* three months. Anyone breaking that rule could end up dead. Each of you is empowered to kill to accomplish this mission. You've been issued weapons, survival gear, and money. If you think we've forgotten something, let me or Coy McWaters know.

"Our first priority is to find the who, what, and where of this threat and here's where we're going to start," Phillips said as he spread out a map.

"Here's the camp in Afghanistan," he said as he put his index finger on the plains of Afghanistan. "As near as we can tell, only two, maybe three, escaped and it looked like they were on a motorcycle, probably an ATV because the engine heat was unshielded. They headed west toward Iran with somebody on their tail. Could have been another terrorist or someone out to finish the job they started on the camp. Here are the four major towns and villages on this route. Four of you will visit them and see what you can find out, then report back."

"Do we have any idea who these two or the one following are?" asked one of the team.

"Not really. You've got to look for some stranger who just came through on an ATV, maybe they were wounded or hurt. They may have shifted to a truck or mule for all we know. You've got to look for anything unusual, anybody unusual, and we don't have much time to get you there before the trail gets cold.

"If we can capture one or more of them then we can get the information out of them, I'll bet," Phillips said sarcastically.

"You all speak Farsi and can pass for Arabs or Iranians, except for you, Carolyn, but it won't take long before the word gets out on you. Strangers asking questions in small towns always draw attention, so your extractions will occur no later than 48 hours from your arrivals. If you don't make the connection, you're on your own.

"Here's the bottom line. We've got to find out who these terrorists are and where they're going. So far, they're the only possible link to the disaster waiting to happen," Phillips said. "If we don't find them there's a good chance that everything each one of us loves will likely cease to exist."

The room seemed darker and began to close in as they focused on the gravity of the threat.

The session continued for hours and yet each member was paying rapt attention.

"Here are your necessary papers and safe houses. Brill, you'll go to Birjand. Mays, you go to the village of Gonabad and then ride a bus into Kashmar to make sure he hasn't veered east. And Jennings, you'll fly out in a cargo plane from Riyadh and land in Isfahan. Coy will go to Tehran and run operations from there. Good luck. Now, get going," Phillips said.

"This is going to be like waiting for the astronauts when they went around the moon," said one of the team members, likening it to the communications blackout that occurs when astronauts travel to the dark side of the moon.

"That's right. We'll be holding our breath. Be there for your pick up on time," Phillips reminded as the four checked their gear to ensue they had the necessary items and moved to the door. Each walked out without a word and quickly faded into the darkness of the night.

"That leaves the rest of us. Brown," Phillips said to Mark Brown, a young, studious black man, "you're the computer expert. Now it's time for you to start hacking. I want you inside every government computer you can find in the Mid-East. Run searches for traffic that might give us a thread on what we're looking for.

"I don't care if it's a location that's mentioned or a mission name or casualty count from someplace or anything else. We don't know what we're looking for so we can't pass up anything."

"Will do," Brown, a recent cum laude doctoral graduate of MIT, said as he opened a metal sliding door unveiling a multi-monitor computer system driven by a new IBM AS400. He seated himself at the console and began issuing commands to the system.

Chapter Four

Mashhad, Iran

Asam awoke to see his old friend staring down at him. Still groggy, it hit him when he glanced out the dirty window into the darkness that it was evening. He bolted up in the bed and gasped, "Abdul! What time is it? What day is it?"

"Calm yourself," Abdul said as he placed his hand on the man's shoulder to gently restrain him. " You've slept for 36 hours. It is only a day and a half later than when you arrived. You couldn't have left sooner. It has taken some time to make the arrangements."

Asam began to relax and lying back, said softly, "I had to leave a man. He was wounded and I brought him with me. I didn't think he could make it here so I left him in a small town on the border, I think it was called Birjand. I promised I would return for him."

Abdul sat silently. "Who is he?" he asked.

"Just a man of the Jihad. But I gave my word. Will you go for him and make sure he receives help? There may still be people after us and I don't know how safe he is."

"Yes, I will do as you ask but now you must listen to the arrangements I have made for you and learn how you'll get to the United States. We have taken care of as many officials as we can but you will have to deal with the U.S. Customs yourself.

"It will not be easy. My sources tell me the customs service has, in the last few days, tightened security measures at all U.S. ports of entry. They are scrutinizing papers more closely and detaining more travelers than ever, especially those coming in from the Mid East."

"I see," Asam said with his brow furrowed.

"It would be much safer to go by boat," suggested Aziz.

"I'm sorry, Abdul, I don't have the time. I must take the chance. The plan is to start soon and without me it won't happen at all."

He could see his friend looking at him and wondering why he was so important that a major operation could not occur without him.

"All right," said Aziz. "Here's the plan. And here's your $12,000. You will leave from here at ten in the morning day after tomorrow and fly to Tehran. It will take about an hour. And then on to Chicago. Memorize this fact sheet. You are a Saudi businessman, Mohammed Al-Lamri, and you own a company in Riyadh named Sajad, Limited. It is a real company and we have people there who will confirm that, if necessary. Here are their names.

"Since I have no idea what you're going to do in Chicago, I cannot do anything but get you there."

"That's okay. It's better that you don't know. Just know you are making a great contribution to the Jihad," said Asam. "What about a weapon?"

"It's too dangerous to try to send one in with you. We could prepare it so it probably wouldn't be detected but you just don't know what might happen with these new security practices of their customs. It is very risky. I suggest you purchase one in Chicago. There are plenty of gangsters there so there should be a good supply," Aziz smiled.

"Here are your new clothes," Aziz said as he opened a closet showing three expensive suits in navy, gray and brown. "They have Riyadh labels. Your passport and visa, everything is from Saudi."

"How did you manage this so fast? You are a wizard," said Asam with a smile.

"I could not have been successful without a special friend, a very important friend," replied Aziz.

"What kind of friend? Who is it?"

"Ah, you have your secrets, I must have mine," said Aziz.

Asam continued to stare at Aziz. "Oh, all right, my friend. You leave no stone unturned, do you? It is a Western journalist. I am a secret source for him on many subjects and he has been able to have important stories because of my inside knowledge. He has won many awards and is highly regarded as an authority on the Mid East, thanks to me. He knows that when I call for favors, he had better deliver."

"Journalists," Asam spat derisively. "They're all the same, aren't they? Whores. All of them whores."

Asam said good-bye to his friend at his apartment and caught a taxi to the airport. The boarding of the airplane went smoothly. The small, dingy terminal was perfect for an unobserved and unchallenged embarkation. The Iran Air 727 had seen its better days. It was dirty and smelled of the staleness of old fabric and poor ventilation.

A few businessmen and oil field workers occupied its worn seats. Asam sat in the back of the plane to avoid those bored passengers who might want a conversation but also because he could quickly escape through he back exit if something happened while they were on the tarmac.

Once in Tehran, he transferred to a newer and more comfortable Kuwait Air plane to Chicago with a stop in Kuwait City. After he was seated, a flight attendant took his order for food and disappeared to the front. Asam carefully scrutinized the other passengers, looking for anyone who might be too interested in him.

It seemed to be an average group—a few vacationers, businessmen, and families. He looked for clean cut men, typical of Interpol or some other law enforcement agency, but found none. Still, he was uncomfortable. He of all people knew that not everybody was always as they appear.

He sat in his seat and read the latest newspapers from Chicago provided by the airline and then watched an old movie, a parody on the old West. He found it impossible to sleep so he just closed his eyes to relax.

The high pitched whine of the engines startled him and signaled he had indeed fallen asleep and now the jet was making its final approach into Chicago's O'Hare Airport. He looked around the cabin to confirm nothing had changed and began to straighten his chair.

"Did you sleep well?" he heard someone to his left say.

He turned to see the male flight attendant standing next to him, smiling.

"Uh, yes. Thank you," Asam acknowledged and began to fiddle with his seat belt. He didn't want to engage anyone in conversation but he didn't want to seem strange, either. All of a sudden his accent seemed overwhelming to him and he became very self-conscious.

"Is this your first trip to Chicago?" the flight attendant asked.

"No, I have been here before," Asam answered knowing he had made a mistake the moment he uttered the words. When undercover, always tell as much of the truth as you can, he remembered, but it was too late.

"Oh, do you like the "L?" the flight attendant asked brightly.

Asam was stunned. He had no idea what the "L" was. He was sure he was about to be caught by a colloquialism. He was about to blurt out something when the plane's loudspeaker cracked.

"Ladies and gentlemen. We're making our final approach into Chicago. Flight crew, please take your seats," the captain said.

The flight attendant smiled and said, "Oops, better go." He quickly went to the back of the airplane and strapped himself into the crew seat.

The plane landed and the group made their way to the customs check point. There were two customs officials at each gate and there seemed to be two also strolling around the entrance giving everyone the once-over.

Asam tried to choose a place with other people who looked as if they were from the Mid East. Maybe they would think he was with them.

The line crept ahead at an agonizing pace. Every bag was opened; each person was scanned with a hand scanner, in addition to walking through the metal detector. He saw at least two men and one woman being escorted away, protesting their innocence, to questioning rooms in the huge airport.

What worried him most was the man perched on a chair and small desk elevated above the floor who appeared to be looking through a photograph book. He would examine the book and then look out onto the crowd. Look at the book then look at the crowd. Asam avoided his gaze.

The woman in front of Asam was lugging a huge carry-on bag and two large, hard shell suitcases. Customs insisted on opening each of them. He noticed the questions were more than just cursory. Instead of the standard, "business or pleasure. Anything to declare" questions, the agents were asking occupation, domicile, place of employment, friends and family to be visited, home of record, as well as any other probing questions that came to mind. Something was definitely up.

"Sir, please step over here," said a customs agent as he walked up to Asam and motioned for him to follow.

Asam's heart sank as he pulled out of line. *At least if I had had a bomb, I could have struck one blow,* he thought. *Now I will be found out and will accomplish nothing.*

Chapter Five

"I'm supposed to do what?" asked Laura incredulously as she stood with her mouth open in front of Strong's oak desk.

"He just wants some help with procedures. You're the operations expert; it's only right that you go," Strong said.

"Wait a minute. You can't tell me that we've ever had a client ask for that. I'll bet you can't tell me that any client, anywhere, has asked for that. Why in the world would we honor such a request?" Laura asked in frustration.

"Because he pays for our time," Strong said curtly. "I don't understand why you're so resistant when it's a chance to earn billable hours for the agency. It's rare that an operations type gets to do that."

By now Laura had plopped down into one of the leather guest chairs, crossing her shapely legs.

"Oh, I'll just bet that guy has another agenda. Guys like that always do," Laura said, staring toward the bottom Strong's desk.

Strong flushed. "Let's get something straight, Laura." His abruptness startled her and she looked up at him. "First of all, not all men are susceptible to your feminine charms. There are some Herculean individuals who may be able to actually resist them and focus on business. Finklestein didn't ask for you. He wanted an 'operations person,' period. I told him you were the one."

It was Laura's turn to flush.

"And secondly, you make $100,000 a year working here and Finklestein and Mark is the only thing that stands between you and me and the unemployment line. I'm tired of you assigning ulterior motives to them. I'm tired of you questioning them . . . their good credit for God's sake! Either get on the team and start thinking positively about them, about what we can do for them, or find another place where you'll be happy," Strong never let his eyes leave Laura. He could see she was fighting back tears but he didn't care. It was time to clear the air.

Laura sat quietly for nearly three minutes and then said in her most businesslike tone, "You're right. I'll be on the first plane out in the morning. I'm sorry, Andrew," and before he could respond she stood up and quickly exited the office.

Laura arose at 3:30 a.m., showered and dressed, and began the 45-minute trip to Will Rogers World Airport. The morning was mild and she enjoyed the soft music from the classical station as she drove along the deserted streets of Oklahoma City.

Where, she wondered, *is this taking me?* She had been highly recruited from the Oklahoma University by Arthur Andersen LLP, one of the planet's most respected consulting firms. Even though she had graduated from the business school she had a minor in drama and often thought she should have gone into the theater. Operations was about as far away from the theater as one could get.

She was quickly pegged as one who would move up fast but it became obvious that the road to advancement was one that would take her away from her little family, an ailing mother and college bound younger brother, and her beloved Oklahoma.

At first, the travel didn't bother her and she found the idea of traveling around the country, living in big cities, exciting. That was before she tired of the upset stomachs of early morning flights, last minute, shabby motels thanks to airline cancellations and having more than one client view her something different than a top notch executive.

About the time she was fretting over the turn of events in her career, she met thirty-five year old Andrew Strong at an arts festival committee meeting. She thought he was witty and charming and by the end of the gathering had categorized him as an astute and up and coming businessman.

The next day, he called her and asked if she would have coffee with him. "I'd like to get your professional opinion of an opportunity occurring within our firm," he said. They met and he outlined the tremendous plans he had for his agency. By the end of the hour, he had asked her to come aboard as his "Number One" at twice her present salary.

She accepted and for nearly a year, all had been great. Trouble hit in February when the agency suffered the unexpected loss of their biggest account. It was not long before the agency was facing financial ruin. And then came Finklestein and Mark.

What a godsend F&M was. Andrew was right; we shouldn't be looking the gift horse in the mouth, she thought.

She parked her car in the airport lot and waited for a sleepy driver to bring the shuttle to her.

"Any luggage?" he asked.

"No, just the briefcase. I'll be back tonight," she said.

The driver deposited her at the Southwest Airline counter and the flight monitor directed her to gate C-1. She collected her boarding pass and waited until her number group was called to get on.

It was a quiet thirty-minute flight; landing at Dallas' Love Field at 7:00 a.m. She continued to reflect on her life. *Why aren't I sitting at home with a couple of kids?* she wondered. She knew the answer. It wasn't as if she hadn't had her choice of plenty of men. There were always plenty. There just wasn't one, to be honest, that was strong enough to keep her attention. *Oh, well,* she thought, *maybe he's out there looking for me today in Dallas.*

Laura disembarked and caught a cab to F&M. Some employees were already there. She hadn't noticed before how tight security was at her earlier visit. Security guards patrolled the building's exterior and the main door was steel and heavily secured. She rang the entry bell and was admitted, finding her way to the reception area where Finklestein's secretary sat.

"Good morning," she said to Laura. "Mr. Finklestein is waiting for you."

"Hello, Ms. Newcomb. I understand you're going to fix our operational problems," Finklestein said as he held his office door open for her.

Eleven words and he hasn't used any profanity. Must be a record, she thought. As she went into the office and took the seat he offered, she noticed there was something different about him.

"Strong says you're the best person to get our operations running smoothly. Is that correct?" Finklestein asked.

Remembering to exude confidence after her last meeting with him, Laura said, "I think so. I was a consultant with a Big Ten consulting firm before I came to the agency so I have several protocols that I think will be helpful."

"That's excellent. I'll go over the areas I want examined and then you can ask for any additional information as you interview the people in that department. How long do you think it will take to compete the study and issue a report?"

"Well, I thought we'd visit today and then I could come back next week and start the discovery," Laura said.

"Sorry, no. That won't work. I want this done immediately. Didn't Strong make that clear? I don't want to wait until next week. I want you to start today and work straight through until you're completed."

"Well, I didn't bring any clothes or toiletries or anything," she sputtered.

Finklestein stared at her and with a small smirk that hinted a trace of disgust, pushed the intercom on his phone. "Megan, go to Neiman's and get Ms. Newcomb enough clothes and toiletries to last throughout her assignment. Make her reservations at the Anatole."

He turned back to Laura. "Tell her your sizes and be back here in ten minutes to start. If you believe it'll cause you trouble at the agency, I'll call Strong. I don't think he'll object," he said and then waited for her to exit.

Laura told the secretary the necessary information and went to the bathroom before returning. She was totally confused by Finklestein's conduct. There was none of the coarse, obnoxious swagger they had witnessed the first time and yet, he was just as demanding and in control as he ever was, but this time he was the model of executive demeanor.

She returned to Finklestein's office ready for another bout.

Brill was parachuted at night outside of Birjand and made his way into the town the next morning. He went to the market to put his extraordinary hearing to work. Part of being a linguist was the ability to discern to the nth degree sounds and nuances of speech.

He was dressed, as were many of the people of the village, in an open collar shirt. He wore a light jacket that had more purpose than warmth and, with the exception of his snow-white beard, fit in easily. As he walked from booth to booth, ostensibly to examine the foodstuffs, he surveyed the speech around him. Even through the cacophony of sounds his trained ear could decipher individual conversations. At the third booth he heard two women gossip about the stranger who was wounded and getting worse. They worried they would be punished if he died.

Brill waited until the women had left and then asked the merchant, "Do you know how the stranger is doing?" he asked in perfect provincial dialect.

The man gave him a questioning look and then, probably because of the familiar way he spoke, replied, "Not good."

"Who is caring for him?" Brill asked.

"I think it is Ishmael," he said.

Brill bought a sack of figs and, wishing the merchant well, wandered down the dirty market to the end of the block. At the last booth, he asked an old woman selling melons, "I am a friend of Ishmael and am passing through and would like to see him. Can you tell me where he lives?"

"Yes," the woman answered. "Go down this street. He lives on the right side of the corner."

Brill thanked her and walked away. He knew he had now asked

questions of two villagers and it would not be long before he would be the subject of inquiries among them. He might have six hours to get finished, maybe less.

He found the humble home of Ishmael and after looking around, knocked gently on the door. When no one answered he tried the door and then gave it a shove, and it opened easily. He looked around and put his hand into his jacket where he had his Glock nine millimeter.

He saw no one so he began moving to the bedrooms. Inside the first bedroom he found nothing but the second bedroom was occupied. He went to the bed and looked down at the scruffy-looking man. He was every bit as ill as he had heard. The man opened his eyes groggily and started to yell when Brill quickly put his hand over the man's mouth.

"Shhh, brother. I am a doctor," he said. The man relaxed and Brill removed his hand. "Let me see your wounds," he continued while uncovering the man's wounds. "How do you feel?"

"I am very hot. My head aches and aches," replied the man. Beads of sweat had formed on his forehead.

"How long have you been here?" asked Brill.

. "What are you doing?" said the deep voice behind Brill. He turned to see a tall Arab with a pistol more suited as an antique than a weapon, pointed at him.

"I am a doctor," Brill said. "I am with the Ministry of Health. Take that gun off of me."

The Arab was shaken but hesitant. "Why are you here? How did you know he was here?"

"I was coming from Tehran and my car ran out of water outside of your village. Then I heard in the market he was here, ill and needed help," Brill replied.

"Did he send you?" the Arab asked, slowly lowering his pistol.

"Who?" asked Brill.

"The one who brought him and promised someone would come for him."

"No, but I must know the details if I am to help this man," replied Brill trying to regain control of the conversation.

"First, how long ago did he come?" Brill asked.

"No, tell him nothing!" said the driver, trying to sit up in bed.

"Now, now, you must rest," Brill said trying to calm him. "Have you anything to make him sleep?" he asked the Arab.

"Yes, I have this," the man said and produced some homemade elixir.

Brill motioned for him to give it to the driver and then stepped out of the room. The Arab followed shortly.

"He arrived four days ago. A man on a desert bicycle brought him. He was armed and told us to keep him," offered the Arab. "He has told us that bandits searched for them and were trying to kill them."

Brill kept talking to him and got a general description of Asam and a handle on the timeframe and direction of his movement.

"Look, I must leave but this man needs care you cannot provide here. Have someone get him to the next town with a hospital. If you don't, he will die," Brill said as he rose to leave.

"But you, why can't you take him?" the Arab asked.

Brill was not prepared for this logical question and stuttered slightly before saying, "I must take water to my car. I am going to Afghanistan. I cannot take him."

Brill went in and took one last look at the sleeping patient, trying hard to remember the features so, hopefully, Sam Mayes' drawing could identify him.

He asked the man for a bag of water for his car and after getting a goatskin of water, he thanked him and left the village. It was not a moment too soon. Already, he could see villagers whispering about him as he walked into the desert. He pulled his GPS from his belt and began the journey to the pickup zone.

After a few minutes of shuffling down the road he looked back at the house where the man was housed. He had put some distance between them in just a few minutes. Just as he stared at it, a flash of light erupted from the ceiling and the windows were blow out by a tremendous blast. The "bandits" had caught up with the wounded man. *I could be next,* Brill thought. He started to run down the road trying to be out of sight before anyone would come to look for him.

☆

"Andrew, Toni Herrod is on line one for you," said the operator at The Idea Group.

Strong reached for the phone and punched the line one button to speak to his banker. "Hi Toni. What's up?"

"Andrew, can you come out today and spend a few minutes with me?" she asked cryptically.

"Well, I can but what's it about?" he asked.

"I'll tell you when you get here, okay?"

"Sure, how about one o'clock?" he asked.

"That's fine," she said.

Strong could have sworn there was nervousness in her voice. He hung up the phone and began to wonder what she wanted. Getting a call like that from your banker was not a welcome event. He had a $100,000 note but he was making his quarterly payments in a semi-regular basis. When he couldn't come up with the payment, Toni would usually let him defer it to the next quarter.

The anxiety about the call began to build. He finally decided he couldn't stand to wait until one o'clock and got in his car and drove over to the small community bank. He went into the lobby and looked into Toni's glass-fronted office. She had been married to a fraternity brother and they had remained close friends even after her divorce. It was she who had encouraged him to start his own agency and had helped him figure out how to come up with the money for it. The biggest part being the hundred grand she loaned him.

She was on the phone but waved at him as he sat down on the overstuffed couch in the waiting area. When she finished she came out with a quizzical look. "I thought you were coming at one?"

"I thought I'd break away sooner. You sounded like it was important," he said.

"Come on in," she smiled and led him into her office shutting the door behind them.

Another bad sign, Strong thought.

Toni didn't waste time with small talk. "Andrew, it's about your loan," she said directly.

"What's wrong with it? I've been paying regularly. Well, almost regularly," he said.

"No, it's not that. This is very confidential, Andrew. I could lose my job if it got out that I told you, so *please*, keep it quiet," she implored.

Now Strong was really getting interested. He realized that anything that happened to Toni or to her bank was going to affect him but how much he couldn't yet tell.

"The bank is being bought by Topperly Bank N.A. No one knows it so it can't get out. But I've already been told by their people that your loan will be called when it happens," she said.

Strong opened his mouth to protest but Toni raised her hand.

"It's not your payment history, Andrew, so don't get uptight. They just don't want that kind of loan. They aren't as lenient as I am about collateral and feel that they'd be criticized by the examiners if they had a credit like that," Toni continued. "They're probably right. But in any case, once they take over you can expect to get a phone call."

"Damn. Toni, I just got this huge account. I can probably pay if off early. Won't that make a difference?" he pleaded.

"Not unless you want to deposit an offsetting balance. That's about all they care about," she said.

There was a silence as Strong stared at her desk. "How long do I have?" he asked quietly like a man getting his death sentence from a physician.

"Could be a month. Could be three. It just depends how long it takes to finalize the deal. I'm sorry, Andrew, but there's nothing I can do. You need to start looking for a place to move the loan," she said sympathetically. "If I were you I'd get it moved by the first of January or you may have a mess on your hands."

Strong thanked Toni and left the bank to return to the office. It was lunchtime but somehow, he didn't feel hungry. He knew what would happen if they called the loan and he couldn't pay. They'd file a lien on everything he had including receivables. Vendors would withdraw credit and his clients would probably leave him if they thought he was a credit risk. It wouldn't take thirty days for the agency to be driven into the dirt. Huge new account or not.

Move the loan? Who were they kidding? No other bank would take that loan. He would have never have gotten it in the first place if it hadn't been for Toni.

There was a balance of about $88,000 left on the debt. Maybe $75,000 would satisfy them as a compensating balance. If everything went right he might be able to clear that from the Finklestein account in 60 to 90 days. His only chance was to make enough cash to make the offsetting deposit she mentioned. And make it by January first.

"May I see your passport?" the Customs agent asked as he gave Asam the once-over.

Asam complied and was certain the beating of his heart was loud enough to give him away.

"And your business, Mr. Al-Lamri?" the uniformed agent asked, his eyes never leaving the passport.

Asam responded promptly. The agent continued to question him and finally, when he had apparently satisfied himself, said almost conspiratorially, "Did you notice anyone who appeared, oh, out of character on the plane? Say someone who looked suspicious?" the agent asked.

"No, but, of course, I didn't see everyone on the plane," Asam replied.

"Of course. Well, you've been very helpful, sir. Have a nice stay in Chicago. Oh, and what did you say the name of your company was?" the agent once again asked.

"Sajad, Limited. In Riyadh . . . Saudi Arabia," Asam responded, fully aware he had never mentioned his company.

"Of course. Thank you, Mr. Al-Lamri," said the agent smiling as he handed back the passport and opening the door for Asam to leave.

Asam walked out thanking Allah for his freedom.

Immediately after closing the door the agent opened a drawer and shut off the videotape and voice recording that had been activated as soon as Asam's questioning began. At the end of the shift, this tape would be transmitted to the appropriate authority, actually, the FBI, who had most recently expressed a keen interest in all incoming international passengers.

☆

At about the same time, a tall, nice-looking CIA operative who had been undercover as an airline flight attendant, picked up the pay phone in Concourse B of Chicago's O'Hare Airport and called a number he had been given. He was one of dozens of operatives placed on international flights in the last week and instructed to make a daily report on the people they observed on incoming planes. When the phone was answered he identified himself by code and gave his account.

"This is Tiger. There were three who might be worth checking out. The first was a guy who was coming in from Stuttgart and seemed to either be drunk or just stupid. Name was Holter, J.A. Flight 1333 this morning.

"The second one was from Riyadh and connected in Stuttgart on the afternoon flight that just landed, Flight 1200. Said he had been to Chicago before but didn't know what the 'L' was. Looked Arab. Name was Al-Lamri, Mohammed.

"And the third one was also an Arab, a woman in native dress, veil and all. I don't know, she just seemed to avoid eye contact with everyone. Could have been her upbringing but I just had a hunch. She came from Tehran. Name was Shala, B.B."

The flight attendant placed the receiver back in its cradle and walked down the concourse into a sea of travelers and out of the airport.

Asam hailed a cab and went to a small, inexpensive hotel in downtown Chicago. He checked in, unpacked and then went to look for a pay phone. He found one a couple of blocks from the hotel and dialed a number which was answered after a few rings.

"Los Angeles is hot this time of year," Asam said.

After a short pause the voice answered with the countersign, "But

New York is cool. Come by today. The apartment building at Third and Lexington. Walk if you can. I've been expecting you," the voice said.

Asam asked a passerby if the address was close and finding that it was, began to walk toward it. When he arrived he climbed the outside steps only to realize he did not know which apartment. As he studied the register a voice came through the intercom, "Come up to twenty-one."

Asam hiked up the stairs listening to the only slightly muted sounds of angry conversations and television dialogue coming from the small apartments, to find the door of number 21 partially open and a wide-eyed old man frantically motioning him inside.

"Welcome, brother," said the old man looking out into the hall before he quickly shut and locked the door. "You are the first to arrive."

"I am the only one to arrive," Asam said and began to explain what happened.

"Are there others who can take up the mantle of those who fell?"

"Not now," replied the old man, clearly concerned. "That was the prime cell for this operation. Because of the secrecy required, the need to know was restricted to only those directly involved. That means a backup cell was only identified, not trained or briefed. That is why your group was assembled and advised of the mission at the very last moment possible. It will take months to coordinate another group.

"You are the only hope we have of this happening and it has to start now. Already, the Americans and Russians search for our leader and us. They are trying to force the Afghans into cooperating with them to capture him," said the old man.

"Spend the rest of the night preparing for your trip and then proceed with the plan. Here is the formula in code. When you arrive, it will be decoded. Memorize it and then destroy this paper," the old man said softly. "May Allah go with you."

Asam left the dingy apartment and returned to his hotel room and spent the next hours studying and memorizing the names, addresses and data, including the formula, and planning for the next leg of his trip. As he studied, he realized he still didn't know the full impact of his mission and wouldn't be told until the last second.

The next morning he took a cab to the bus station and boarded a

Greyhound for Springfield. It took just under four hours to travel the 202 miles to the small town where he went to a rental car agency. This constant changing of travel modes was necessary, Asam felt, to ensure he was not being followed. It made tailing him difficult and allowed him the greatest chance to detect anyone surveilling him.

The person at the car rental was courteous but Asam was uneasy. He had never rented a car before and the constant questions and demand for documentation made him nervous. At that moment a Chicago police car pulled into the parking lot.

"Will you be taking the car out of the state, Mr. Al-Lamri?" she asked.

Why would she ask that? If he said yes would he have to provide more information, perhaps more insurance? He wanted her questions to end and for him to get out of here.

"No," Asam replied.

"Thank you, sir. The car will need to be back in three days with a full tank of fuel," she said.

"Yes, thank you," he replied absentmindedly. He looked out the window to see the police car turn around and exit the parking lot. He inwardly sighed a sigh of relief, took the papers, found the rental car and began the next leg of his journey.

Chapter Six

"Here's the list that contains the different areas I want you to examine. We believe, with the proper advertising and promotion, we can move several extra tons of vitamins first quarter alone. We expect your agency to accomplish that level of sales for us," Finklestein said as he reached across the desk to hand Laura the list.

"That amount is three times our current volume, so, in order to accommodate that increase, we must have every system at its most efficient. We are, as you know, sold directly to the consumer. No distributors, so our marketing efforts are all we have."

"The first area is ordering and shipping. Find out how much we can expect from them and what it will take to get them up to speed. The second is manufacturing. I think we can keep up but I want your opinion, and third, accounting, billing and such. Any questions?" he asked.

"Just one," said Laura with one of her award winning smiles. "I have to admit that your demeanor today and the one of the person we interviewed is quite different." It was time to disarm this man and her friendly, pleasant approach had never failed her before.

Finklestein smiled slightly but was clearly unmoved by her charm. In a voice that was deep and soft yet distinctly condescending he said, "I, like most people, change when the occasion calls for it to extract the most from any opportunity. Please understand, I am the same person . .

. I am the client." He rose and led her to the door. "Megan will get you anything you need. We'll talk later," he said as she felt the door close behind her.

Laura had been dismissed before but never that stingingly. *She was off base with this guy. Not only was he not going to make a pass at her, she wasn't sure she could even get him to like her.*

Laura began her investigation as instructed with the shipping and ordering department. She examined procedures, volume handled, response times and return rates as far back as there were records, which was about two years. It had taken her the rest of the day and would consume at least a full day tomorrow before she could move on to the other areas that had been assigned.

At about seven in the evening, she decided to call it a day. She didn't want to be stranded in this part of town. She picked up the phone and called a cab company only to be told that they didn't service that portion of Dallas. After three fruitless tries—it seemed nobody wanted to come into the area—she finally connected with a company that would send a cab. She waited inside the front door until the taxi appeared and then quickly ran out to the car, hearing the heavy steel door's dead bolt lock slam shut. The surly driver, who reeked of body odor, took her to the luxurious Anatole Hotel and after a tip, drove away without a word.

Her electronic key was waiting for her at the desk and she made her way to a well-appointed suite with welcoming flowers. She went into the bedroom which was decorated with antique furniture, old Persian rugs and expensive wallpaper, and opened the closet door to find it fully stocked with a striking array of dresses and pant suits, shoes, scarves, the whole shebang. And all in her size and, amazingly, all in her taste.

She was still in shock when she went into the bathroom. Not by the Jacuzzi or the multi head shower, she had seen those before, but by the toiletries that awaited her. Fine perfume, make-up, everything she could possibly need for a several day, or several week, stay.

But something was wrong and she couldn't put her finger on it and then it hit her. Everything . . . everything was exactly as she would have bought it. The same brands, the same colors, the same sizes. She had only given Megan her sizes not her preferences. Her mouth dropped open when she looked under the sink and found a discretely placed new box of tampons. She had started her period that day.

Shaken, she picked up the phone and dialed the agency's number, hoping someone would answer, even at this late hour. Sure enough, Andrew's voice announced the agency name.

"I'm glad I got you," she said relieved. "It looks as if I'm going to be here a lot longer than I thought. He wants me to do complete audits now with no if, ands or buts."

"Then stay as long as it takes to make him happy. When do you think it'll finish?" Strong asked.

"I don't know. If he wants to be a jerk about it, it could take months. I'm staying at the Anatole, which he provided, with a full wardrobe of clothes and necessary items, which he provided. All he hasn't done is give me spending money."

"You can't be talking about Finklestein," said Strong in amazement. "The kick ass monster who hired us is doing that for you?"

"One and the same," Laura replied. "This is not the same guy we met at first. He's articulate, poised and businesslike. He's still very much in charge but it's much more like working for a Fortune 500 company than we thought.

"He really wants to maximize his resources. He's clearly expecting a tripling in sales so I hope our campaign is a barn burner because if it falls short, he'll know in a hurry and we'll be toast."

"It will be a barn burner, don't worry about that," responded Strong.

They talked for a few more minutes and then Laura rang off, promising to keep Strong informed as she progressed. She watched television for a few minutes, enjoyed a relaxing bath and prepared to get in bed when she saw a small envelope on the bedside table addressed to her. She opened it to find five hundred dollars in cash with a note from Megan that "Mr. Finklestein thought you might need some spending cash."

☆

At seven o'clock in the morning the elevator doors opened and Laura walked into the expansive, ten-story high lobby of the Anatole Hotel. Before she could make her way to the doorman to ask him to summon a cab, a muscular, swarthy looking man approached her from the paneled reception desk. He was dark and had pockmarks on his cheek.

"Ms. Newcomb? I'm Eric from Finklestein and Mark. I'll be your driver while you're here," he said.

She looked at him and was not sure whether to be reassured or tense. He was pleasant enough looking with a neatly trimmed beard but he had piercing eyes and a jaw that was set with a serious twist. His callused knuckles told Laura he had plenty of experience in taking care of himself. He led her outside to a pearl Cadillac SLS and, after getting into the Central Expressway traffic asked, "Was everything satisfactory at the hotel?"

"Very much so," she replied. "How did you know when I would come down? I haven't told anyone when I would be in."

"Well, actually, I've been here since six. Mr. Finklestein thought the odds were good that you wouldn't leave before then."

"This is pretty VIP treatment. What's the occasion?" Laura asked.

"Not really. Mr. Finklestein said you had some difficulty getting a cab home last night and doesn't want that to happen again. He says your work is too valuable to have you distracted."

They pulled up to the front door of F&M and Laura went directly to the shipping and ordering department, offering the standard "good morning" to the few staffers on board at this early hour. She was deeply immersed in the sequence for processing orders when a voice broke her concentration.

"Sorry for the difficulty with the cab last night. We should have thought of that," said Finklestein, standing at the door.

"How did you know I had trouble with the cab?" Laura asked, quickly looking up from her records.

"Actually, Megan was doing a routine review of the calls and put two and two together. She was here later than you but was in a different part of the plant."

"I hope everything else was to your satisfaction," Finklestein said.

"Of course. I can't accept the cash, though, there's no reason for that," said Laura.

"Don't be ridiculous. You will have certain expenses that you'll need cash for. I expect to cover those expenses. Frankly, I want you to have it and that's reason enough," Finklestein replied staring her straight in the eyes with one of his icy stares. "I'll leave you to your work." He turned and left the room. Laura was used to going head to head with ego dominated males and wasn't afraid of such a confrontation but Finklestein seemed to render her helpless. He was as intimidating a person as she had ever met.

Laura continued her investigation and finished at about four. She immediately went to the next department, manufacturing, to begin the process there. She quickly noticed the records only went back two years, again.

"Sir, the last one has checked in. They should all be here by tonight," said the communications specialist. "Brill was picked up on schedule and Mays, Jennings and McWaters are already in country."

"Set a briefing for twenty hundred," said Michael Phillips. "I want everyone here."

"Yes, sir," the specialist answered.

At 8:00 p.m., Phillips shut the door and looked at his team, together again, and awaited the information each had to report.

"Welcome back, all. Brother Mays, let's hear from you," Phillips said.

Mays stood and put one foot on the chair. "I found zilch. I went to Kashmar and it's such a damn small town, no one would talk to me. It was more like walking into a commune where everybody knows everybody . . . except you. I would try to stop people in the street to ask directions and they just ignored me. It was frustrating. Sorry."

"Don't worry, Sam, we knew it was a risk. Several of the others have sketches that need to be done. Since your report is so short perhaps you can start working on those so we'll have them while we're all here," said Phillips.

"Sure," replied Mays. Brill gave him a gesture and Mays went over to him.

"Jennings, how about you?" continued Phillips.

"Well, I had a little better luck in Torbat-e-Heydariyeh. We did find that a man had been through on an ATV at about the right time for our guy. By himself, Uzi strapped to his back, but that's it. Headed north, but no indication of where. That's pretty much it. Lot of work for nothing," Jennings said.

"Maybe not," Brill spoke up interrupting his conference with Mays. "I was in Birjand and I found that he had indeed been there and deposited a wounded buddy. The wounded man wasn't very helpful, in fact he was almost dead, but the Arab taking care of him was willing to talk.

"He gave me a decent description of the other terrorist and I just gave Sam my notes so we should have something in a minute. Apparently, the guy was on his way to Mashhad and said he had to get there by sundown. That was four . . . five days ago. He's on the move and he's in a hurry," he said.

"Shit. That means he probably has his marching orders and so the plan is operational. " Phillips said, rubbing his forehead.

"They claimed that bandits wounded the man and that they were after them. I don't think it was bandits but whoever it was, blew him to pieces just as I left the village," Brill continued. "Somebody wanted him dead besides us."

Mays interrupted, "Do these look like the bad guys?" he asked as he held up two rough sketches that so closely resembled Asam and the wounded truck driver that Brill exclaimed, "That's the wounded one and the other one looks exactly as the villager told me."

"Get those out to all our sources and Brown, start running searches," Phillips said.

Brown immediately took the sketches to his multi screened console and began scanning the documents before dispatching them over the secure net that was established with all agencies participating in the search.

"Mike," said Coy McWaters, "this insertion went okay. We're all back, but I don't think we can pull off another one. I've never seen such security in Tehran; checks are random as well as planned. It reminded me of Hitler's Germany. I didn't realize it was such a risk."

"I'm afraid going back may not be an option. If this terrorist is moving I have a feeling he doesn't plan to stay in Iran. God knows where he is now," Phillips said.

"Carolyn, tomorrow night is a reception at the Iranian Embassy. You're on the guest list. Here's the cover," Phillips said as he handed a sheet of paper to Carolyn Zudi. "See if you can pick up something. By the way, any psychic pictures yet?" he said, only half kidding.

"Nothing I'm ready to share with you," Zudi said, deadly serious.

The team continued to review the facts they had and the new ones they had accumulated.

"Here's where we are. One terrorist is dead by now and the other is on the loose. If he had connections and support, how far can he get in five days?" Phillips asked.

"To our front doorstep," said McWaters and the room became very quiet.

"Then we have to assume he's either at, or close to, his final destination. Start checking U.S. ports of entry," Phillips said just as Brown came up huffing.

"This guy was identified by an agent on a TWA flight coming into Chicago yesterday. Here's the agent's report and they're downloading a video and voice track of him right now," Brown said.

The group huddled around the large monitor as Brown manipulated the controls. Soon an image began to fill the screen. At Brown's command, it began to move.

"Damn, Mays, you do good work. Your sketch was perfect," said Brill as he noted the details portrayed on the videotape as the same ones the artist had captured from his description.

"Okay, this is our guy and we have him in Chicago yesterday. Get this stuff to the Bureau, ATF, CIA and the state police in the surrounding states. We need them to check cabs, planes, buses, the whole stroke, for someone who saw him. We can't lose him now," ordered Phillips.

The week had been frantic. Especially after Laura's warning, Strong had pushed the staff constantly to fine-tune the advertising campaign's creative approach and to make sure the media selection was sound. He had demanded the organization put in long days and work on weekends but he had led the charge, working harder and longer than anyone.

His day had started at six a.m. and wasn't over yet. He had gone home at eight that night, changed clothes and gotten something to eat. Then he worked on the computer at his townhouse. He'd tried to get some rest at midnight and couldn't sleep so, after tossing and turning for two hours, he got up and decided to go back to the office. It was easier than lying there worrying about what had to get done tomorrow. At least this way he could get started on it.

He drove up to the east side of the office building. Even though his office was on the opposite side, it was this entrance that his access card would unlock after the building had closed. Strong walked through the dimly lit atrium. It was somehow surreal the way the shadows danced between the plants as his footsteps echoed on the stone floor. He entered the hallway that housed his suite of offices. Then he saw it and his heart stopped.

It was 2:30 in the morning and there was a light on. Perhaps someone had a deadline that had caused him or her to work all night. Perhaps the cleaning people left a light on. Perhaps not. He quietly walked to the entry, opened the glass-paneled door and slipped in, gently shutting it behind him.

He stood silently for a moment to see if he could detect any noise but the only sound he heard was a faint tapping. He carefully walked through the reception area toward the clicking until he was outside the room that housed the master computer. As he inched to the door and slowly eased into the entrance so he could see, he was shocked to witness a man he did not know working away at the terminal.

Without thinking, Strong shouted, "What the hell are you doing?" moving fully into the doorway.

The man, average-sized with long, stringy hair, turned around and jumped up, gave a quick look to each side and realized he had no escape route but through Strong. He bolted toward him. Instinctively, Strong widened his stance. He took the same position he had in high school to stop a runner on the football field.

Strong and the intruder slammed together. Strong's shoulder absorbed the blow. He pushed it into the man's waist and began to churn his legs to drive him back.

Suddenly, Strong felt an excruciating pain pierce his shoulder blades. It instantly worked its way down his spine. The man was driving his elbow into Strong's back in solid, repeating blows. In reaction, Strong momentarily released his grip on the man's legs and felt the trespasser's knee slam into his face. It knocked him to the floor. The burglar jumped over Strong, as he crouched on all fours, and ran out of the office.

Strong struggled to get up and fell against the desk. He righted himself and followed the man out of the office as fast as he could. He picked up speed. Adrenaline coursed though him and erased the pain in his back. He wasn't thinking about doing the safe thing. He was thinking like a Marine in combat. He raced through the foliage in the atrium and could see the man struggling with the door. He had to push the red release button for it to open but he didn't know that.

Strong caught up and grabbed him by his shoulders. He turned him around and wrestled him to the ground.

"Give it up, buddy. You're caught," Strong said between clinched teeth. He hoped the guy believed him. Apparently, he did not.

The man struck Strong in the eye and, in the moment that Strong reached to his face, pulled loose and tore out though the plant packed entrance hall. Strong got to his feet and gave pursuit with eyesight out of only one eye. He stepped into the soft soil of the plant garden sinking up to his ankles. When he found his way back to the flooring, he slipped and slid with the moisture on his shoes. The man had run to the other side of the building. He had obviously figured out how to unlock the door because when Strong arrived the corridor was empty.

He pushed the release button that opened the door and went out to see if he could spot his assailant. There was no one to be found. Strong had the presence of mind to hold the door open to keep himself from getting locked out.

Satisfied he had missed the intruder, he turned to re-enter and was face-to-face with the burglar. The man flew out of the shadows from which he had been hiding. He hit the entrance and literally ran over Strong. Slammed against the door as it flew open, Strong was knocked to the ground and completely disoriented. *The clown had been waiting for me to unlock the door for him.*

His head cleared several minutes later and he found himself locked out of the office building in tattered clothes with multiple scrapes and bruises.

He made his way back into the building but was so wobbly the best he could do was to place himself in the guest chair in the master computer room. He picked up the phone and called the police.

As his head cleared he focused on the monitor of the computer screen in front of him. It was still downloading information, to where he didn't know. He quickly went around and interrupted the activity.

Who was that guy? What did he want and where was he sending the contents of his office's computer system?

It was a quiet night in Oklahoma City and the police arrived within minutes. "Was anything stolen?" the policeman asked as he looked around the offices.

"No, he was just downloading data from the computer," Strong replied dabbing his scrapes with a wet paper towel.

"I wonder why they didn't just hack into your computer and get what they wanted that way," said the patrolman, flipping on lights in the various office spaces. Strong followed the cop down the hall.

"Our computer system has a state-of-the-art intruder shield just for that purpose. Maybe he tried and couldn't get through," Strong thought out loud. "Maybe he figured this was the only way he could get it.

"But I don't understand what we have that he would want. It's not like we have some big defense contractor as a client."

The policeman filled out his report, noting the description of the man from Strong but quickly losing interest when it was confirmed that nothing but data was stolen. He asked Strong if he had any other information and once satisfied that he had a complete report, left his card in case he thought of anything and left the office.

Strong had a feeling that this would be the last time he would hear from the Oklahoma City Police Department on this issue.

☆

Laura finished the manufacturing department a week later. Each evening she had been chauffeured to the Anatole and greeted with fresh flowers and a special weekly gift of increasing value. She didn't like it but Finklestein had made it clear that one didn't question his methods. She was still making herself believe it was just a generous way of thanking her for going above and beyond. She decided to make a call to Strong.

"Well, I've gotten a start on the first couple of departments," she said when she reached Andrew.

"Jesus Christ, what the hell are you doing?" Strong asked.

"Classic Arthur Andersen protocol. He's demanding, and getting, a complete evaluation. I haven't done one this thorough since I worked for Arthur," she said specifically not mentioning the continuing gifts.

"Have you found anything out I need to know?" Strong asked. "Surely you're enough of a snoop to be able to uncover something."

"Yes, I have, but it'll have to wait. I'm not sure what it means or how it might affect the business," she said.

"Whoa, hold on! I want to know anything that might affect the business. What is it?"

"Nothing yet, but if it turns out to be anything, I'll call immediately," Laura comforted.

"Please do. Call tomorrow and give me an update, okay?" Strong said with an edge of nervousness in his voice. He thought about telling her of the break-in but then dismissed the idea. *There was no sense in distracting her. She couldn't do anything about it anyway.*

"Yes, I'll talk to you tomorrow," Laura said as she put the handset on the cot.

The next morning, she took her notes to the accounting department and began examining every document she could get her hands on and asking questions of the people working there. She couldn't find anything, including employees, that went back before 1999. Finklestein had specifically told her the company was fifteen years old. *There was no reason for him to lie,* she thought. *I'll ask him when I make my summary presentation.*

Strong went by Laura's office on his way to see Finklestein. His weekly meetings with Finklestein, while not particularly welcome, were necessary to work out the myriad of details and obtain the countless approvals required to complete a campaign of that magnitude. Disappointed to find her normal workspace empty he went back to the reception area and patiently waited. Laura wasn't normally a high maintenance person but he had a feeling that was going to change if he wanted her to stay where she was.

Within moments he was summoned into Finklestein's office and, after cursory greetings—never any small talk—they got down to a long list of discussion items.

The meeting went amazingly well with Finklestein agreeing to most every point. As Strong began to leave he decided now was as good a time as ever to ask the unanswered question that had been popping up.

"Incidentally, Mr. Finklestein, I ran up against an interesting item," he said. "Our Dallas phone book is a few years old and I couldn't find Finklestein and Mark in that book. You didn't operate under another name years ago, did you?"

Finklestein glared at Strong as if he had asked if his mother were married. "Get a new phone book, Strong. Worry about tomorrow for us, not yesterday," he said and turned to walk to his desk signaling that Strong was dismissed.

Strong's face was burning and he looked at Finklestein without making any signal he was going to leave. "Actually, Mr. Finklestein, I don't think that is an unreasonable question to ask. Things that have happened in the past with the company can dramatically influence the advertising efforts of today," he said trying to control his anger. "If we're going to achieve our objectives, we've got to be able to ask salient questions without worrying about giving offence—when it's not intended."

Finklestein looked at Strong as if he were going to pounce. Then suddenly, his face softened and he said, "Of course, you're absolutely correct. I can assure you there is nothing we haven't told you that might affect your advertising campaign. Please, feel free to ask any questions you deem important," he said.

He still didn't answer the question, Strong thought. "Thank you," he said. "I'll be in Oklahoma City for the rest of this week and then back next week." Strong was so angry that he quickly left the office and headed back to Oklahoma City without even checking with Laura to see how she was progressing. If he hadn't had his back to the wall, that would have been the last time Finklestein would have seen him. He was starting to calculate in his mind how long he had to keep the account before he tell Finklestein to go to hell.

Laura closed the books on the accounting department two weeks later. She had been though every record and tested every system the department had. She had added checks and balances to protect against employee fraud. Additionally, she had instituted redundant systems that would ensure that no matter what, the company always had an accurate picture of their financial status. It was, if she said so herself, a hell of a piece of work.

She called Andrew to report the news. "Andrew, I'm finally through Accounting. This has to be the hardest one," she said. "Andrew, you've got to get me out of here. This guy is grueling to work for."

"I'm fully aware of what he's like. You may remember I meet with him quite regularly. But Laura if you can hold out and finish it, we can get through the first campaign we can make some personnel adjustments then. Right now we've just got to make it work until we're out of the woods financially," Strong said. Look, Laura, we're not going to ever have this guy as our friend. If we're lucky, we might be able to extract some respect from him so don't think that there's something wrong because he isn't the friendliest client we've got."

"I guess you're right. Well, I'll start on the next department and by the time we break the campaign this will be one smooth running company," she said resignedly.

"Atta girl. I'll talk to you in a few days," Strong said and hung up.

She signed off and went back to straightening her desk and planning the assault on the next area.

"You *have* made a lot of progress!" Finklestein said as he entered the department. "Do you have a minute?" he asked and motioned for her to come into the hall.

"Yes?" she asked when they were outside the department.

"I appreciate your hard work. I know you've been putting in long hours and I'd like to take you to dinner at the *The Old Warsaw* tonight. It'll be a nice break for you. It's one of the finest restaurants in Texas. I'll pick you up at about eight?" he asked rhetorically. Before she could answer, he was gone and she was beginning to suspect the worst.

Thank you, Andrew, for your great insight into the male animal, she thought. *Some Herculean individuals actually focus on business,* she remembered him saying. *Yeah, right. They're all hard-ons waiting for a place to light. Now this guy is looking for the payoff for all the gifts and courtesies. Well, he'll have a surprise,* she thought.

She finished work early, about six, and arrived at the hotel twenty minutes later. As had been the case throughout her stay in Dallas, there were fresh flowers in her suite and a small package on the coffee table. She took off her high heels and sat down to open the package. She wondered what it would be this time. She had so far received a *Mont Blanc* pen, a *Gucci* handbag, and a bottle of *Chanel Number Five*.

She tore open the wrapping paper, not noticing the subtle logo from one of Dallas' most elite jewelers and was shocked to find inside the box a black pearl necklace. The thing was gorgeous and had at least 20 perfect pearls. Laura knew it must have cost at least $20,000. *He's really trying to make it hard to say no,* she thought, *but this has got to stop. I'll return this tonight, offend him or not,* she thought.

Laura bathed and put on a new dress that had miraculously appeared in her closet. Like everything else, it had materialized without as much as a request from her. At precisely eight o'clock the phone rang. It was Finklestein.

"Good evening," he said. "If you're ready, perhaps you can join me in the lobby."

"Thank you, I'll be right down," she answered.

That was not the move of a guy trying to seduce me. He couldn't have been more correct in his behavior.

Laura had heard of *Old Warsaw*. It had been a Dallas icon for fifty years, but she had never been there. She'd eaten at *The Mansion, Ruth's Chris Steak House* and some of the other upscale Dallas restaurants but somehow, *The Old Warsaw* had eluded her.

She was impressed by the grace that greeted her.

"Ah, Mr. Finklestein, welcome," said the Maitre D' who could have easily passed for Telly Savalas' double.

"Good evening, Salim," Finklestein replied.

They were led to their table, one nestled in the corner, shielded by dividers of slatted wood and silk and across from the string quartet that was filling the restaurant with the elegant sounds of Tchaikowsky violin concertos. The small bowl of rose petals on their table and the rich mahogany ceilings and walls exuded grace and warmth. She could have been in Warsaw for all she knew. It couldn't have been any more European or more chic.

From the opening presentation of their food by the tuxedoed staff, Finklestein conducted himself in an entirely proper, in fact, charming manner.

Finally, as they were enjoying the special blend of coffee, he spoke.

"Ms. Newcomb, Laura, you've done a wonderful job. Even though I don't have your final summary I have been watching you and you've asked all the right questions. After a great deal of thought, I've decided to offer you a place on our team."

"Well, I didn't expect this," she said, trying to hide her astonishment. *I wouldn't work for this guy for all the tea in China. The truth of the matter is he scares the hell out of me,* she thought.

"If my information is correct, you currently earn $100,000 a year with The Idea Group and the income stream that funds that pretty much depends upon our business, isn't that correct?" he asked.

Once again, Laura was astounded how much he knew about her and wondered how he found out all the personal things. Her silence was the only acknowledgement Finklestein needed.

"You also are responsible for your mother, whom I understand has been identified as a high risk for Alzheimer's." His voice softened. "That disease is a curse because it debilitates the victim and then destroys the finances of the loved ones. You have a younger brother, Jack, isn't it, in school at Oklahoma State University? That's quite a load you're carrying on $6,000 a month take home pay."

That does it. How dare he quote back to me facts that are none of his business!

"How do you know these personal things about me? That is private information! Who would release that to you?" she said angrily.

Finklestein ignored her outburst, showing no emotion. "If you join our company, you'll find we have one of the finest security departments in the corporate world. The proprietary information we use is every bit as secret as the formula for Coca Cola. Perhaps you've noticed the facility is very secure. In fact, as secure as any top-secret military base.

"The proprietary formulas and manufacturing processes for our vitamins are worth millions and we are obligated to protect them. It's necessary in our business that we know everything about each person who works here as well. And we pay them handsomely for that slight invasion of privacy."

"Well, you can't pay me enough for invading *my* privacy. I think someone else should be working with you and I'm going to tell Andrew tomorrow," she said, her face red.

Finklestein smiled. "I'm prepared to offer you a very generous financial package, Ms. Newcomb. At least hear me out," Finklestein said.

Laura said nothing.

"First, your salary will be $20,000 per month."

Laura gulped silently. Her quick mental calculations came up with $240,000 per year. A quarter of a million dollars! She would be more than doubling her salary.

"Second, we will issue you a health insurance policy that'll cover your mother if that hideous illness progresses. She'll have the best care available and it won't cost you a penny. And finally, I'll personally arrange for your brother to receive a full scholarship at OSU. All in all, that's about a $350,000 a year package."

Laura was flabbergasted. She was not only worried about the future of the agency and her job but also about how she would care for her mother as her condition deteriorated. That occupied her thoughts far more than how her brother would get his education but this opportunity solved both problems and almost tripled her salary. She couldn't imagine what she could do that would be that valuable to the company to warrant such huge compensation.

"You're right. That's a very generous offer, Mr. Finklestein. And one that's hard to decline," she said conversationally. Her drama classes were paying off here, as she outwardly appeared calm. "I have to ask, though, how can I possibly justify so much money?"

"You will not quit your job at The Idea Group. You'll continue to collect your salary from the agency but you'll be our employee and you'll be looking out for our interests. You have the best chance of gathering intelligence if nobody knows you're on our payroll. This advertising campaign must work and I want to know in advance if it appears to be weak in any way.

"You'll continue the work I assign you and report to Strong that I insist you remain. Tell him you convinced us to make a partial advance payment on production. That should make him happy."

"How long would I have to maintain this charade? It seems really duplicitous," she asked.

"Approximately six weeks. By then the new advertising campaign will be going and the threat will have passed. At that point, you can simply announce to him you've received an offer from us that you can't refuse and Strong will, of course, acquiesce because he wants to keep the business." Finklestein said.

Laura was quietly looking at her hands.

"If you're concerned about taking the agency's money, we will, I'm sure, be billed for your time. Rest assured that will more than compensate them for your salary," he finished.

"Can I think about it?" Laura asked.

"Of course. Take the next sixty seconds."

"Please. Mr. Finklestein, this is a big decision. I can't make a choice like this without some thought. I'd like to talk to my Mother actually. Plus, Andrew has been very good to me and I feel as if I would be . . .well, you know . . .betraying him."

"I understand. You have forty-five seconds," he said never altering his expression.

"It's a lot of money and it would mean that I would have to live in Dallas and the whole reason I'm in this business is so I can be close to my mother," she sputtered, seeing the opportunity slip away.

"Move her here. You'll be able to afford it. Thirty seconds."

"What happens if I decline?" she asked.

"You can be out of here tomorrow and I'll have a new agency on board within a week. Fifteen seconds."

"I . . . I . . . accept," she responded with eight seconds to spare.

Chapter Seven

Asam drove his rental car down the lush four-lane highway that led south from Springfield. Expansive farms on each side of the highway flaunted their bountiful harvests. Thriving small towns dotted the landscape.

He had never been to the United States and marveled at the abundance and cleanliness of the countryside. No animal carcasses rotting by the road or dirt streets constantly generating dust that penetrated everything and everyone. The wealth and prosperity overwhelmed him.

Islam has been in existence for thousands of years and yet, we have nothing; they have been a nation only two hundred years and they have everything. It is only right that we take something of value. We will take their tranquility, he thought.

He stopped for gas and noticed the continuing procession of people with personal automobiles buying what, he realized, was cheap fuel compared to his own country. He filled his tank, calculating the 729 miles to his destination would be well within the range of three more tanks full.

He pulled back onto the highway and drove with an urgency that was almost beyond his little rental. Several times he looked down and was exceeding the speed limit by fifteen miles per hour. He was a man, he felt, on borrowed time with a mission that could not be denied.

The trip continued, uneventfully, through Illinois and he was soon greeted by the famous St. Louis arch. His resentment of this country grew. *How many of our children could be fed by the money used for that monument to Infidels,* he thought angrily. He turned southwest across Missouri, hitting the Turner Turnpike outside of Tulsa and plunging south again.

Stopping for more fuel and a quick bit of food, he examined the other patrons of the Oklahoma truck stop. It gave him a strange feeling of power to know that in a short period of time some of those customers, and many of the people he passed on the highway, would be dead, thanks to him. He was used to taking life but not in such a detached way.

He tried to identify those who looked as if they should die. There was the unshaven truck driver busily smoking and drinking coffee. The tired, middle-aged waitress who was busy slinging plates on the counter and into the booths while the dark-skinned laborer two seats from him ate silently but hungrily. He finally gave up, concluding they all seemed to be just peasants and, as in his own country, no one carried more sins than the other. It was the *comfort* of America he wanted to attack and there didn't seem to be much luxury here.

He picked up I-35 north of Oklahoma City and continued south, slipping onto the infamous NAFTA corridor, named for the latest trade agreement between Mexico and the US. The route had resulted in a continuous flow of illegal drugs though the heartland states on their way to Canada and was patrolled heavily.

As a soldier of twenty years, Asam could sense trouble before others were aware of its existence. He heard that instinctive alarm in his mind and began to search around him as he traveled down the highway. Within moments the threat emerged and he saw a stream of frenetically flashing red, blue and white lights behind him.

Asam was confused. The flashing lights were on a vehicle that had no markings and was not identified as a police vehicle. He suddenly realized the danger was that the police car was unmarked. The late model Ford Crown Victoria was equipped with blackened windows hiding the hyperactive emergency lights, until they unveiled themselves to the unsuspecting violator.

He pulled over, once again cursing himself that he had no weapon.

He was not prepared for this and knew he had limited options. *Had the police been notified about him?* He sat in the car and rolled the window down.

"Good afternoon," the tall Oklahoma Highway Patrol Trooper, said pleasantly as he bent down to look in the car and at Asam. "May I see your driver's license and insurance verification?"

Allah protect me, Asam thought. I do not know what is insurance verification. Asam fumbled in the rental papers trying to decide what to do next when the trooper's two-way radio blared. He straightened up, pulled the microphone from his epaulet and acknowledged the message. He quickly bent back down into the window.

"It's your lucky day, sir. I'm being called to an arrest. Drive carefully and watch your speed," the trooper said and ran to his car, activating the siren and screeching around Asam, tearing onto the highway with smoke pouring from his spinning rear tires. Asam didn't quite understand what had happened but as soon as the patrol cruiser was out of sight, he carefully pulled back onto the Interstate. Within five miles he had his answer.

Oklahoma's highway patrol had pulled over a motorist, probably a suspected drug trafficker, and had the driver out of the car lying face down on the slope of the underpass. Other patrol cars, including the one that had stopped Asam, were beginning to appear suddenly from nowhere and assemble around the arresting officer. They were in normal colors, blue, red, brown. They were almost impossible to detect. *So, this country also has a secret police.*

Flabbergasted, he could barely decide which fork in the road to take as I-35 quickly branched off to Dallas one way and to Amarillo on the other. He swerved at the last minute and worried that one of the unmarked cars might think he was a drunk but when no cascade of lights erupted, he relaxed ever so slightly.

He continued his trip, careful not to break any traffic laws. Now alerted, he spotted five different unmarked vehicles. He drove well within the speed limit and after four arduous hours he reached his destination. *My God, how big is this country?* He struggled with the intertwining highways that greeted him as he searched for the motel located on the outer loop of the city.

It was dark when he arrived. After several aborted attempts and much backtracking, he located the inn and registered under the name Shandez. *One more item to throw off anyone who is tracking me.*

He settled into this room, locked the door and, instead of finding a pay phone as he had in Chicago, made a call from his room to a predetermined number and, after a series of intermediaries, spoke to his contact.

"Los Angeles is hot this time of year," said Asam and received the proper counter password, "But New York is cool."

"I am here. When do we meet?" Asam asked.

"In the morning. Someone will pick you up at 10 a.m. and deliver you here. Bring your belongings. You will not be returning to that location. Turn in your car tonight and get some rest," the voice said.

Asam did as he was told and then went back to the motel to rest but couldn't. He was a soldier and it bothered him he had no weapon. He felt naked and vulnerable. Perhaps he would be able to arm himself here.

"Damn it. If we don't get something soon, he's going to be gone," said Phillips. "Do we not have *anything*? No sightings? No intercepts? No leads from interviews?"

"Well, here's something," replied Coy McWaters as he approached holding a sheet of paper. "The video tape and the sketch of our suspects has made the rounds and it seems that our guy is a known follower of bin Laden and a member of the al-Qaida. Name is Benjamin Asam, Mohammed Al-Lamri is a cover. He's the son of a peasant farmer in Iran, went to the university and graduated in Chemistry. Has been one of bin Laden's top field commanders since the Gulf War. Extremely adept at close quarter fighting. I don't quite know why that skill would be needed for this mission."

"If the cell were annihilated then he may have had to take charge by the process of elimination," replied Phillips.

"That's true," continued McWaters. "The person that Brill saw in the village doesn't show up at all. He was probably just some soldier."

"Okay. What do we have? Benjamin Asam is a terrorist who has made his way to the U.S. disguised as a businessman. He lands in Chicago and then we can't find him. He hasn't left by rail or air?"

"No, " said McWaters. "We've had agents watching all the airports and railway stations. He might have slipped through, but I doubt it."

"What about rental cars?"

"We're checking but there are a couple of hundred places he could have rented, bought, borrowed or stolen a car," said McWaters.

"What if his final destination is Chicago?" asked Brown.

"It could be but it's unlikely. It's too easy. We have Chicago PD searching for him while we're looking for his trail if he left the city. If he's in Chicago, we'll know quickly because the area is just so big."

"If he's on the move, though, the job is much more complicated. We don't know how much area he has covered or in which direction he went," answered Phillips. "I want random traffic stops in all surrounding states. Concentrate on interstate highways."

"Right," said McWaters. "I'll see to it."

Most of the next two hours were spent coordinating a perimeter of checkpoints in the surrounding states.

"Listen to this! We just got a voice intercept from a call made in downtown Chicago about two days ago. It matches Asam's voice profile," Brown said as he commanded the computer to play the track.

After listening to each word of the password and countersign and the instructions that followed, Phillips yelled, "Jennings. You and Brill get over there and bring his contact back here. Bring him alive and make it fast."

"Why not just have the Chicago police pick him up?" McWaters asked.

Phillips' face was cold when he turned to McWaters and said, "Because he may not live through this and I want that information to stay with the team only."

Hearing that, Jennings and Brill hit the road in their Dodge SUV and drove directly to a vacant lot where they were met by an unmarked UH-60 Blackhawk helicopter. Once on board, the pilot turned to a heading of two niner zero degrees and flew toward Chicago at its maximum speed of 163 miles per hour. The crew landed on the Gulf Petroleum Building in downtown Chicago. They were met with another Dodge SUV with the navigational guide operational and set to Third and Lexington. Within 15 minutes Brill was standing at the front door of number 21 and Jennings had scaled the back fire escape and was pressed against the bricks next to the window.

Without hesitation, Brill slammed into the door with his shoulder and ran through with his pistol drawn. Simultaneously, Jennings crashed through the glass and within seconds they were on top of the old man in his bed. Quickly, his mouth and hands were secured with duct tape and he was dragged to the floor.

Jennings ransacked the small apartment but found nothing. They pulled the old man out of the apartment, shutting the door against the shattered doorsill. Throughout the fracas not one door opened, not one person looked out to see who was terrorizing their neighbor.

The helicopter was waiting and they were back at the undercover operation center before the hour had passed. Two hours later they emerged from the windowless room that was being used for the interrogation of the old man.

"We aren't getting anywhere. He's clammed up and I'm afraid if we get too rough with the old bastard, he'll croak," said Brill.

"What about drugs?" Phillips asked. "Can we shoot him up and get anything?"

"It's too dangerous. If he's on any medication, and I suspect someone his age is, it could cause a stroke. We may have to take the chance, though," said Brill.

Phillips thought for a moment and then looked up. "Wait a minute. There may be a way we can get the information we need."

In 15 minutes Carolyn Zudi walked into the dark area of the interrogation room to see an old but defiant man sitting in a wooden chair in the center of the room illuminated by a single light. His hands and feet were tied with plastic cords. Brill and Jennings sat across from him in chairs turned backwards.

"He can't see us," Phillips whispered to Carolyn as they entered. "He has no idea where he is or how long he's been here."

"We know that Asam was at your apartment. Where did he go?"

Brill demanded. The old man remained mute.

"Bring over the eye cup," said Brill. Jennings rose and returned wheeling a small metal table over by the old man.

"Ever use one of these?" he asked as he held up a small glass eye cup. "Normally, you put a little Visine into it, place it on your eye and it takes away your pain. In this case, however, we put a little hydrochloric acid in it and, well, I'm afraid it will cause a little pain. We don't have to do that if you'll just help us. Tell us where Asam is. You know we'll find him eventually."

In his only burst of outward defiance the old man whispered in heavily accented, but very satisfied, English, "Eventually will be too late."

Carolyn Zudi studied this aged, defiant Arab and wondered what savage tribalism would make him endure such pain and fear. She began to concentrate. As she stared at him she suddenly started receiving mental pictures. At first they were frightening, nonsensical images. Then, slowly, they became more understandable. She could see a tent, then a man she knew as Asam. Intermittently she saw flashes of fighting and then she made out Asam again. She got a glimpse of the old man and Asam looking at a map and drawing a line down the map as if planning a route.

Carolyn signaled to Phillips to go into the hall. Once there she said flatly, "Asam isn't here. I can't tell you exactly where he has gone but I think it's south."

Phillips eyes grew wide. "That, at least, gives us a direction. Good job, Carolyn. Tell Brill to keep at him and not let him have any sleep. If he goes to sleep, slap him awake; kick him in the balls, whatever they have to do. We can break him with sleep depravation without killing him but it takes awhile and I don't know that we have the time," he said as he strode down the passageway.

Chapter Eight

There was a murmur of voices in the Finklestein and Mark conference room as Andrew Strong watched while the agency's account team set up for the presentation of the new ad campaign. Weeks of work, long twelve and sixteen hour days had gone into it, not to mention hundreds of thousands of dollars. It was complete in all respects and an effort that, if left alone by the client, could, Strong believed, set record sales for the vitamin company.

Finklestein rose at the head of the conference table. "We're here to view the upcoming campaign created by our new agency, The Idea Group. This marks a major shift and commitment for our company and will result, we expect, to move us into one of the top five vitamin producers in the country. Now, I'll introduce Mr. Andrew Strong, the president of the agency, to tell us how we will achieve that goal."

It flustered Strong. Finklestein was exactly as Laura Newcomb had said. Contact with him had indeed demonstrated his new found demeanor. Finklestein bore no resemblance to the overbearing jackass who had tried so hard, and succeeded, in intimidating them at the first meeting. Strong didn't know all the people in the room, although Laura seemed to be quite friendly with each of them. *I guess that's what happens when you live at the client's company*, he thought.

He scanned the room during Finklestein's remarks and figured that most in attendance were department heads and, of course, Finklestein's personal assistant, Megan. Each was seated around the table with a few in chairs along the wall. Strong's staff was strategically placed to operate the various recorders and projectors.

He began his presentation. "This campaign has one purpose, and one only. To convince over 1% of America, and with the latest population figures at 276 million, that's two point seven million people, to become monthly subscribers and consumers of Zaner vitamins. We think the message we've devised will compel people to change their lifestyles. Not only theirs, but the lifestyles of their children and loved ones by becoming devotees of these miraculous supplements you market as Zaner vitamins."

A series of screens came alive with charts and graphs assembling themselves in graphic color.

"The effort begins with the base medium, direct mail, going into every home in the country. Blue-collar homes will be addressed with a sweepstakes offer that allows them the chance to win a cash prize, such as the magazine clearinghouse promotions, while at the same time, have an introductory package of vitamins to get them started. Your chemists believe that the improvement they will feel in just two weeks will convince them to continue with Zaners."

Strong nodded to a staff member who flashed images of the All American family on the main screen.

"White collar and upper income homes will receive a well-reasoned approach that shows the good health they can expect from using Zaners and a special child's package will be an added incentive. For each family that subscribes, we will provide the children's version of Zaner so their children can enjoy healthier lives as well. There is no charge for the first year of the child's vitamins."

A series of photographs of nice looking men and women wearing telephone headsets sitting in front of computer monitors fill the multiple screens.

"An army of telemarketing specialists will make follow-up contacts and should increase our sales by 7-9%.

"The 8-week campaign is supported by national television and radio commercials and a series of appearances by celebrity spokesmen, try Alan Alda and Candice Bergin, on such highly rated talk shows as

Oprah and Rosie O'Donnell and radio shows that include Larry King Live. Their presentations will be highly seasoned with testimonials from satisfied Zaner users.

"The orders will be driven to the company and the F&M Internet site and be processed within 24 hours. The customer should become an active participant within three days. We're spending a little more money to have expedited shipping to ensure the first order is there fast.

"Outdoor signs are also a secondary support medium."

At that moment, the conference room door opened and a hard looking man, appearing out of character in an ill fitting suit, quietly slipped in and took a seat against the wall. Strong smiled at the newcomer and continued.

"The creative that will drive this campaign has tested extremely well and we think will move people to action quickly and efficiently," Strong said as he signaled for the television commercials to begin running featuring the powerful "Give The Gift of Health" theme.

The audience was awed by the convincing and persuasive message and the unrelenting frequency with which it hit consumers over and over. Even the unidentified stranger seemed to marvel at the synergy of the communications effort.

After Strong had finished the presentation, the group applauded enthusiastically. He saw a small "thumbs up" signal from Laura and Finklestein began walking toward him. The room was almost clear when Finklestein made his way over and said, "Excellent, Strong. However, there's something you haven't told me, isn't there?"

Strong looked apprehensively at him.

"The budget! That campaign can't be done for $4.5 million can it?" Finklestein asked.

"Ah, Mr. Finklestein, I did tell you ... in our first meeting. Remember, I said $4.5 million wouldn't begin to touch it?" Strong retorted.

"So you did. Let's sit down here and get straight on what it will cost," said Finklestein. "Oh, I'd like you to meet a friend of mine," he said as he ushered the unidentified latecomer to shake hands with Strong. "Mr. Mohammed Al-Lamri, may I present Andrew Strong.   Mr. Al-Lamri is an associate of mine from Riyadh, Saudi Arabia." The two men shook hands. Strong noticed the callused feel of a hand that was short and vice-like. They then turned back to the issue of budget.

"So, how much?" Finklestein asked after they were seated.

"$6 million," Strong answered but quickly injected, "but half of the cashflow you'll need will come from the fast response of the campaign and then the remainder will easily be covered by the increased volume. But if you want immediate results, it can't be a penny less." He pulled out a spreadsheet and displayed it on the conference table.

"As you can see, Mr. Finklestein, you have to fund the effort out of existing cash until here," he said as he pointed to a spot about two months away, "then the income will begin to out pace the expense. By three more months you'll have positive cashflow. I know the acquisition cost may seem high at $2 a subscriber but just one year's subscription should average $600 per subscriber in income. That means annual revenues of over a billion a year.

"The second campaign would simply expand the market."

Finklestein studied the figures for a moment and then passed them back to Strong.

"Very well, Mr. Strong. The campaign and budget are approved. When did you say it is programmed to start?"

"The first of November through Christmas," said Strong. "By not long after New Year's Eve there should be two and a half million Americans faithfully following the Zaner regimen for better health." He looked at Laura and smiled.

Laura suddenly felt very sullied.

"Well, what did you think?" asked Finklestein.

"Quite impressive. But do you have that much money, $6 million?" asked Asam.

"No, but as Strong said, the increased volume will take care of it. Our credit rating is so outstanding we can probably stretch payments to suppliers to ninety days without any consequences. In any case, we'll be gone after the first of the year. We'll do it under the guise of a lengthy business trip and the employees will run the company.

"Now, down to the issue at hand. Do you have the formula?"

Asam took a piece of paper and wrote the formula he had been given. Finklestein looked at the data and fed it into his personal computer then watched as it decoded and printed out the deciphered instructions.

"You haven't been told the entire story because there was too much chance of you being captured but now it's time to fill you in," said Finklestein and he walked to his office door and locked it. Asam sat, eager to learn the plan.

"Four years ago, our leader decided that only a massive strike would bring the Great Satan to its knees. Many plans were considered. Nuclear, which is now within our ability, had too many global implications. Outright terrorist attacks are possible but result in harsh and immediate reprisals.

"The Reis had to solve the problem of exterminating millions of Infidels without being detected and having retribution taken against him before he could finish the task. Chemical and biological weapons held promise, but again, there was too much danger it would spread beyond the U.S. and the delivery systems were not dependable.

"Then, he had a flash of genius. Why not infect the population with a virus that would lay dormant and be activated at different times for different people? This would allow for an escape and would severely hamper, and extend, the effort to stop the virus," said Finklestein.

"What kind of virus?" asked Asam in amazement.

"Actually, it isn't a virus. It's an incredibly potent agent created by our own chemists. I had half of the formula and you have delivered the other half. It lies dormant in the system and collects each day until it is activated. Sometimes it happens quickly, sometimes slowly but in every case, it's deadly.

"And of course, the delivery system is the Zaner vitamin. That's why we started this company two years ago. The distribution must take place swiftly; hence, this big marketing push. If we take a lot of time to disseminate the toxin, the Americans would surely discover it. But by compressing the process we'll have 25 million infected and just waiting for the poison to be activated," Finklestein said.

"What is it that activates the poison?" Asam asked, his chemist mind becoming curious.

"Coffee."

"Coffee?" repeated Asam.

"Coffee is the lifeblood of the American workforce. Nothing happens in this economy until these people have their morning jolt of caffeine. By the end of the day they will each have consumed five to seven cups of the stuff. Even the children of this godless country are addicted to the caffeine in their drinks. Cokes, Dr. Pepper, Pepsi Cola are all staples of the American children's diet. What simple names for such an addictive drug.

"Once someone begins taking Zaner vitamins they begin to build up poison in their system. When the caffeine level in the body reaches a certain level, the poison begins to activate. It gives fake symptoms and once the person dies, no one can tell for sure what he died of. Some people will die instantly. Some will have seizures while driving and their deaths will become traffic fatalities. The homosexuals will become just another victim of AIDS. Others will become ill and it may take a week or two to just to get a diagnosis. By then they are dead."

"Isn't there a government agency that monitors the content of the vitamins you sell?" questioned Asam.

"Of course. The Food and Drug Administration is the inspecting agency. And we have complied with every possible requirement they have in the production of the vitamins we've been producing for the last two years. We have an excellent reputation with the agency."

"But what happens if they check on the batch with the new formula?" Asam asked.

"Vitamins aren't regulated the way prescription drugs are," said Finklestein. "It is a huge hole in their system."

"This is all very extraordinary. Now that I have delivered the formula, what can I do for the mission?" Asam asked.

"A great deal, my friend. I want you to take charge of security. Only you, Eric and I are members of the al-Qaida. The rest are simple employees happy to have a job that pays them 20% above the market. They think the company is fifteen years old and well established. That's to throw off anyone who might get suspicious. They are focused only on their job and know little of anything outside their own areas."

"You mean no one knows how it all works but you?" Asam asked.

Finklestein nodded. "There's one exception. The advertising agency has had access to every part of the company and there is a certain exposure with them. We've taken steps to cut off any chance of a leak by entering into a secret agreement with Laura Newcomb from the agency that has put her on our side. We've compromised her so now she can't divulge what she knows without implicating herself. You'll meet her, quite attractive. And greedy.

"After this advertising campaign has begun and we are well into the distribution of the Zaners, we must be able to escape before the mission has been detected. The company will run fine for weeks, even months, with the employees doing what they have always done. If we're lucky, by the time the deaths are traced to Finklestein and Mark, we'll be back in Tehran."

Asam sat quietly. He had waited for the specifics of the plan to be unfolded for him but he had no idea it was this unconventional. After he had absorbed the strategy he asked, "Finklestein? Why did you choose a name like Finklestein for a cover?"

Finklestein laughed. "Perhaps for the irony of it. I thought our leader would enjoy having a Jewish name spread all over the newspapers as a suspected mass murderer."

"And who is the Mark in Finklestein and Mark?"

"Just my imagination. I thought it gave the impression of a larger firm. I think it sounds older and more established, don't you? And we'll certainly leave our *mark*!" Finklestein laughed.

"Yes," Phillips barked into the receiver as he grabbed the black phone.

"Mr. Phillips?" a voice asked.

"Who's calling?"

"This is Deputy Commissioner Smipes of the Illinois Highway Patrol," the voice responded firmly.

"This is Phillips, Commissioner. What can I do for you?"

"Well, the governor called me in a few days ago and gave me a top-priority assignment to set up roadblocks and begin canvassing car rental agencies in Chicago," he said in a quizzical tone. "There are damn near a million of them and I've had most of the patrol and CPD working on it for several days.

"The governor also directed me to contact you at this number if we found anything. I am complying with his orders. This afternoon we found a lady in Springfield, Illinois who recognized the suspect from the photo we got from Washington. He used the name Shandez, though. She remembered him because he stated that he did not intend to take the car out of state."

"Where was he going?" asked Phillips, motioning for Brown to come over.

"That's just it. He said he wasn't going out of state but she got a message today that the car had been turned in, in Texas. Customer claimed he told the agent and that she must have made a mistake. She was pissed because now it reflects on her and . . ." Smipes said.

"Where in Texas?" Phillips interrupted.

"Why, Dallas at D/FW airport," answered the Commissioner.

"Great! Thanks, Commissioner," Phillips said.

"Sure, but do you mind answering one question?"

"What?" Phillips asked impatiently.

"Who the hell are you people? I've never seen such pressure come from above in my 35 years in the patrol. Who are you that you could command such influence?" the commissioner asked.

"Commissioner, trust me, we're just working stiffs like you," said Phillips and hung up the phone.

"Get me a map of Dallas, the whole metroplex," he said to Brown while he waved over Mays and Jennings.

"Mays, you and Jennings are pulling the duty on this one again. We've tracked Asam to Dallas at D/FW airport. We don't know where in Dallas he went or if that's his final destination. We've got to get a noose on him now. He can't be far away from doing what he came to do.

"Get to Dallas, go to the rental agency where he turned in the car. He had to leave from there somehow. Did he walk, take a cab? We'll put the Dallas & Ft. Worth P.D.s on it, too. Find him quick and find out what the plan is. Remember, if you kill him, we may never know what they're doing," Phillips said. "They'll send someone else and we'll have to start all over again."

The two met their helicopter and were transported to a small regional airport where an unmarked Gulfstream executive jet was idling on the runway. Within minutes they were cruising toward Dallas at 42,000 feet. Already, the Dallas police had begun their second series of interviews with the rental car agent and cabbies that operated in that area.

Strong drove his convertible up to the as yet empty office building. It was seven in the morning and the other tenants had not yet arrived to begin their day. The Oklahoma Autumn was in full swing and the trees had turned gorgeous shades of red and orange. He paused a moment to reflect on how beautiful the foliage was.

It had been only two weeks since The Idea Group presented the campaign that was supposed to vault Zaner Vitamins into the forefront of America's diet and only two weeks left before it hit the airwaves. While the mechanics of producing and placing the advertising was going well, he had noticed in his daily conversations with her and weekly trips to Dallas, a subtle change in Laura's attitude.

It was a transformation he didn't understand and had attributed it to the fact that she was, in essence, being forced to stay in Dallas and work on the systems that Finklestein wanted. Finklestein and Mark operated seven days a week and she had been required to stay in Dallas, non-stop, for nearly 90 days and it looked like she still had two weeks to go. The short breaks that had been offered had been for a day or two at a time. They weren't even enough to allow her to come back to Oklahoma City.

Finklestein's thinking was sound, Strong knew. It would be stupid to mount a huge selling effort without the systems in place to fill the orders when they started coming in but asking the agency to provide that direction and then dictating that it be carried out non-stop was, well, unusual to say the least.

Maybe her difference in attitude was a result of being tired — and mad at Strong. Perhaps he should have been more assertive in demanding that she stay in Oklahoma City but without this account his management skills would be a moot point. No Finklestein and Mark, no Idea Group. *He would make it up to her once this campaign broke,* he promised himself.

Strong was proud of what they were accomplishing for the client. He was doing it right. He didn't want to change anything because it was going to work.

His divorce months before had been devastating. His college sweetheart had left him for an older and wealthier man. His ego had reeled from the blow of being abandoned by someone he had loved and trusted but he was a resilient person and had committed to rebuilding his life. Finklestein and Mark had given him the vehicle to do that. It was more than just an account to save the agency. It was saving him as well.

Asam got into the Ford Taurus SHO that Finklestein had provided. "It can't be traced to us and there are a million of them on the road," Finklestein had told him. "We bought it at an auction of rental cars and paid cash."

Asam had decided he had been without a weapon for long enough. He drove to a grimy pawnshop in the little suburb of Grand Prairie. He parallel parked on the narrow, crowded Main Street, went in and was greeted by the proprietor.

"Whadaya need pard?" asked the unshaven, beer-gutted owner.

"I want to buy a pistol, please," said Asam.

"Well, we got 'em. What are you looking for? Big caliber? Automatic or revolver?"

"I want a 9 millimeter Glock with Black Talons, if that's the best you can do," Asam said and looked straight at the man.

The owner narrowed his eyes at Asam. "And if we can do better, what would you be looking for, ole buddy?"

"An Uzi for starters. In fact two of them," Asam said.

"Well, pardner, those are illegal but if you want to come in the back I might have something you'd be interested in." He walked to the front of the store and locked the door and then pointed for Asam to go into the back room.

Asam walked back though a stained curtain and sensed fast movement behind him. He turned to see the owner on the down stroke with a steel backed SAP aimed for his head. He instinctively blocked the blow but was off balance and fell sideways. The owner moved quickly for a man of such bulk and was on top of him. Asam could barely breathe under the weight, not to mention that the man had his hands around his neck squeezing with all his might.

Asam rammed his strong palms up and grabbed the fat man's ear and tore with all his strength. The man screamed and the bloody, jagged piece of ear came off in Asam's fingers. He didn't wait a second. He drove his elbow into the pawnbroker's face and with the sound of cracking bones, sent him rolling over backwards with blood gushing from his head and face.

Asam was at once on top of the owner with his arms twisted around the man's head preparing to deliver the coup de gras when his assailant yelled,

" Please, no! I thought you were a cop! Don't kill me!"

Asam hesitated. "Honest, mister, I thought you were here to bust me. I've got hardware, plenty of it. I just had to be sure you were okay," he pleaded.

Carefully, Asam relinquished his grip and the man stumbled to his feet, grabbing a rag to stop the bleeding. "Goddamn, man, you nearly killed me. So what are you looking for, really?" the owner asked breathing heavily.

"I want two Uzis, four magazines, 500 rounds of Black Talon rounds, a pound of C-4 explosive and an M-79 Grenade Launcher," Asam said, as he stood ready for a second attack.

"Whew! Man, you do want some firepower. Do you want some armor, too? A flak jacket or two?"

Asam had a slight smile as he said, "No, no armor." He knew if he had to use these weapons he would probably end up with Allah, anyway.

"Well, that's a pretty big order. It'll cost you about $10,000," the owner said.

Asam reached in his pocket and pulled out $5,000 and laid it on the small desk where the man was sitting, still nursing his wounds.

"Five now and the rest on delivery. But I want the Uzis now," Asam said.

"Aw right! Now we're doin' some bidness," the man said suddenly oblivious to his wounds. "I'll get the Uzi. I've only got one here. I'll have to find another one. But I can give you the M-79 as well."

He left the room and returned huffing with a handled case. He opened the container to show a shining Uzi submachine gun. It was so new the Cosmoline, the shipping gel, was still evident on the barrel. Next to the Uzi was a new M-79 with four rounds. He shut it and pushed it toward Asam.

"I'll have the rest this time next week. Same day, same time. Okay?" the man asked.

Asam mumbled his approval and the man walked with him to unlock the front door. He went directly to his car, placing the case in his front seat, and prepared to cautiously ease out of the parking place into the street.

"Hey, Bill, did you see that?" Grand Prairie Police Officer Tom Whittle said as he and his partner drove by the small pawnshop as part of their routine patrol.

"Naw, what?" answered his partner.

"There was an Arab guy coming out of the pawn shop with a big case. It could have been something."

"Shit, Tom, we've been staking that place out for four weeks looking for weapons and nobody's gotten a damn thing. Now you're seeing terrorists everywhere. It's probably just some rag head redeeming his suitcase," said Bill. "But alright, if you want to harass his ass, we will."

The officer hit his brakes and quickly turned right and into an alley, reversing and heading back to Main Street.

Asam kept his eyes on the police car as it passed and instantly saw the flash of the patrol car's taillights. He saw the officers check their rear view mirrors before making the unplanned reversal. He knew that, for whatever reason, those police were coming to talk to him and he could not be discovered with an illegal weapon.

He slammed the car into gear and did a complete 360-degree turn from the parking space to the blares of horns from oncoming pickups.

He swerved around cars waiting at a stoplight, fishtailing and almost losing control. The tires screeched as he went from the hard-packed gravel of the shoulder to the asphalt of the road. By now the police were in hot pursuit. They had lights flashing and sirens screaming. Worried he couldn't outrun the police car, he kept his foot on the floorboard. The response he received explained to him why SHO stood for Super High Output.

They crossed the concrete bridge outside the Naval Air Station at 130 miles per hour and, as he weaved in and out of the lanes, he could see the pursuers bearing down on him. Other cars were forced off the road behind him.

Entering the turn into Dallas, Asam's car began to slide as he fought the steering wheel to keep the acute angle at the high speed. He careened sideways into a woman in a Mitsubishi, and then righted himself as the other car went flying off of the thoroughfare into a highway sign that collapsed with a shower of sparks.

Asam pulled back on the highway as if he had been thrown from a slingshot. The black and white stripes on the two-foot high retaining wall to his left looked like flashes of light.

The police car was gaining. He looked ahead as the flyaway overpass began to rise and with horror realized that all three lanes were jammed bumper to bumper. There was no place to go. He was traveling too fast to stop.

Asam closed his eyes and used all his might to turn the steering wheel to the left. He heard a dull crumpling sound. His tires were forced nearly flat. He felt a jolt and grimaced at the scraping sound of metal on concrete. The car jumped the highway curb and crashed through the railing on the side. Then there was a silence with only the whistling of wind. The car tilted, riding on air. It sailed down the 10 feet to the median below.

The crash sent Asam's head against the steering wheel, nearly knocking him unconscious. He opened his eyes. Horror was the first emotion he experienced. Jerking his head around, his pupils opened to adjust to the bright environment.

He saw the flashing lights of the police but they were mired a mile back in the rush hour traffic jam. He could make out people leaving their cars and coming to see if he was hurt. Scooting out from under the driver's seat, he grabbed the case and recognized his only chance. He ran across the buzzing interstate, dodging three streams of honking, oncoming cars until he reached a tall fence. He threw his case over it and clamored to the top, dropping to the other side. He looked back long enough to see the policemen throw up their hands as they saw him disappear into Six Flags Over Texas, a gigantic theme park where he would join 300,000 other visitors packed together in a mob of humanity squeezing in the last holiday before the park closed for the year. It was a crowd that would make detection or capture nearly impossible.

Asam wove his way through the multitude and ducked into the first public restroom he could find. Inside a stall he caught his breath and planned his escape. He carefully looked out of the door and took off his jacket and stuffed it in the trash. Within minutes a young maintenance man with an earring and tightly cut hair appeared to empty the container.

"Excuse me," Asam said to the young man. "I am not feeling well and I would like to go home. I do not feel well enough to call or wait for a cab. I don't want to ruin the holiday for my family, though.

"Would you consider driving me to my home? It is not far from here. I will pay you two hundred dollars now and two hundred when we get there," he said as he offered the boy two one hundred dollar bills.

There was no hesitation. The young man quickly stuffed the bills in his pocket.

"Is there a special gate only for employees?" Asam asked.

The boy nodded and said, "It's right down this fence about a half a mile."

"Take this case and meet me at that gate," Asam said. The boy agreed and sped off in his golf cart.

Asam, now stripped of his case and coat, rolled up his sleeves and blended in with the other revelers. He calmly walked to the prearranged location. The boy was already outside the gate with the case. He started walking to an old Dodge and Asam followed. They got in the car and Asam gave him instructions on how to get to Finklestein and Mark.

When they arrived in the area, Asam directed him to a deserted area only a block from the Finklestein and Mark building. The boy looked around and said, "You want out here? This place is …" He was interrupted by a flashing palm that slammed upwards into his face. The blow was centered on his nose and drove his nasal cartilage into his brain. He was dead instantly.

Asam pushed the trunk opener and drug the body to the rear of the car. With sheer strength he loaded the lifeless form into the trunk, reaching in the dead boy's shirt pocket and retrieving the two hundred dollars he had given him. He shut the lid and locked it. He hurriedly slipped into the driver's side and drove to Finklestein and Mark, parking the car behind the building and carrying his case inside.

He went directly to Finklestein's office and explained to him what had happened.

"Don't worry. I'll have the car disposed of tonight. You're sure they don't have a lead on you?" he asked.

"I am certain," Asam said.

"Grand Prairie PD just reported they had been involved in a high speed chase with a suspect that they think was buying arms from a known trafficker.

"Description was a Mid East looking male about 5 foot 6 or 8, hundred and fifty pounds, about forty to forty-five. Believed to have escaped with an unknown number of weapons," McWaters said to Phillips.

"Escaped? How could he have escaped?" Phillips asked.

"Abandoned his car, which was untraceable, and went to Six Flags,"

McWaters said whimsically.

"Oh, my lord. What next?" Phillips wondered. "Get someone over there to see if they can learn any more."

Chapter Nine

The first television commercial aired at 8 p.m. on November 5th, 2001 during a professional football game between the Dallas Cowboys and the Miami Dolphins. The telephones began to ring and continued unabated until 11:00 Central Standard Time. When the evening's business was totaled that one spot had generated over $100,000 in orders for Zaners from every state in the Union.

Laura was ecstatic and so was Strong, who had flown down for the premiere of the first spot. Yet, the joy she felt with the early success of the campaign was eclipsed by her growing guilt at deceiving Andrew.

"Excellent, Mr. Strong. Our bargain seems to have worked. We left you alone to do your work and you've delivered the business. If the rate continues, you'll certainly hit our goal. And if that happens, you can be sure you'll have the next campaign," Finklestein said knowing there would never be any further campaigns and that it was unlikely The Idea Group would ever be paid for this one.

Once they left Dallas, the company would function for a while and then begin the spiral into bankruptcy, leaving The Idea Group one of the hapless unsecured creditors. *Greedy capitalist bastards*, he thought.

Finklestein indicated he wanted a word in private so he and Strong left the conference room and slipped into one of the vacant offices close by. Finklestein shut the door and sat on the corner of a desk. "Strong, I want to thank you for allowing Laura to remain here. Her help was absolutely critical to this being a success. As you can see, if any of the areas she's been working on were not up to speed, we couldn't have performed tonight," he said.

"That's all right," Strong said. "I think it was very shrewd to make sure the operational aspect of the plant was in good shape. I know, though, that Laura is ready to come home and we'll be happy to have her back full time at the agency."

"Actually, I'm going to ask you to bear with us a couple more months and let me keep her until I'm sure the systems are solid. I'm happy to pay her hourly rate but I would like a monthly rate instead of a daily one."

"Quite candidly, it isn't an issue of money. This has been very hard on Laura and it's time to get her back. If you feel you need more support, we can send someone else who is familiar with the account, now that the initial work is done."

"That will not be acceptable, Strong," Finklestein said. "I want her here. And if you're worried about how she feels, ask her. I think you'll find she is quite comfortable with the idea."

"All right. If Laura is amenable to the idea she can stay but for only one more month. Will that work for you?"

"That will be fine."

Laura is not going to like that. I know she's got to be sick of being here. I'm not even sure paying her a fortune will make her want to do this. I'll get through tonight and then figure out how to handle it.

Laura was busy trying to decipher how the traffic was handled and if the orders were being properly logged and transmitted to shipping. After she was satisfied there, she went to the manufacturing and stocking department.

"How are we holding out, Malcolm?" she asked the manufacturing head.

"I think it'll be fine, Ms. Newcomb. You hit it on the nail, quantity-wise. How much more do we have to go?"

"Oh, Malcolm, this is just the beginning. We'll be reaching nearly 100 million American families before this is over. Remember, we set up those red flags to warn us when our orders might be exceeding our capacity. That's when we go to a second shift. Just watch those and we'll be okay," she said.

She couldn't help being proud of herself. She had thought this out to the very last detail. Every eventuality had been considered and redundancies in systems had been built into every step. If they didn't attract two and a half million new subscribers, it wouldn't be her fault.

But there was one thing of which she was not proud. She had sold her integrity. She was no better than a common Judas. She had tried to rationalize it every way she could. It didn't work.

Last week she had called the agency and talked to Strong about the areas of the campaign he thought were the weakest and if it were to fail, where would it show up first. He had carefully analyzed the entire campaign and was keenly aware of where there could be trouble, as well as having an emergency plan to deal with it. Then, after he had sworn her to absolute secrecy, she wrote a confidential memo to Finklestein alerting him.

Try though she might to ignore her inner voices, she felt dirty. She wasn't a dishonest person and the deceit she was practicing was wearing on her.

Throughout the night Strong had been praising her and telling everyone how important she was to the agency. Just before the spot aired, Strong stood up and asked to say a few words.

"In a few minutes we'll experience the most important 30 seconds in the life of not only Finklestein and Mark but The Idea Group as well. I promise you, none of our lives will ever be the same again," he beamed. "And a lot of the reason for that is Laura Newcomb. She took on the toughest job in the agency and, as I think you'll see, did it perfectly. Laura, this is from The Idea Group, to the best idea we ever had—hiring you."

With that he handed her a handsome sterling silver bowl from Bergdorff Goodman with an appreciative message engraved on it. That didn't do much for her sense of ethics. It was all she could do to keep from crying.

As the evening wore on, most of the people drifted home. Finklestein and Strong left after the sales tabulation was completed. She remained and continued Finally after midnight, when the orders had subsided, she rang for Eric, her driver.

"I think I'm ready, Eric," she sighed.

"I'll be at the front door, Ms. Newcomb," he responded.

The car was waiting and Eric was quick to open the door for her. She settled into the backseat and almost fell asleep on the way to the hotel. She went directly to her room and undressed as she walked to the bed, letting her clothes drop to the floor where they fell, getting in and falling asleep without even taking off her makeup.

It was a happy scene. The rolling meadow was a carpet of green punctuated with explosions of color in dozens of patches of wildflowers. Clouds of monarch butterflies swirled and dived, softly pumping their delicate wings, silent playmates on a playground that had to have come from Heaven. She delighted in the way they hesitated until the last moment, then smoothly swerved out of the way of the running kids. The children were dressed in new play clothes, laughing and romping and she was taking such pleasure in watching them. She laughed as they surprised each other, rolling with laughter and playful screams.

"Come on, Mama," the little girl yelled to a partially obscured parent. "Play with us. Catch us!"

The child ran up, eyes bright and face eager with anticipation, touched her mother quickly as if she were a hot stove and then, in an eruption of giggles, ran away as fast as she could. The boy followed her lead and escaped the mother's grasp with cascades of yelps.

Laura couldn't resist the temptation to join in the fun, and jumped from her place on the blanket, chasing after them through the flowered pasture. The wild flowers were so big they masked her view and she could only guess that she was running in the right direction. She followed their little voices as they taunted her, saying, "You can't find us, Laura," in a singsong rhythm.

She ran laughing and yelling, pledging she would find them and when she did, promising them the tickling of a lifetime. She loved playing like that, had missed it so much. It was so much fun, she and her brother all happy and waiting for their mother to find them.

She burst through the high grass and suddenly found the children in a clearing. They were sitting in a semi-circle with their backs to her but something was wrong. The wildflowers had been replaced with nasty, dismal clouds that formed a shroud about the clearing. There was no laughter; instead a peculiar, unhappy sound resonated from them.

Was it groaning? What was it? She had heard it before, many times. Then they turned to her and she remembered the sound. They were crying.

Rivers of tears flowed from their little eyes, red now from the salt, their small noses emitting streams that ran down their faces. But they had been so happy just a minute ago. What's wrong? She asked so she could fix it but they didn't answer, they just pointed to the center of the circle and then moved apart so she could see the focus of their pain.

She wanted to vomit when she saw it.

Her sweet, loving mother lay lifeless, broken on the crushed flowers and trampled butterflies of the meadow floor.

How had this happened? Who did this? As she looked in anguish at the helpless dead form she realized there was another shape looming over her. Her gaze was slowly forced upward to the figure standing over her dear mama, peering down at them. As her head and eyes moved up over the form, she reached its face and saw a hard, demanding countenance. She couldn't quite make the face out, but she thought it was a narrow, bearded face. Suddenly, the features dissolved and glowed red and Laura began to cry, and finally to howl in agony and terror as the red thing grew larger and larger.

She screamed, and at that instant her eyes snapped open, her heart racing and her face was wet with tears.

The red message light on his phone stared back at her and continued to throb like a single eye in the darkness of the room. She sat upright in the bed where she'd fallen asleep, drenched in sweat.

"My God," she said, breathing hard from the nightmare. She shook her head to clear it, then picked up the phone and dialed the front desk.

"Yes, Ms. Newcomb," the night operator said. "How may I help you?"

"My message light," Laura said. "It's on."

"Oh, yes, ma'am," the operator said. "Your mother called from

Oklahoma City. She left a message to tell you that she knew tonight would go well and that she was so proud of you."

"Thank you," Laura said. She gently replaced the receiver in its cradle and turned on her side, took a deep breath and buried her face into the pillow, and cried.

☆

When Laura arrived at the office the next day Strong had already called. She returned his call with a certain amount of trepidation.

"Great night last night wasn't it?" he asked.

"Certainly was," Laura responded, trying to sound believable.

"I spoke to Finklestein last night. He wants you to stay another month. Can you stand it?" Strong asked.

"Sure. That's fine," she responded.

"Really?" he asked. "If you don't mind, it would sure help. I'll tell him it's a done deal." He sounded skeptical but didn't push the issue. She wondered if he was suspicious.

She hung up the phone and felt herself slipping deeper and deeper into an abyss of deceit.

☆

Strong stared at the phone. *What's wrong with this picture?* he thought. *Laura Newcomb has been agitated that this project has gone longer than expected and that she has been separated from her home and her mother. Now, all of a sudden, she is ever so casual about extending it another month.*

Strong was an astute businessman in an industry that was filled with incompetent entrepreneurs. He could spot blips on the radar screen and this was clearly a big blip.

Chapter Ten

The promotion was going "swimmingly" as Strong liked to say. For three weeks the campaign machine had been churning out the message and the American public had been responding. The factory was now into a second shift and FedEx was making four pickups stops a day. America was becoming "Zaner Country," just as it had become "Marlboro Country" forty years before. But the latter was far more fatal than the former.

Strong had arrived in Dallas for an early morning meeting with Finklestein and stopped by to see Laura before he went in.

"Hi," he said cheerfully. "How's it going?"

"Great," she replied, cringing with the lie she was telling. "How is everything at the office?"

"Good. We got a partial check for the television production this week so that has helped. Will you see if you can get our invoices moved to the top of the stack? It would really make a difference."

"Are they not paying on time?" she asked, surprised.

"Well, they are a little slow. They were late on the last set of invoices and as you well know, we have little reserves to cover a hole like that in cash flow." Strong smiled.

As attuned to the financial condition of the agency as Andrew is, he has got to be panicking, she thought.

"Does Finklestein feel like the campaign is as great as I think it is?"

he asked, changing the subject.

"He seems to be happy. Let's just hope it continues," Laura said, her mind still on the unpaid invoices.

"It will, just wait til it gets some momentum," Strong grinned.

Poor Andrew, he's so dazzled by the excitement, he can't even see what's being done to him, she thought.

Strong went to his meeting and waved good-bye as he left the building with his set of marching orders from Finklestein.

The whole encounter had been unnerving for Laura. *She had to talk to Finklestein. She couldn't keep on like this. Her attempts to rationalize her actions by thinking she was ensuring that The Idea Group kept the account weren't working. At the very least she had to resign from the agency. She felt like a thief. No, a liar. No, a tramp. Hell, all of those things.*

She finished the report she was working on and got up from her chair and walked down the hall to Finklestein's office.

"Is Mr. Finklestein in, Megan?" she asked.

"I'm sorry, Ms. Newcomb. He's in with Mr. Al-Lamri. Has been all morning since Mr. Strong left and said he was not to be disturbed."

"Call me when he has a moment, will you?"

"Of, course," Megan said.

Laura walked back to her office. *Maybe, it's not all me. Now that I think about it, there are some pretty strange things around here. Its not just the two year thing, although that's not been explained why everybody here thinks the place has been around for 15 years and yet there's not a person or record that goes back over twenty-four months.*

Or take the bank account. When I went through accounting, there wasn't enough cash, or assets that could be turned into cash, to finance this expansion. Plus, I didn't see one payroll check to Finklestein.

And, his telephone is a separate line and is charged for a scrambler service. And another thing, who the hell is this guy? He's never said where he was from, where he worked before and where is this Mark guy we never see? It's time I got some answers.

☆

The next morning, by the time she reached her office, Laura was wound up tight. She had spent a sleepless night beating herself up for what she was doing. She picked up the phone and called the agency. She needed to talk to Strong. All of a sudden, she didn't care if she lost this job. She had to get out.

"Is Andrew there?" she pleaded when the receptionist answered.

"No, Laura," the girl said, recognizing her voice. "He went to the bank. Should be back today. Is there a problem?"

Laura thought for a moment. It would be unwise to give the impression there was trouble. Andrew would surely overreact.

"No, of course not. Just have him call me, please, as soon as he gets back."

She hung up and looked up around the room. *She had allowed herself to ignore the warning signs that something was not right. How stupid could she be? There was something seriously wrong with this company and it was time to follow the threads and find out what it was.*

She went to the Accounting department and sat at one of the empty consoles. Entering the passwords, she called up the bookkeeping system on the computer.

Seeing her, the supervisor walked over and asked, "Can I help you with anything, Ms. Newcomb?"

"No, no, Marjorie. I just needed to check some figures," she stuttered and turned back to the screen.

Clearly uncomfortable with her unscheduled appearance, the supervisor shrugged but walked away.

Laura ran the payables report back to the first, January two years ago. She ran the receivables back to the same date. She pulled a financial statement from the beginning and it showed retained earnings but no record of where they came from.

She double-checked the bank accounts. Clearly, there wasn't enough cash to pay for this multi-million dollar advertising campaign and there had been no capital injection, save the sales income, since the ads started and now bills were being moved from "on receipt" pay to "60-day pay" classification.

We're starting to borrow from the vendors. And that includes

Andrew. She signed off and left the department, walking with a new urgency in her step.

The Shipping and Ordering Department was also into a second shift and had tripled in size and staff. She went into the windowed alcove that served the manager as an office and asked if she could check a few records.

"Sure, Ms. Newcomb. I need to go out on the floor anyway," he said. He excused himself and walked out onto the floor to supervise a forklift.

As she suspected, the orders started coming in two years ago in January. They came from all over the country, and not just one or two orders but dozens all at once. And every order was a full order indicating the subscription was a new one.

She left and walked to the manufacturing area. After checking in with the supervisor she sat at his offered desk and started going through records, finding the same thing. No increasing volume. Just start day one with a full load. She continued to review the records until the manager interrupted her.

"Scuze me, Ms. Newcomb, but I was getting ready to head home and needed to lock my desk," he said apologetically.

"I'm sorry, I didn't realize it was so late," she said glancing at her watch surprised it was 6 p.m.

She got up from the desk and began hurrying down the hall just as the phone rang. She heard the manager pick it up and say, "Yes sir, she's here." By the time he turned to call her to the phone, she had disappeared. *They were looking for her and she didn't want to be found.*

Back in her office she had just begun to review her notes when the phone rang.

"Hey, kid," said the voice on the other end.

She exhaled an audible sigh and rested her forehead in her hand. "Andrew, I'm so glad you called. I've got some things I need to discuss with you."

"Sure, I've tried to return your call all day but could never get you," said Strong. "What's up?"

"I'm not sure," she responded, looking around her to make sure she was alone.

"Nothing's wrong with the campaign, is there?" he asked, a trace of panic clear in his voice.

"No, but other things. There's something not right here. You remember all the things I was worried about at the outset? The fast pay, the no past history to speak of?" she said.

"Yeah," Strong said cautiously. "I thought we had resolved all that."

"No, I'm afraid not. Andrew, there is something going on that makes me think this company is a sham. They're running out of cash fast and there's no capital injection taking place." She knew that would get his attention.

"Uh, oh. If they default, we're history. Why would they be a sham? I don't get it."

"I don't completely, either. But I think they aren't out to make a profit. I think there's another agenda. They want to move vitamins, for sure. But they're not running the place like they want to stay in business.

"And if you think about it, I've been here for weeks and I still don't know anything about Finklestein. I mean nada. Plus, he hasn't taken a salary, ever. How about that? For two years. Not stock options, zilch. And I know a lot about this company.

"I've looked at enough operations during my days with Arthur to spot a shell when I see it." Suddenly, her line went dead. She tapped the phone button but the line remained dark.

She looked up. Al-Lamri was standing in her doorway.

"Ah, Ms. Newcomb. I wonder if I might have a little of your time?" he asked in a heavily accented voice.

"Uh, of course, Mr. Al-Lamri. What can I do for you?" she said as she gently placed the receiver on the cradle.

"Actually, I'd like to show you a restaurant a friend of mine owns. You and your firm have done such a wonderful job here, I wonder if you might be able to help him. You see, he is new to this country and doesn't quite understand the nuances of marketing and his operation, while providing a top-notch product, is not enjoying the success he had hoped. He is from Saudi and is quite wealthy so he could easily afford your services," Al-Lamri said smiling.

Just as she was beginning to deliver a spur of the moment story explaining why the agency had decided long ago to avoid restaurants, her phone rang.

"Excuse me," she said, happy for any distraction to buy time as she picked up the handset. "Yes?"

"Ms. Newcomb," Finklestein's cold voice echoed over the line. "Mr. Al-Lamri will be visiting with you concerning a favor. I would appreciate it if you would accommodate him and at least evaluate his friend's place. If you can't, or don't want to handle the account, you can pass it on to a competitor but I know he would be grateful for the professional opinion."

"He's here now and, of course, I'll be happy to help," Laura said, knowing she was trapped.

"Thank you so much," Finklestein said unemotionally and rang off.

How did he know where I was? How did Al-Lamri know where I was?

"That is excellent," Al-Lamri said after listening to the conversation. "I had hoped you would consent to help and have taken the liberty of telling your driver, Eric, that I would escort you from the office tonight. Say seven o'clock?"

Laura gave the powerfully built Al-Lamri a weak smile, feeling more and more apprehensive about what was ahead of her. All she could think about now was getting out of here and making things right. The dream about her mother had awakened her to her ethics. She'd do what she had to do to not tip her hand but as soon as she could flee, she'd be on a plane back to Oklahoma City and *nobody* would get her back here again.

Al-Lamri returned to her door promptly at seven. Laura had tried to call the agency twice but each time got a busy signal. She hoped that it was only trouble on the lines. The trunks sometimes got jammed out of Dallas.

Al-Lamri drove them to north Dallas and parked the car at a nondescript restaurant in a strip shopping center on Royal Lane. They were greeted by the owner and taken to a secluded table in the back corner of the dining room. The dimly lit room looked like a thousand other neighborhood cafes she had seen and wondered why he was worried. These things always did well, if the food was only marginal. Even on a weeknight he had a respectable crowd.

"Please, I would like your opinion on the menu, the food, the atmosphere—everything," Al-Lamri said. "Permit me to start the meal with a special wine that is made here on the premises."

Smiling, the owner appeared with two generous goblets for both of them. "To you," said Al-Lamri and clinked his glass to hers. Laura didn't want to drink but felt she must at least have a sip to keep from giving offense and actually, the wine was excellent.

The evening progressed with Al-Lamri ordering the dinner and asking questions about The Idea Group, who was involved and how deeply. The food was good enough but she hadn't paid attention to the steady sipping she had been doing on the wine. Suddenly, she had trouble focusing on Al-Lamri. His voice seemed to be coming from underwater and she thought she was going to throw up. Then, the room darkened.

Finklestein told Megan to hold all calls. He closed the last of his desk drawers and locked it. He looked around the office searching for anything that might give a clue as to his destination or plans. He opened the wall safe and withdrew a Smith & Wesson .357 magnum without serial numbers and $100,000 in cash. The cash was bulky and he carefully placed it in an aluminum briefcase and locked it, dropping the key in his pocket. He stuffed the pistol in his leather attaché case and set both cases on the chair by the door.

"Ready to go?" Asam asked as he entered quietly.

"Almost," Finklestein replied, his eyes scanning the room once more. "How did it go with Laura Newcomb last night?"

"It was easy. She passed out quickly and we got her out of the restaurant without anyone even noticing. Anyone who did see would have thought she was drunk.

"She's secured in the place you recommended. You are very clever. It is so out of the way that she won't be discovered for months and by then, she'll be dead. How did you know she had learned of the secret?"

"Oh, I don't think she had totally figured it out yet, but the telephone monitors were showing she was getting very suspicious. Her last call to Strong had to be disconnected and blocked. That's why we couldn't wait any longer," Finklestein said.

"Won't she be missed?" Asam asked.

"I'm taking care of that. We have enough of her voice tracks that I've synthesized a message from her to Strong's answering machine. Listen," Finklestein said as he entered a command into his computer.

Suddenly, Laura's voice, or what certainly sounded like her voice, said "Hi, Andrew. Sorry I got cut off today, the phones were acting strange. Anyway, I'll be out of the office for the next week, maybe two. Finklestein is sending me to Los Angeles to visit a couple of pharmaceutical labs that might be able to save him some money in making the vitamins. It's going to be crazy with the time changes so don't worry if you don't hear from me. I'll call you next week. Bye-bye."

"That's amazing," Asam said. "You can do all of that with your computer?"

"Easily," Finklestein answered. "That takes care of the agency for a week anyway, and the people here won't even miss her. They expect her to come and go. She's been checked out of the hotel and anything that is connected to her destroyed. In a week you and I will be in Tehran where no one can touch us.

"I wasn't expecting that you and I would have to leave for another month but given Ms. Laura's little investigation, I suppose we should make our exit now. I don't expect anyone to even begin to look for us for a thirty days if then."

"What if someone comes searching for her?" Asam asked.

"Eric," Finklestein replied.

"Eric?"

"Yes, you've met him. Newcomb's driver? But he's more than a driver. He's our assassin. You should identify with him." Finklestein flashed an evil smile. "He'll take care of anyone who threatens the plan. He's to stay here until we are in Tehran then escape if he can and if not, gladly give his life for Allah. You didn't think I would leave her to die a natural death did you? Eric will take care of it and it won't take months.

"My assistant has been briefed that I'll be spending Christmas in Canada and then staying until New Years. She is to hold all messages and I'll deal with them when I get back. Everything else will operate as always, until they run out of money, of course."

"Where did all of that money come from?" Asam asked pointing to the briefcase.

"Skimmed profits. We may need to buy our way into or out of a couple of places on our journey so we'll be ready. Otherwise, it goes to the Reis. It was his money that started this.

"Let's get started. I've got to clean up a few loose ends and make sure there's nothing left at my condo. I want to be at the plane by three."

They walked to the door, switched off the light and locked the office as they left. They passed by Megan without speaking.

Chapter Eleven

New Canaan, Connecticut

Becky Henderson walked quickly to her BMW. The cold New England winter was in full force and she wanted to get her Christmas shopping finished to avoid the crowds and the harsh weather. Ever since the Asian flu had hit her the year before, causing her to actually pass out on her bathroom floor, she had been especially careful about her health.

At 51, her immune system wasn't what it used to be and she shivered as she pulled her suede coat tight around her. She got in the car and placed her coffee cup in the holder in the console.

Like so many other Americans, Becky was diabetic and that made her particularly susceptible to infection. Those limitations were part of the reason she had started on the new, powerful vitamins, Zaners. This year she wasn't taking any chances.

She drove to the short and fashionable Main Street in the small commuter suburb and circled for ten minutes before she found a parking place. She got lucky and slipped her car into a space in front of the Starbucks Coffee House. She had finished her cup of coffee in the car and decided to have another before she started shopping. Becky didn't ask for much but she did demand a constant flow of hot java. It woke her up and kept her energy level elevated.

"You can take away my husband, but leave me my coffee," she often joked.

She ordered her regular brew and sat down to enjoy the steaming cup before going to pick out the Christmas dance dress asked for by her 16-year-old daughter. As she sipped the coffee she experienced the warming effect of the liquid move throughout her body. Renewed, she drained the Styrofoam cup and headed out of the store to attack the seasonal shopping.

Once on the cobblestone sidewalk, she stopped at an intersection to wait fifteen seconds on a traffic light to change. By the time the light had gone from red to green, Becky Henderson had fallen to the concrete, her heart stopped, never to beat again.

☆

Strong pressed the rewind button again on his answering machine. He listened to the message for the third time and still, there was something out of place.

Sorry about that, but he wasn't buying that he's cut off in the middle of a telephone conversation with Laura telling him something is screwed up and then gets a voice mail that says everything is peachy! Bullshit. He had tried to call her back and all he got was someone telling him she had already left the building. More bullshit, he had just talked to her. He turned off the machine and called Southwest Airlines.

He got on the early flight to Dallas the next morning and had a chance to consider all that had occurred. *Had he been in denial? Was it because the account was so desperately important to him that he had ignored the warning signs and let a person be put in danger?*

Laura had been trying to tell him but he hadn't been listening. She was isolated in Dallas totally under the control of this Finklestein. And he had let it happen, looking the other way because he wanted the business. *This bullshit was about to stop, big account or no big account.*

He was going to find out whatever was going on. It had been years since he had been in the Marine Corps but the admonition to "Take care of your troops and your troops will take care of you" was still an integral part of the way he managed his company and his life. Maybe he had strayed a little from it because of the almighty buck but he was going to make a comeback. Once at Love Field he rented a car and went straight to Finklestein and Mark. He entered the reception area as he had done dozens of times before.

"Hello, Mr. Strong," said Megan cheerily.

"Hello, Megan. Where can I find Ms. Newcomb?" he asked matter of factly.

"She's on the west coast on an assignment for Mr. Finklestein," she answered without the cheerful tone and no longer maintaining eye contact.

"I see. Where can she be reached?"

"Well, she didn't leave a number but said she would call in," Megan said.

"How about Mr. Finklestein?"

"Mr. Finklestein is out of town until after Christmas and can't be reached," she said.

It didn't take long for Strong to figure out that no answers were going to be coming from Megan. He left her with promises he would return. As he drove to the Anatole Hotel he realized that the whole scheme that Finklestein had set up was one that would allow him to control, even confine Laura. For all he knew she could be locked in a closet. But why? He knew with her concern for her mother she wouldn't put herself in a position where she couldn't be reached for an hour let alone days.

If he had been wrong, then he would have gotten a lot more answers from Megan and she would have been far more eager to help. Being able to read people was one of his strengths and he was reading Megan completely. She was hiding something. One thing Strong had learned over the years was that you don't have to know what is wrong to know something is wrong.

He arrived at the Anatole and parked the car. The manager on duty knew Strong, so it was easy to find out that Laura had checked out. No, nobody saw her or talked to her. Eric, her driver, did it all.

Strong didn't like this one bit. He thought for a moment to decide the best way to handle the situation. He couldn't stand around and wait in line until someone would listen to him. He could go to the Dallas police and get put in line with everyone else and wait for the system to work. The Marine Corps was the only system he trusted.

By this time he was convinced that Laura was in real danger and the longer he waited, the greater the jeopardy to her.

Strong believed it's not what you know but who you know. True to that, he wracked his memory to try to come up with someone who might be in a position to help. Being in Dallas made it tough because he didn't have as many contacts as in Oklahoma City and then he remembered a fellow that had been the featured speaker, recently, at the black tie dinner for one of his favorite organizations, The Fifty Committee. Devoted to supporting the law enforcement agencies, the group contributed thousands each year to families of downed firefighters and police and was highly revered by the law and order agencies in the region.

He dialed the number of the FBI field office in Dallas and asked for the director, Richard Otis. When questioned by the receptionist as to who was calling, Strong said, "Andrew Strong with the Fifty Committee in Oklahoma City." Otis finally answered after five minutes of holding.

"Hello, Andrew. How are you?" the stern voice said.

"Mr. Otis, I didn't know if you'd remember me, " Andrew started and was interrupted.

"Of course, I do. I'll never forget that great steak that you bought me at the Oklahoma City Country Club," and then with slightly more urgency, "How can I help you?"

Strong sensed the impatience in his voice and cut right to the chase. "I have a friend who is missing and I suspect foul play. I don't know anyone in the local police and I don't want to waste time wading through paperwork. I thought you could give me some advice and maybe a head start on finding her before I had to go to them.

"I know something like a missing person is not an FBI matter but I need some help. Will you give me a few minutes of your time?"

"I'm sorry, Andrew," the Field Director sad, "but we're in the middle of an all-consuming project right now and I'm very strapped for time."

"Please, Mr. Otis, I won't take but a moment. I'm really concerned she may be in danger," Strong pleaded knowing that he was calling in every favor he might ever expect of the man.

There was a pregnant pause on the line. Strong chewed the inside of his lip. He knew this was the only shot he had. "Is this something that we can do over the phone? I really am quite busy."

Strong hesitated. It would be easy to tell him everything but, no, he wanted to be face to face to make sure something happened. Conducting business on the phone made it too easy to hang up and forget it. "Actually, I'm afraid this needs to be done in person," he said.

Again a call and a hint of a frustrated sigh, "All right, when can you be here?" Otis said, the annoyance evident in his voice.

"Give me half an hour," Strong replied.

"Very well. We're in the Cabell Building on Commerce. Do you know it?" Otis asked.

"I do. I'll be there in thirty minutes," Strong said and flipped his cellular phone shut.

"I'm afraid I don't have much time," Otis smiled as he entered the small room where Strong had been seated and told to wait. He was about fifty-five, with a receding hairline and graying hair. At 6 feet and over 200 pounds, he was an impressive figure even at his age. "You say you have a missing person?" he said as he offered his beefy hand to Strong.

Strong relayed the whole situation, how they got the Finklestein and Mark account, how F&M had asked for Laura, and once she was there never let her come back. He told of her bizarre telephone call and the subsequent message she left for him. Otis listened quietly only occasionally asking questions. The more Strong talked the more it began to sound to him as if he might have exaggerated the seriousness of the clues.

Finally when Strong had finished, Otis said, "So something was wrong with the message, huh? Is it still on your answering machine?" Strong nodded.

"Okay, well, we have people, analysts, who can quickly determine if a person is under duress from a recording. We don't normally have them in the field offices but I happen to have one here today on a demonstration visit from the FBI Academy in Quantico. If I have him listen to your message, run it through the system and conclude that your colleague was just leaving a simple message for you, will that satisfy you that she's all right?" Otis asked.

Embarrassed, Strong stuttered, "Yes, of course."

Otis called in an assistant. Strong gave him his phone number and code for the answering machine. Before the man left, Otis said, "Give the agent the names of the key people in this client company and we'll have them run through the computer just to make sure none of them have a record." Strong complied a short list of Finklestein, Mark, whom he had never met, Eric and the new guy, Al-Lamri. He handed it to Otis who passed the names to the agent who then left the room.

"I bet we'll have this mystery solved for you in about twenty minutes," Otis smiled. "If you'll excuse me, Andrew, I really am pressed for time. Agent Pinon, the man you just met, will be back with the results of the inquiry."

"Thank you, Director. This means a great deal," Strong said as he once again shook Otis' hand.

Strong sat and waited in the mini-room and, as the minutes ticked away, began to worry that he had overreacted and was making a fool of himself by taking up the time of a man who was obviously overworked and highly stressed. Then, to his surprise, Otis and the agent reentered the room. With a startled and concerned look on his face, the Field Director exclaimed, "We have a problem."

"What is it?" Strong said, standing up.

"You were right. There *was* something wrong with the message. It was totally synthesized. They must have had her voice tracks," Otis said.

"That means they've been recording her!"

"That's right. But here's the kicker on who 'they' are," Otis said. "None of the names you gave me exist in any of our databases. No driver's licenses, no tax returns, no military service, no bank records, nothing. Except for your Mr. Al-Lamri and, while it seems he has only existed for a few weeks, there are quite a few people looking for him. There's something going on here for sure and I'm afraid you may have reason for concern.

"We'll need to ask you some questions. Agent Pinon will work with you. In the meantime, I need to call some folks in Washington who are going to be very interested in this. You'll excuse me," he said as he left the room.

Strong's heart began to beat rapidly.

Chapter Twelve

The air was damp and heavy. There wasn't a scintilla of light anywhere and Laura had to feel her own face to convince herself she wasn't dead. Her head ached and her shoulders had piercing pains resulting, she realized, from having her hands tied behind her back for how long?

The last thing she remembered was sitting with Al-Lamri at that damned restaurant. She had been a fool. They knew she was on to them and were simply going to take her out and she played right into their hands. But something was missing. They wouldn't have gone to all this trouble to have her escape and blow the whistle on them. Clearly, they were going to kill her and she just wasn't sure why they hadn't done it already. She wondered if they were distributing illegal drugs and she just hadn't figured it out yet. *My God, it's probably some damn drug cartel.*

She tried to pull herself to a sitting position to figure out where she was. She felt so tightly confined. "Hello? Is anybody there?" she screamed. Her voice sounded frail and the words seemed to be muffled as soon as she uttered them. She tried again with the same results.

She struggled to her feet only to slam her head against a strange-feeling ceiling that forced her back to her knees. Unable to free her hands, she slowly raised herself again until her face could feel the rough surface of the overhead. *Where am I? What kind of hellhole is this?*

She sank back to her knees and began to carefully move until she hit an obstruction. Oddly, it had the same feel as the ceiling. And both had an unusual smell. *What kind of box had she been put in?* The barrier continued as she made her way around the cubicle, gently feeling the walls with her cheek. Her knees were aching painfully and finally she had to slump to a sitting position. *I've got to get my hands free,* she thought.

She struggled to pull her hands out of the plastic cord that held them together behind her back. Pull though she might the cords simply cut into her flesh. She could feel the warm blood dripping from her cuts and her hands swelling, making escape difficult and unlikely.

She realized there was only one way to get out. With a huge effort she arched her back over and pulled her wrists under her buttocks in an attempt to slip her hands through. It didn't work. She was now caught in a ball with her shoulders in extreme pain from the added pressure. She couldn't move.

Her first reaction was panic and then, as quickly as it surfaced, she dismissed it. *I got myself into this disaster because I didn't do what my mother taught me. By God, I'll get myself out and fix this mess!*

With a massive effort, she writhed like a contortionist in the darkness on the hard wooden plank floor, summoning all her strength to pull her hands to the front of her body. She screamed as she felt muscle and sinew tear and shoulders dislocate. With a colossal push she brought her hands over her twisted legs. But the strain was too much for her body and she passed out from the searing pain and fell flat, her bound hands pulled close to her breasts.

Laura opened her eyes and for a moment was frightened that there was no light. Remembering her situation, she tried to sit up. It was easier with her hands in front. She must have been out for hours. The air was stale and it had gotten much warmer in her diminutive chamber. She touched her wrists' binding with her tongue and concluded it was a simple plastic tie used for packaging. She began to chew on it and within an hour had gnawed through the restraint.

Once she had freed her hands she rubbed her wrists, careful of the deep gouges that the tie had made, and then began to examine the surrounding walls.

I know that texture! It's burlap! She continued her exploration and detected a substance below the burlap. As she rubbed it between her fingers she realized she had cotton in her hands.

Good Lord! I'm surrounded by cotton bales! That's why no one can hear me! That's why there's no light. I must be in a cotton compress where they bundle and store this stuff! She tried to move the bales but quickly realized nothing short of a tractor would budge the 500-pound cubes. Sweating from the rising heat and exhausted, she sat back and tried to devise a plan to gain her freedom.

Unaware that the oxygen was becoming thinner, she began to feel lightheaded and drifted into unconsciousness. She couldn't hear the rumbling ignition of the diesel engine of the compress' forklift outside her prison as it moved close to her cell.

"They've found him!" Coy McWaters said as he read the dispatch to Michael Phillips. "The Dallas FBI field office had a man come in with a missing person report. Don't ask me why he came to them — and it seems Al-Lamri was tied into it.

"They also found enough strange stuff connected with him that we may have found the operation and remainder of the cell. A company called Finklestein and Mark. They make Zaner vitamins and —" Coy stopped abruptly and looked up at Phillips, alarm in his face. The silence was deafening. Their eyes locked.

"Oh, my God," Phillips whispered. "All this time we thought it was an explosive threat. Get everybody in here right now!"

The team quickly assembled in the main room. Phillips relayed the information hurriedly to the group. "If they're using Zaner vitamins to transmit a virus or something, no telling how many people are being infected. Mays, Brill and Jennings, get to Dallas now and try to take those guys out. Brill, there will be FBI and Dallas PD personnel already organized into teams. Take command of them. See what the FBI and DPD have on them. Brown, you go with them and tap into the computers at that company and see how many people and who they are that have taken the stuff. Carolyn, set up a command post in Dallas. We're moving."

Brill and his team were a block from the Finklestein and Mark Building in two hours. The SWAT team comprised of Dallas PD and FBI personnel were awaiting their instructions as to what to do. Brill ordered them to cordon off the area and begin closing down the perimeter until they had a tight noose around the building.

"That place is pretty secure," Mays said looking through his binoculars from the car. "It's got security and steel doors."

"I don't want to give them time to destroy anything. I'm going to try to finesse my way in. Listen, and if you need to mount an assault, do it in a hurry," Brill said.

He checked his flak vest and body intercom and left the car and walked up to the front door, ringing the bell. After identifying himself as Mr. Brill with the Food and Drug Administration, the door buzzed and he walked right in.

He marched straight to the receptionist and pulled out his badge. "I am federal officer Brill and this facility is now under federal control. Unlock that door immediately!" the receptionist was terrified and quickly pushed the unlock button.

"Occupy the facility," Brill ordered to the waiting officers as the door buzzed incessantly as the lock was held in check. He scanned the room to ensure there was no resistance.

The police quickly flooded into the building and began isolating the different areas.

"Please have your people begin the interviews with all the personnel. Let's see what we have here," Brill said to one of the FBI agents.

With military precision, the factory was secured and each person began a series of intensive interrogations, or the more politically correct word "interviews," by professionals who could extract information from subjects who were unaware they held the information. Within an hour the reports pointed to a plan that Finklestein had hoped would not become public for months to come.

"Where is this Eric fellow? He seems to be the only other one who is directly connected with Finklestein and Al-Lamri," Phillips asked as Brill briefed him on the results of the interviews.

"We think he's still in Dallas. He left an hour before we got there."

"Find all three of them! I don't want them to get out of the country," Phillips demanded.

Coy McWaters picked up the phone and in an instant was connected with FBI Field Director Otis. McWaters issued the orders to find the trio and listened for a moment to the reply.

His face reddened and the normally contained man erupted into the phone, "I don't give a fuck what kind of problems you have. I don't care if their trail is cold. I don't care if they're invisible. You goddamn find them within 24 hours or you'll be out of the FBI, period. You got it, Otis?" After hearing the answer, McWaters slammed the phone down and stood panting.

The room was quiet and then the flurry of noise quickly returned.

"I may be wound a little tight," he muttered to Phillips.

"You had better be. We all had better be," replied Phillips.

It hadn't taken long for Director Otis to call in every asset the FBI had in the area and put them on point to find Finklestein and Al-Lamri. Agents were combing every possible exit within a three-state area. Telephones were busy, the Internet was buzzing, state and local police were alerted and their governors appropriately informed by the White House.

"Director, we may have something on the one called Eric," an agent said as he handed a message to Otis. "His car has been spotted in McKinney."

Otis looked at the dispatch and said, "Let's get over there."

Strong got up and began to walk out with Otis.

"Hold on, you can't go. You're a civilian. This is too dangerous," Otis said as he put his hand on Strong's chest.

"No way I'm being left out of this, Director. My friend is still missing and that guy was her driver. And besides, you wouldn't even know what was going on if I hadn't brought this to your attention. You owe me," Strong demanded.

Otis hesitated for a moment and then said, "Well, maybe you're right. In any event we may need some background information and right now you're the only one that can provide it. Just keep your head down." They poured out of the office at a run headed for a point in a suburb northeast of Dallas.

In less than forty minutes they arrived at the Federal Compress, a huge 100,000 square foot building that contained a massive bailing machine for cotton and acres of storage space for the thousands of bales of cotton that were to eventually be shipped throughout the world. Eric's Cadillac SLS was parked outside.

"McKinney PD hasn't shown up yet and we can't wait on them. Go ahead and call Phillips and his boys and let them know where we are," Otis said to an agent on the radio. "I'm sure they'll want a piece of this but they're going to have to take seconds."

He turned to Strong. " Let's go, but be careful."

Laura coughed. She seemed to have something in her throat and her head ached with a pain worse than any migraine she'd ever experienced. She opened her eyes and the light caused her to squint until her pupils could adjust to the new brightness level.

When she could make out the blurry sight that was moving toward her, her blood went cold. It was Eric walking with a pistol in his hand. *Ah, now I see. He's in it, too. He came back to kill me. He didn't want to take a chance on me just suffocating.*

"Well, Eric, it turns out that you're more than just a driver, aren't you?" she said, getting to her feet. "You can tell me now, what's going on? Is Finklestein and Mark just a front for the drug cartel?"

Eric's mouth twisted into an evil smile as he raised the barrel of the weapon toward her. "Actually, Ms. Newcomb, it has nothing to do with the drugs. I'm sorry you're awake. This would have been much cleaner if you had stayed passed out. Turn around, please."

I'll be damned if I'm going to make this easy for him, she thought.

Chapter Thirteen

"When did you begin to feel bad?" Dr. Michele Lum asked the middle-aged woman seated before her on the examination table.

"I don't really know. Maybe three days ago. I just thought it was the flu so I started taking Echinacea and sucking on Zinc tablets but nothing has helped. I just kept feeling worse and . . ." the woman said before breaking into tears. "I just feel so depressed."

"We're going to run a few tests and see if it really is flu, so don't be worried. We'll take care of you," Michele said comfortingly.

The doctor turned to the nurse and issued instructions and then went into the hall of the Emergency Room. She was troubled and she didn't know why. She walked to the unit clerk's desk and began to look at charts when the open newspaper on the counter caught her eye. It was turned to the obituaries and the face staring at her from the page was one she recognized. She put the chart down and picked up the paper. She read the column and then waved over her colleague, Dr. Sam Wallace.

"I've been working emergency for the last three weeks and I'm starting to see more and more flu-like patients but none of them have the flu. Most of them go home but we hospitalized two yesterday, and then today, I pick up this paper and see this," she said and pointed to the picture.

Before Sam could answer she said, "This thirty-seven-year-old guy was in here two days ago. We treated him for the flu because we weren't sure what it was, even though he was depressed as well. He broke down while we were examining him and squalled like a kid. He had a slight heart condition but it was well under control. His last five physicals were perfect. Now, in 48 hours he's dead."

"That could be coincidence," he pooh-poohed.

"Oh yeah? Sitting in there I've got a fifty-two-year-old female with the same symptoms including the depression and crying fits. This is *not* flu and our tests are not pointing to anything and the people are dying."

Sam started at Lum. She was the best diagnostician in the city and she may have uncovered something important.

"Let's call the Chief of Staff. If we've got an epidemic on our hands," he whispered, "he'll want to know."

Lum nodded and returned to the woman in the examination room. "How are you feeling?" she asked.

"Oh, a little better, I guess," the woman answered.

"I think we're going to keep you for a day or two, just to watch you and make sure you're alright," Lum said. "Do you have anyone you want us to call?"

"Well, I live by myself but I do have a son in school at OSU and a daughter who's currently working in Dallas. You can call her company and they can get a word to her and then she'll let my son know."

"Sure, what are their names?"

"Laura and Jack Newcomb."

"Mike, we have another problem," Coy whispered to Michael Phillips. "We need to talk."

Phillips looked up and walked with McWaters to a secluded section of the room. He kept the folder open that he was looking at and did not look up. "Are you going to tell me what I've been worrying about for the last week?" he asked.

"I'm afraid so. I just got off the phone from Dr. Blasingdale, the Surgeon General. He says the National Public Health Service is noticing a sharp increase in admissions in hospitals all over the country for everything from flu to heart attacks. In each case the diagnoses are not completely certain. He says there are also deaths occurring from conditions that aren't normally fatal.

"I've been talking to him since we discovered the Finklestein and Mark connection. It isn't sure yet but it appears most of the latest patients have been taking Zaner vitamins. Some for years, some for just months. Why the variance in reaction times, we haven't been able to figure out."

"But it isn't for certain that Zaner is causing the problem is it?"

"No, not at all. It could be something else entirely but the preponderance of the evidence is pointing toward Zaners," Coy said.

"I think we need to be careful not to overreact. We could pull Zaners off the market and then find out they aren't the problem at all. Plus do we want to tip our hand to what the poison is before we even have an antibody for it?" Phillips said.

"I don't think so."

☆

"Come on, Eric. At least let me have a little dignity. You can let me get put together so they don't find me in a heap. Let me put my shoes on, straighten my dress and at least be in a decent position when you take my life," Laura said coyly, staggering a little as she tried to stand.

Eric was baffled at her coquettish, but seemingly undisturbed, attitude. "Are you crazy? You want to get dressed up before I kill you?" he asked. Their voices seemed to have a tinny echo in the cavernous warehouse.

"I know it sounds stupid, but you know me. You've been with me every day for the last few months. You know I don't like to look slovenly ... at anytime. Here," she said as she crossed her leg to put on a high heel shoe. As she shifted to the other foot she appeared to lose her balance and fell toward Eric.

Reacting instinctively, Eric reached for her but as he did, Laura raised the shoe in her hand and brought it down hard, driving the sharp spiked heel into Eric's eye. Blood gushed out and the screams were loud and animalistic. He raised his hands to his eyes and his pistol clattered to the floor falling between an inch and a half interval in the floor planks. Laura bolted, running as hard as she could on the rough wooden floor in a rambling building that seemed to go on forever.

She was afraid to look back and continued to sprint until she could feel her body giving out. Her legs were getting heavier and heavier and her breath was coming in short gasps. She looked back and could see Eric far back, staggering, but still coming after her. She spotted a stack of bales ahead and a huge pile of unbundled cotton. She veered toward it and realized she had reached the baler. She could go no further.

Her lungs were shooting pains across her chest and she had picked up large splinters in her feet as she raced barefoot across the floor. She leaned against one of the thick posts holding up the roof to catch her breath and didn't realize she was propped against the control panel of the baler.

Her weight kicked the simple switch and the machinery of the massive baler came to life. She jumped when the racket of the moving walls started to slowly compress the reservoir of cotton that filled it.

She looked back. Eric was still coming. She made her way behind the surrounding bales and searched frantically for the kind of sanctuary her little cell had given her so unwillingly just moments before. She couldn't go any further. Her body was extended to its capacity. She found a crack between bales—about 13 inches—and nestled between the bales, hoping Eric would pass her by. She could hear his shuffling as he came closer and the low, guttural whining that he made as fought the pain in his eye while forcing himself to keep going. He was moving out of hatred and rage and she had no illusions about what he would do when he found her.

She heard him come closer until he sounded as if he were right beside her. Then the noise stopped. She held her breath and tried to see between the bales. She could see nothing and carefully let out a little breath. She began to relax and turned her head to look behind her.

The bloody face and blinded eye of Eric stared through the bales at her only 24 inches away. She screamed as he reached his arm in to try to grab her. She squeezed herself out from between the bales on the other side but before she could run, she saw him crashing around the corner of the cotton. In panic, she began to climb up the five-tier mountain of stacked cotton bales. He was close behind her, clawing at the bales, spittle and blood spewing from his mouth.

He grabbed for her leg and missed but continued after her. Just as she made the last push to the top, she felt his hand, sticky with blood, clamp down on her thin ankle. She wrapped her hands under the metal bands holding the bale together and screamed as he tried to pull her down and himself up. The metal began to cut her fingers. She held on but she could see he was grappling his way to the summit. In a moment he would be on top of her with his hands around her neck.

She kicked as hard as she could just as he came over the top and landed a terrific blow to his mouth. Blood, teeth and flesh spewed out. *Don't stop now! Hit him again before he can recover,* she thought.

With every last bit of strength she could summon, Laura kicked again, this time pushing his head back. She stared as he lost his balance, almost in slow motion, and fell backwards, tumbling into the jaws of the baling machine, burying himself up to his waist.

He struggled desperately but there was nothing to hold on to. The walls of the machine continued to close around him the engulfing cotton like a pool of white quicksand. She watched in horror when his eyes began to bulge as his breath was methodically squeezed out of him. The horrible vision of Eric's torso protruding from the tightly compressed package of cotton gave her no satisfaction, only relief.

The rapidly increasing sounds of footsteps turned her attention to the north end of the compress. She sighed as she recognized the group of men with guns drawn running toward her as law enforcement. And best of all, Andrew Strong was in the lead. She had never been so happy to see someone in her life.

"When did you first suspect?" Laura asked Strong as they sat on top of a cotton bale.

"When we got cut off. Then I started putting all the isolated things together—the unexplained thirteen year gap in the company's existence, the fact that the agency was broken into and the data was stolen—"

"The agency was broken into?" Laura exclaimed.

"Oh, yeah, I didn't tell you did I? Well, I didn't want to distract you," Strong replied. "Anyway, the fact that they knew all about me – and you—and all the other things. One by one I ignored them because I wanted the account so damn bad but when we got cut off and I couldn't find you I started facing reality and it all came together."

"But I don't understand why. Do you know what was going on?" he asked.

"No, at first I thought it was drugs but Eric said it wasn't. He didn't have any reason to lie at that point. Do you know anything?" Laura asked Director Otis.

"Not yet, but there's something big time going on," Otis said. "Do you have everything you need?" he asked the agent that had been getting the story from Laura.

He nodded affirmatively and the group walked slowly into the car at the same time the McKinney police arrived.

Chapter Fourteen

Finklestein and Asam drove the Bronco out of Dallas. The traffic was bumper to bumper even though it was midday. The Dallas-Ft. Worth Metroplex had become so congested that savvy travelers actually bypassed the city on trips that had it in their path.

Asam busied himself with inspecting the weapons he had acquired and ensuring they were ready while Finklestein negotiated the frantic multi lanes of automobiles.

Finklestein turned the Ford onto the two-lane state highway leading to the small regional airport. After a few miles the facility came into sight. "Why did you choose this airport?" Asam asked.

"It's the smallest I could find that can accommodate the kind of plane we needed. We need at least 5,000 feet of runway," Finklestein said as he sped up to right under the speed limit. "Also, this little field is in financial straits and were much more eager to look the other way for a large customer."

Asam looked puzzled.

"All they have here are a few small private planes. Mostly single engine. They rent tie down space. Or they have an occasional visitor like that target puller over there," he said as he pointed to a perfectly restored F-86F Saber Jet looking every bit as new as it did in 1956 when it came off the assembly line. The plane was used to tow targets for the military to shoot at. "That kind of business doesn't bring in much revenue.

"We, on the other hand, lease an entire hanger and maintain a new airplane here. We buy fuel, pay for maintenance and service, and we pay fast. They love us," Finklestein explained. "They didn't even balk when we started doing some strange things like modifying the plane. You'll see what I mean."

Finklestein slowed and turned through the gate into the airport and went directly to Hanger Three. They honked and the heavy metal doors opened slightly, just enough for the Bronco to enter.

Asam couldn't believe what stood before him. Bathed in the blue-green light of the hanger stood a beautiful twin engine Learjet 35A business jet. But instead of the markings typical of such a craft, this one was totally painted in Navy colors with military insignias and numbers.

"Like it?" Finklestein said, slightly smiling as the saw Asam's mouth open in surprise. "There's a Naval Air Station in Grand Prairie. They have aircraft like this flying in from time to time. They're called the C-21A. This one, however, has been modified. It has greater range with the extra wing tanks, ceiling and speed than its Navy counterpart. And, we're much less likely to be questioned in this airplane."

Asam remembered the air station as he had sped by in his most recent escape from the police.

A pilot appeared from behind the plane dressed in the uniform of a Navy Commander. He was pre-flighting the aircraft and gave a half-salute when he saw the two men. Finklestein handed him a message. "Scramble this and transmit it as soon as we're airborne. It's our insurance."

He turned back to Asam. "We've had it for the last year as a corporate plane but I had it repainted last month in anticipation of today," Finklestein said. "We've even equipped it with UHF radios so it can receive and transmit on military frequencies. We have all the military call signs and clearances that'll allow us to bypass customs and have free access to overseas routes. And, as you can see, we even have the correct costumes.

"We'll refuel in Cuba and be in Tehran in twenty-four hours," Finklestein chuckled. "Stow your gear and we'll get out of here."

The sound of screeching metal as the small entry door of the hanger swung open caused both men to turn. Scurrying in was a worried looking man in an open collar shirt.

"Mr. Finklestein, I think we've got problems," he said quickly as he approached Finklestein. "There's a cop, a federal man, in the office asking about all the planes and wanting to see ownership papers. Says they're checking all the airports. We've been putting him off but I don't think we can hold him much longer."

The man looked around to make sure no one was coming.

"You had said not to ever tell anyone anything about the plane unless you said so, so I wanted to warn you," the man said.

Finklestein's face darkened and he reached out and grabbed the man by his throat. "Stall him. Tell him whatever you have to but keep him out of here!" he barked. "If you fail, I promise I will kill you and your fat wife. Do you understand?"

Finklestein glared into the airport manager's eyes. There was no question that he would make good on his promise and the man, on the verge of hysteria, knew it. Horrified, he uttered his understanding. Finklestein pushed him toward the door as he said, "Get out and keep him away from here until we can take off!"

"Let's go," he shouted to the pilot who quickly pulled the chocks and ran to the wall of the hanger, pushing the power opener for the huge hanger doors.

Slowly, the gates began to open like the jaws of a sleeping monster. The pilot bounded up the plane's ladder, pulling it up behind him and letting it slide inside the bottom half of the door as it closed. He jumped into the left seat and started the engines.

He maneuvered the plane to the hanger doors, waiting on them to create enough of an opening to free the craft. Finklestein looked out the round window and could see an official looking man burst out of the airport office being chased by a pleading airport manager.

He pulled the .357 Magnum from his briefcase and dashed over to the airplane's door. Unlocking it, he pulled it open. The split door separated and the upper half receded into the fuselage. He dropped to his knee and took aim and rested his forearms on the door's unretracted lower half.

When the aircraft cleared the huge hanger doors and began accelerating toward the active runway, he saw the agent draw his weapon. The whine of the turbojets was deafening but the flash from the agent's barrel confirmed to Finklestein that the agent had fired.

Finklestein began to crank off rounds and before he had loosed his third shot, saw the agent fall. Just for good measure he continued to fire and watched as the fleeing airport manager was thrown face-first into the tarmac by the impact of a hollow-point bullet in his back.

Finklestein slammed the Learjet's door shut and was thrown into his seat as the plane sped down the runway. When the speed hit 100 knots the pilot pulled sharply on the yoke and the plane vaulted toward the sky, quickly turning to a heading that would take them out of U.S. airspace as fast as possible.

"When did this come in?" Phillips asked, holding up the piece of paper and looking around.

"Brown's scanners just picked it up off Waxahachie PD's 911 line. We've been monitoring all of the 911s in the Dallas-Ft. Worth Metroplex. The woman was hysterical, screaming that her husband and a federal agent had been shot. It's a small airport about 50 miles away," said McWaters.

"How long to get there?"

"It will take us about 30 to 45 minutes but Otis is a lot closer."

"Good, put him on it. We'll get there as soon as we can," Phillips said.

The men left to join the group in pursuit. They were stopped at the door.

"Sir, there's a call on the secure line for you," said Brown. Noting the quick look of irritation in Phillips face he added, "You're going to want to take it. It's the President."

Phillips went to the desk and sat down, composing himself. He picked up the phone. "This is Michael Phillips, Mr. President."

"Mr. Phillips, I'm sitting here with FBI Director Nall and Surgeon General Blasingdale. The cases of infection and death are rising sharply across the nation. Our normal daily hospital census is a little over

660,000. In the last week we have had 25,000 admissions. That's double the normal rate of illness reported. This is clearly tied to the activities that you have uncovered in Dallas. There hasn't been any media attention yet but it's just a matter of time if these figures keep climbing.

"If we declare an emergency, we tip our hand to the fact that something is wrong, and that could lead to a general panic," the President said. "On the other hand, the longer we wait, the more cases we have and the less we can do to cure them. We seem to be on the horns of a dilemma. I have two advisors sitting here who sharply disagree on a course of action.

"What is your counsel from the field? You're the man on the front lines."

"Mr. President, if the public finds out that Zaner vitamins are causing them to die, we'll have panic in the streets. We don't know yet that they are the cause and, even if they are, what we can do to stop the infection. The investigators at the Finklestein and Mark plant haven't discovered anything yet and, on their own, it may take months before they do.

"Our only chance is to capture the two remaining terrorists and force them to tell us what is in them that can cause the illness. We're closing in on them and if you can give me some time I think they can be caught.

"Mr. President. Once we let the news of an epidemic out, we've opened Pandora's Box and I believe every fear that Director Nall had, that I'm sure he has articulated to you, will be realized. Right now we have a chance to control this but once it's out, I can't guarantee we can do anything. Please, just give us some more time," Phillips pleaded.

"Very well," the President said. "I can't guarantee you any set amount of time, however. This situation is far too volatile and fluid. There may quickly come a time when we'll have to declare an epidemic. God knows where that will lead us. Use what time you have and I hope you can give us an alternative, Mr. Phillips," the President said and then the line went dead.

"We've got to get those bastards and fast," Phillips said to Coy McWaters as they ran out of the secret headquarters.

Chapter Fifteen

The call came in just as Otis was leaving the Federal Compress. They immediately turned on the flashing lights in the grill and sped toward the small airport in Waxahachie.

Otis' car was full with Laura, Strong and another FBI agent in it. It scraped bottom as they hit the rise entering the airport and skidded to a halt, throwing gravel against the wall of the little airport office. There was already a Waxahachie policeman talking to a dowdy, overweight woman who kept dabbing her eyes. Crime tape had been placed to rope off the scene and Otis quickly identified himself and took control of the investigation.

"I recognize this place," Laura said to Strong as they sat in the car. "Not from being here but from the records, the bills. Finklestein and Mark has an airplane here. They spend thousands on it every month."

"That's what she says. They've painted their plane like a Navy plane and have taken off," Otis said coming back from talking to the officer and the woman and overhearing Laura's comment.

"Can't you send someone after them?" she asked.

"We can try to get a jet scrambled but that'll take at least thirty minutes. We can't get through the red tape any faster. It wouldn't matter if the President called them," Otis said rubbing his head trying to come up with a solution fast.

"Well, hell, give me a plane and I'll catch them," Strong said. Everyone looked at him as if he had lost his mind.

"I'm not kidding. I flew F-4s in the Marine Corps. I can damn sure fly one of these."

"One of these puddle jumpers wouldn't catch them. They left in a jet," Otis said.

For a moment there was silence and then Laura said, "Well, what's that?" pointing to the jet sitting unobtrusively off the runway.

"Damn, an F-86! I'll bet it's a target puller!" Strong exclaimed.

"A what?" Otis asked.

"A target puller. They're owned by private companies and on contract to the government to pull targets for target practice," Strong explained.

"That'll sure catch them, if it doesn't fall apart first," Strong said and began running toward the plane. Otis started to yell for him to stop and then thought better of it and ran after him. "Is that plane fueled?" Strong shouted as he ran past the airport manager's wife. She nodded it was.

Strong pushed a ladder to the plane and scampered up, pulling off his coat and flinging it to the ground. He slid into the cockpit and strapped himself into the parachute and ejection seat, all the while scanning the instruments to locate the essential ones. He grabbed the helmet off the ledge of the canopy and put it on, connecting the oxygen mask hose into the appropriate outlet.

Otis was right behind him on the ladder leaning into the cockpit. "This is crazy but I don't think there's a choice. We've got to find them. I've already got one man down. If we wait too long, they'll be out of our airspace. Do you think you can catch up with them?"

"You can bet they're flying straight for the nearest coast. That means the Gulf of Mexico. This thing has a top speed of nearly 700 miles per hour. Theirs can't top much over 530 so if— " and Strong stopped.

"If what?" Otis asked.

"If this thing can still *go* 700 miles an hour I may have a chance of catching them. I figure I have thirty minutes because, like you say, once they're out of U.S. airspace, they can't be stopped. If I can find them, then I'll vector in a military escort from Corpus Christi and we'll force them back," Strong said. "When I'm airborne, scramble the Navy jets from NAS Corpus! I'll give you a position as soon as I locate them."

"Okay. But don't take any chances" Otis yelled, pointing to the machine guns mounted in the wings. "These old guns aren't loaded, you know! All I want you to do is locate them and radio their position, understand? Don't even let them see you, just let us know their position."

"Fine, fine. I'll just spot them and let the Navy jocks from Corpus take them out," Strong said and began looking for the big red button that would start the engine.

Otis quickly climbed down the ladder and the agents pulled the staircase away from the Saber Jet. He waited as Strong started the jet engine and pulled the lever that lowered the canopy. The agents watched as the jet quickly taxied to the runway.

Within seconds, the FBI agents were busy alerting the authorities, while the vintage aircraft was screaming down the runway and lifting into the air on the same path Finklestein's' jet had taken.

"Director Otis, there's a call on the secure line for you," the driver said to Otis as he and Laura drove back to downtown Dallas and the field office.

Otis took the cell phone and after saying "yes" listened intently. "I see," he said and pushed the "end" button. He turned to Laura and she could tell by the look in his eyes there was trouble.

"Laura, that was my office. They just got word that your mother has been hospitalized in Oklahoma City. They don't have a firm diagnosis but she's very ill. I can get you on a plane in thirty minutes if you want," Otis said softly.

"Uh, yes, of course. Please do," Laura said, stunned. Suddenly she was flooded with the old fear she had had since her father died. Even though she was grown, she was scared to death of becoming an orphan.

The car sped up and Laura was delivered to Love Field where a Southwest Airlines flight was being held on the runway for her.

As the car left the airport the phone rang again for Otis. This time it was Phillips, and within minutes the Field Director was headed to his headquarters.

The old F-86 was performing like a brand new plane, Strong thought as he climbed to cruising altitude. Even if it was an antique it was exhilarating to be behind the controls of a fighter again.

For the first time, Strong began to carefully look around the cockpit. While simple by F-4 Phantom standards, the forty-six year-old fighter was amazingly sophisticated. He began to familiarize himself with the controls, knowing that in a few minutes, if he had guessed right, he would hit his interception point.

He had the jet at full military power and, while the plane had to pass all the FAA requirements and was certainly airworthy, it *was* nearly a half-century-old.

How much can this baby take? Strong wondered.

He continued to nervously check his instruments. He hadn't yet decided what he would do if he caught the fleeing plane. He had no guns and wasn't totally sure he would have any help. Even if the Navy did send jets, he didn't know if they would be able to get there in time.

He took a minute to organize his thoughts before he began an intricate exchange with the air controller in Dallas and then pressed the button on his joystick that activated the microphone in his oxygen mask.

"D/FW departure this is Saber Eight-Six November Alfa off Pope Regional Airport; VFR heading is One Niner Zero climbing to flight level 120. Request discrete frequency with you to explain my intentions. I have UHF equipment on board."

The Dallas-Fort Worth Air Traffic Controller responded promptly, "Roger Eight Six November Alpha, squawk zero-four-two- zero. Standby for frequency change."

Strong complied and confirmed with the tower. D/FW located the F-86 on radar and instructed a frequency change.

"D/FW," Strong began, "I am on course to intercept a Lear with Navy markings. He is approximately ten minutes ahead of me and is a suspected murderer attempting to flee the U.S. You may confirm with Corpus Naval Air Station."

The controller acknowledged.

"D/FW— I also need clearance to a 6,000 feet block altitude at 40,000 plus or minus with a southerly heading. Please advise if and when you have a contact with the Lear. I am unarmed and will require vectors to complete the intercept," Strong said.

D/FW cleared Strong to a block altitude and a heading and diverted air traffic from him. Strong continued to talk and arranged the necessary change in frequency as he passed into Ft. Worth's Center. He knew they would have the best chance of locating the Lear and pointing him to it.

"Eight Six November Alpha radar contact," crackled Strong's headphones. "We have your unidentified aircraft at your 11 o'clock position—50 miles with a heading of One Seven Zero—ground speed 430 knots—no transponder and no altitude read out—continue at your discretion –vectors available at your request."

Strong now knew where his quarry was and he was closing fast. The Lear was trying its best to slip undetected from the U.S.

The air controller signed off and Strong called for Naval Air Station Corpus Christi. The FBI agent in Corpus, who had already settled in the NAS tower, greeted him. Yes, the jets were scrambled. What was his position and the Navy jets would be vectored to him. As Strong was transmitting the coordinates, he caught a glimpse of a white dot to his left.

He quickly looked again and as he closed on it from two miles out, could see it was the Learjet. *Where were the jets from Corpus?* He pulled back on his power and carefully eased in behind the Learjet. He was confident that he hadn't been spotted.

Strong looked at his watch then twisted in the cockpit and scanned the sky around him. There were only a few minutes left before the planes crossed into international airspace and there was no sign of any help from the fighter jocks at Corpus.

Strong was going to have to do something fast or they would be invulnerable. By now, he was thinking like a fighter pilot again. He remembered a ramming maneuver that the Russian pilots were famous for in WWII. *Maybe I can come up with a variation that will let me stay alive.*

The F-86 had drawn closer, unnoticed behind the fleeing plane. Strong dipped under the Learjet and then, edging the plane forward, abruptly pulled up and in front of the aircraft, just missing it by sheer yards. The tactic had the desired effect of causing panic in the Learjet's cockpit as well as setting up a raging tornado of turbulence for the plane to pass through. When the terrorists' plane hit the jet wash, it began to roll and yaw, the pilot struggling to keep control. Strong could see him pulling back on the yoke to put some distance between the two.

Strong climbed and slipped to the port side and throttled back to stay even with the plane and signaled the pilot to descend.

"What's happening?" Finklestein screamed as he staggered into the cockpit.

"We're caught," the pilot said as he pointed to the Saber Jet. "That damn old relic nearly took us down."

"Who is it?" Finklestein demanded.

"I don't know. I don't know where it came from either but it's clear he wants us to land," the pilot said.

"Ignore him! We can get out of U.S. airspace if we can buy a few more minutes," Finklestein said.

At that point, the F-86 disappeared from the Learjet's vision and, within moments, suddenly appeared again in front of the plane disrupting the airflow and causing the plane to become uncontrollable.

"Damn, we can't take any more of these. If he doesn't hit us by mistake the aircraft will break up. It wasn't designed for this kind of turbulence," the pilot shouted as he fought to keep the plane out of spin.

Strong was pretty proud of himself. It had been a few years since he had flown a jet but it still gave him a thrill to pull a trick like that and shake the hell out of those bastards in the Learjet. Just about the time he had figured one more shake-up ought to do it, he saw a flashing red light on his fuel flow indicator. Other flashing lights followed with each dial hand dropping into the red zones on their gauges' faces.

It was clear he had a flame out on his hands; the engine had quit and the fire alarm lights were indicating a fire. The Saber Jet began to lose airspeed and altitude. Strong pushed the nose down to keep his air speed up while he struggled to find the ejection handles. He reached down and began feeling for the handles. They weren't where he thought they were! The plane was accelerating and dropping altitude fast.

Where are they? he thought as he frantically searched the cockpit.

This isn't an F-4, dumbshit! It's an F-86 and the levers are in the armrests, he remembered. He looked down and found the two armrests and built-in triggers that, he hoped, would blow the canopy off and send the ejection seat clear of the falling aircraft. He pulled on them as hard as he could and prayed they would work and that the parachute he was connected with wasn't just for show. Just then an ear-shattering explosion rocked the plane.

"She's lucid, sometimes, and then sometimes she doesn't make any sense," said Dr. Lum to Laura as she sat leaning close to her mother's inert form in the bed.

"We're trying to find a common thread with your mother and some other cases that we've had recently. The symptoms aren't exactly the same but we're investigating to be sure there's no connection," Lum said. She continued to probe Laura to explore her mother's health history and habits.

"She's diabetic, you say?" Lum asked. "When we talked to her she didn't indicate she had diabetes."

"That's probably because she's forgotten she has it. It's been under control for years. She takes medicine and her blood sugar has been normal for at least the last five years. She goes in for check-up every six months. I honestly don't think she even thinks of herself as diabetic anymore," Laura explained.

"I think we'll start looking harder at her blood work. If she's having some sort of diabetic incident, that might help explain things," Lum said. "Anything else?"

"I'm afraid so. Last year she was screened for early Alzheimer's. She showed up as a high risk candidate," Laura said.

"I see," Lum said. After exhausting her other questions, she left with promises to return. "We're going to pursue some different areas with her to be sure we're not missing anything. If you think of anything else, please let me know."

Laura sat quietly watching her frail mother for nearly two hours. She had never seen her so helpless. Suddenly, her mother opened her eyes and seemed to look around. Laura stood up and leaned over her bed.

"Mama? Are you okay?" Laura asked. "Can you hear me?"

A smile came over her mother's face. "Hi, baby. What are you doing here? Where am I?" she asked.

"You're in the hospital, don't you remember?"

"Oh, yes. I guess I must have been asleep," she replied weakly.

"Mama, when did all of this begin?" Laura asked. Her mother tried but couldn't come up with any definitive answers. Nothing out of the ordinary had happened, she said.

"I think I just have the flu," she argued.

"Will you check on the house, honey? No one has been there since I came here and I worry I left the coffee pot on," her mother said. "The house keys are in my purse."

"Sure, I will. You just try to get some sleep," Laura said as her mother turned over and snuggled into her pillow.

Laura waited awhile, sitting, looking at her mother and remembering special times when she had guided her as a little girl. Finally, she decided to go ahead and check on the house. There wasn't much she could do here and she'd promised to call her brother and let him know what was going on. He was going to come home from OSU but she'd waved him off. He was in finals and he didn't need to leave until she had determined how bad the situation was.

She went to her mothers' purse and began to search for the house keys. She shuffled through her bag and then happened on a familiar container that sent alarm bells tolling in her head. She saw the Zaner vitamin bottle and suddenly it all made sense. *Murderers who didn't want to make a profit but wanted to move tons of vitamins. Of course!*

"Mother!" she said. Her mother turned over slightly dazed having just slipped back to sleep. "How long have you been taking these vitamins?" she asked, holding up the bottle.

"Well, ever since you started your advertising campaign. I thought it was the least I could do. Support my little girl, you know," she said, smiling.

I better not send people into a panic, especially mother, she thought.

"Did I do something wrong, Laura?" her mother asked.

"No, no. Of course not. I just wondered," Laura said. "Go back to sleep and I'll check on the house."

She left the room and went straight to a pay phone and placed an emergency call to Director Otis in Dallas. Otis answered and Laura quickly explained her suspicion. Otis promised to get back to her after instructing her to tell no one, including her mother's physician, in the meantime.

"She said *what*?" Phillips said into the phone as he waved McWaters over. Otis continued to explain what Laura had just reported.

"Who is she, again?" Phillips asked. "You mean she knows the Finklestein and Mark company? Everyone we've talked to there only has limited knowledge about the operation. We need someone who knows where the bodies are buried. Get her back here."

"That won't be easy, sir. Her mother is very ill," Otis said.

"Well, tell her if she'll come back and talk to us, we may be able to help her mother recover."

Otis was confused. "What now? How can I tell her that?"

"Look, our chemists are going nowhere. They don't know where the records are; they can't find any of the documentation of the manufacturing process. In short, they have their hands tied. If she knows the entire operation, then she may very well be the key to unraveling this damn Gordian Knot," Phillips said.

Realizing Otis had no knowledge of the Zaner vitamin scheme, he quickly continued, "You may not understand all of this because you don't have the necessary clearance but here's the bottom line, Otis. Tell her whatever you have to, but get her back now!"

Otis hung up the receiver and waited a moment then picked it up again and began to dial.

Chapter Sixteen

Strong was tumbling like a T-shirt in a clothes dryer. All he could see were patches of blue and white. His cheeks were being buffeted by wind, his eyes were burning and his back felt as if it were broken. He was dizzy and couldn't seem to stabilize himself when all of a sudden he was jerked as hard as if the airbag had deployed in his car.

The sharp pop of his parachute opening straightened him and he began to sway at the end of the harnesses. He pulled up the visor on his helmet and saw pieces of fuselage and wing fall past him in flames.

What happened, he wondered?

Slowly, it came to him as he floated down under the white canopy. Apparently, the Saber Jet had exploded at the same moment he had pulled the ejection handles. He had been shot out of the cockpit only milliseconds before the ball of fire had erupted and engulfed he aircraft. He was at over 40,000 feet when he ejected and he estimated he was still well above breathable atmosphere. He hoped he could hold his breath till he got below 18,000 feet and could stay conscious.

He tried to examine himself to see if there were any obvious injuries. He appeared to be okay although he hurt all over. Then, he craned to try to spot the Learjet, but all he saw were clouds. *They must be crossing over to the Gulf of Mexico by now,* he thought.

He heard a strange ripping sound and looked above him. Horrified, he saw a small tear opening in the aging nylon of the parachute. If it continued to get larger he would begin to fall faster and by the time he hit the ground it would be like he had no parachute at all. He glanced down and saw thick trees and some small lakes. *Maybe if he could guide himself over the water he would have a softer landing.*

He pulled on the right set of shrouds and began to circle to the right. It was hard to determine where the wind was coming from but he judged from his movement relative to the ground he was being blown away from the trees.

He heard the rip again and looked to see the tear enlarged by several inches. The ground began to come faster. He struggled to maneuver the chute. Control was becoming soft and the canopy was unresponsive. He wriggled to try to influence the direction of his fall but nothing worked. He heard the ripping sound again and wondered if he would live through the descent as he saw the trees lurching toward him.

Otis had escorted Laura into a conference room in the Dallas FBI office and briefly introduced her to Phillips. She wasn't eager to leave her mother but after several minutes of coaxing, plus promising that it could speed up her mother's recovery, she consented. She had hastily left the hospital and caught a last-minute flight back to Dallas.

She was clearly anxious and had already explained to Otis her theory of why she thought her mother was ill.

Phillips signaled for her to sit across from him at the conference table. "Ms. Newcomb, I'm going to have to take you into my confidence. What I'm about to tell you is classified at the highest level of government. If you divulge this to anyone, you can be prosecuted and imprisoned and let me assure you I will prosecute you to the fullest extent of the law," Phillips said very matter of factly.

"Wait just a minute," Laura interrupted with fire in her eyes. "Before you start threatening me about divulging information, which you are so gracious to bestow on me, you had better listen to me, Mr. Whoever you are!

"You dragged me away from my mother who is deathly ill with

some sort of half-ass promise that you could cure her, only to inform me what I can do and can't do before you tell me anything."

Phillips was taken aback at this reaction. He was a man not used to being talked back to.

"The only reason I'm here is because of Mr. Otis. He saved my life, not you. And let me tell you something else. If you know something about my mother's illness, you damn well better not withhold it or I'll have the *Dallas Morning News* crawling all over you."

Phillips looked at Otis who gave him an *I don't know what to do* look and then turned back to Laura. The silence was palpable. Clearly, he had muffed this. He lowered his head and after a pause of several moments looked up at her.

"I haven't done a very good job of this, Ms. Newcomb, and I'm sorry," he said giving her an apologetic smile. "I've been running a breakneck operation for the last five months. We're all exhausted and frightened and sometimes I forget who works for me and who doesn't. Can we start again?"

Even though Laura seemed unmoved, Phillips began softly, "I think when you hear this story, you'll understand my abruptness," and began to unfold the events that had led them to Finklestein and Mark. Laura listened raptly and began to relax and her expression slowly changed from anger to concern.

"So you see," Phillips said as he concluded, "it's not just your mother we're worried about, but the thousands of cases that are pouring in every hour all over the country.

"We can't be sure that Zaners are causing the illnesses and, until we can put some facts together, we can't even begin to come up with a vaccine, if that's what's needed. We already may be too late. We just don't know."

"How can I help? I work for the advertising agency," Laura asked.

"You're the only person we've found who understands what goes on in every department at Finklestein and Mark and how they all tie together. They've been very effective in not investing anyone with the overview of the operations.   "We have to find out how the vitamins are made and see what's different with the ones from, say last year, and this year. You've got to help us. We're running out of time."

"Oh, my God. I was right," Laura said almost under her breath.

"Yes, you could be. That's why we had to get you here. And if *you* figured it out, it won't be too long before the media does, once they latch onto the rise in illnesses. They won't hesitate to air it or publish it, regardless what impact it has on the country. We know that," Phillips answered.

Laura ran her hand though her hair. She seemed to have a distant look in her eyes. "Yes, of course, I'll do whatever I can. How can I help?" she asked, a worried tone in her voice.

"I'd like you to return with me to our headquarters and then I'll go with you to Finklestein and Mark. We'll work with you to discover the information we need. There are areas in every department that we don't understand. Okay?"

"Let's go," Laura said quickly and the three left the office to waiting cars outside on Commerce Street.

"Ride with me, would you?" Phillips asked Laura as they entered the car. This was not the time to even think thoughts like this but he couldn't help being impressed with her. It wasn't until they got in the car and began to drive to the headquarters that he noticed how beautiful she was. He hadn't seen freckles on a grown woman in years and had forgotten how appealing it was.

"Where is he?" shouted Finklestein. "Where'd he go?

"I don't know, it looks like we lost him," the pilot said.

"Good. Drop down lower and try to evade the radar until we can hit the coast," Finklestein commanded.

"Right," the pilot said and began to adjust the trim for a fast descent.

"What's happening now?" Asam asked as he made his way to the front of the plane.

"We've somehow lost the old jet and we're trying to evade anyone he might have told of our location. If we can stay below radar, we can make it out of U.S. airspace. They can't touch us then," Finklestein said malevolently.

Asam went back to his seat and returned with the Uzi and a couple of fully loaded magazines.

"Five minutes," the pilot said as he eased the throttles forward to 100% power, "and we should be in international air space."

Finklestein scanned the sky from the cockpit trying to see any other aircraft. The sky was clear.

☆

Laura and Phillips arrived at the Finklestein and Mark Building and went inside to find operatives, FBI agents and experts from who knows how many other government agencies, pouring over every record and searching every department.

"Here's where Finklestein hung out," Laura said as she led Phillips into the office Finklestein used.

"Here's his computer. Maybe there's something in it." Phillips called Brown over and he immediately began to examine the computer, calling up files and directories.

"Nope, he cleaned this baby out not long ago. He even erased the programs," Brown said.

"I thought you computer experts could recover deleted files," Phillips said sounding a little irritated.

"Not when they've so totally eliminated them. There's nothing to recover," Brown said.

"Well, check all of them. Laura, are they on a network?" Phillips asked.

"Yes, they are. The server is in accounting," she said.

"Check it," Phillips ordered Brown.

"We've done that. It's the same thing on the mainframe. The server has been totally erased of anything but accounting information," Brown responded.

"Well, keep looking," Phillips said brusquely and Brown left the room.

Phillips paused for a moment, rubbing his thumb in the palm of his right hand. He looked around the office, going to the tattered couch, and then spoke. "Let's look at this office from here. Just look at it and see if it says anything to us."

Laura wasn't quite sure what he meant but moved to the couch and sat next to him.

"It's an exercise I devised that seems to help in remembering details and formulating questions. I'm going to sit here and look at every part of the room and ask myself questions about it. Why is this here? Why is that there?

"You, on the other hand, since you know him and this room, might focus on the things he did here. Did he look at a particular item or area differently than others? Is something missing now that was here when he occupied this space? Those kinds of things. Willing to give it a try?"

"I'll try anything to catch that bas— sorry-so-and-so," she answered.

They sat in silence for about twenty minutes. She could see Finklestein in her mind moving from the desk to the door but that was about all. Her few face-to-face meetings with him in this office had resulted in her being so intimidated she didn't really remember details.

"Any luck?" Phillips asked finally, turning to face her.

"I'm sorry, it just isn't working for me. I guess I'm not very observant," she said apologetically.

"It's alright," Phillips said. "Sometimes it takes a little while for the association to hit. Let's go to other areas of the plant."

"Okay," Laura said and they moved to the door. Once outside Laura stopped in her tracks. She was staring at Megan's desk. Megan! She remembered first arriving and being told that Megan had been conducting a "routine survey of the day's phone calls."

"Wait a minute. Finklestein knew everything that went on. He knew things about people that were so personal he could only have done it by listening in on conversations and by visual surveillance.

"What did Megan, his personal secretary, tell you?" she asked, her eyes wide.

"Let's find out!" Phillips said and quickly spoke into a two-way radio. Phillips earphone prevented Laura from hearing but she could tell by his face that he was getting a report from the interrogators.

"Where is she now?" he asked. "Keep her there."

He started walking and waved for Laura to come with him. "She's claiming she was just an employee like everyone else. Says she just did her job as a secretary, did what she was told and never asked any questions. The agent questioning her says she seemed scared to death of Finklestein."

"That doesn't surprise me. He was very intimidating. That's why I think she knows more than she's telling. I'll bet she was scared to death of screwing up. I'll bet she's still scared of him.

"Everyone in the company was overpaid. I noticed that when I reviewed the accounting records. When you do that, people realize it and begin to be afraid they'll lose their gravy train if they make a mistake.

"Mike," Laura said, "you've got to make her more afraid of you than she is of Finklestein. I'm sure she knows something. I think she was involved somehow with the surveillances and wiretapping and all of that.

"In looking back at it, I think they had my apartment searched. It's the only way they could have known some of the things they knew."

"Okay, Laura," Phillips said looking her straight in the eyes. You're a good judge of character. I've already figured that out. You tell me. What will scare her?"

Laura thought for a moment and then looked at him with a funny kind of smile. "I think I know," she said, putting her finger to her mouth. Then she waved at him to follow her down the hall.

The last loud rip sounded like a huge zipper and it seemed to go on forever. Strong began to plummet. He knew he couldn't survive a fall from this height whether he landed in a lake or was impaled on a tree. *God, isn't there something I can do? Am I forgetting something?* he thought as he fell through what could likely be the last twenty seconds of his life.

The chute was now in tatters, the rip having made its way across the top of the shroud, leaving it with strands of flapping silk that had little ability to catch air at all. The ground was racing closer like an image through a zoom lens. Strong knew he was going to die. He let go of the guide cords and held himself with his arms across his abdomen.

His hand hit an exposed wire that gave him a momentary prick and caused him to involuntarily look to see what caused the sharp sting. His mouth dropped open. He had hit the ripcord of the emergency chute! He had never had to bail out in all those years in the Marine Corps. Besides, true military parachutes didn't have emergency packets. The company that owned the F-86 must have replaced it with a civilian model. He snatched the handle as hard as he could. The secondary parachute popped out of the small pack on his stomach and quickly deployed. He took three swings under the full canopy before he splashed into the water of a Texas lake at 30 miles per hour.

Chapter Seventeen

"Stinger Six, this is Stinger Five."

"Roger, Five, go," answered the wingman in the Navy F-14 Tomcat.

"We should have intercept in forty-five seconds," the lead pilot said.

Within moments the two planes were within missile range of the last reported position of the fleeing Learjet.

"I don't see them on the radar scope. Have you got a fix?" radioed the wingman.

"Negative," responded the lead.

The radio hissed from flight control Corpus Christi. "We have a bogey below you at five thousand. They're crossing into the Gulf of Mexico at this time."

Phillips' radio jumped to life and caused him to stop in mid-stride as he and Laura hurried to the interrogation room.

"Go ahead, Corpus," Phillips said. He listened intently. "Where's the Learjet now?"

"They're crossing into the Gulf of Mexico," said the agent in Corpus Christi. "I think the F-14s can catch them now that we have them located but they're going to be in international airspace by the time they get there. What do you want them to do, sir?" the agent asked.

Phillips thought for a moment and realized that an incident could attract press attention and increase the chance reporters could uncover the entire threat. *To hell with it. This is no ordinary situation,* he thought.

"Bring them down. Don't kill them if you can avoid it. We need them back here but *don't* let them escape," Phillips said.

"Sir, that's a violation of international air space," the agent said nervously.

"Do you have a witness to this transmission?" Phillips asked.

"Yes, sir, you're coming over the speaker in the tower," the agent replied.

"All right, listen up. I'll take full responsibility. Do you understand?"

The agent looked around the tower at the other air controllers, all turned and looking at him. They nodded, affirming to him they heard the transmission. "Yes, sir," he answered.

"Very well then, execute the order," Phillips said and signed off.

The two Navy jets hit their afterburners and within moments were hurling toward the terrorists' plane that was crossing into international airspace.

Finklestein bent over and looked around from the cockpit and then walked back into the cabin and down the aisle, bending at the waist and looking out each side to be sure no planes were in sight.

"We may have ditched them," he said to Asam. "We're in international airspace now, so we're safe."

He sat down, strapped himself in, put his head back and exhaled a sigh of relief. He casually looked out the window again. The pilot of the Navy F-14 stared back at him. He snapped his head to the other side only to see another F-14 fully armed with Phoenix missiles.

At that moment the intercom came alive with the pilot's voice. "We have Navy fighters all over us and they're signaling us down. We need to comply."

Finklestein was into the cockpit in a flash.

"They can't do this. We're in international airspace," he screamed.

The airplanes radio came alive.

"Learjet, land immediately. You will follow us back to Corpus Christi. If you resist, you will be shot down. Acknowledge."

The Learjet's pilot reached for the microphone and responded, "Navy Tomcat... be advised we are in international airspace and you have no authority over us."

"Negative, Learjet," the answer came back, "you are obviously a Navy aircraft. We have complete authority. If you do not comply, we will attack."

The pilot was at a loss on how to respond. Their disguise had come back to haunt them. He started to key the microphone and Finklestein stopped him. "Execute evasive maneuvers!" he commanded.

"Don't be ridiculous. They can shoot us out of the sky at 20 miles! It's over. I'm not going to die," the pilot said and once again reached for the microphone.

Finklestein turned gray with rage. He reached in his belt and pulled out the .357 Magnum and placed it against the pilot's head.

"Oh, you'll die, alright. It just won't be from a machine gun. Now, start evasive action!" he said.

"If you're wondering what we would do if I killed you, it's simple. We'd die. But either way you'll be dead. At least this way you have a chance, however slim, to stay alive. Now do what I told you," Finklestein said as he pushed the barrel of the revolver harder into the pilot's temple.

The pilot didn't have to be told twice. He pulled back hard on the yoke and the Lear jumped into a steep climbing turn. Finklestein was thrown against the bulkhead but he kept the pistol pointed at the pilot.

"He's making a break for it!" the flight leader barked over the radio. "I'm in pursuit."

The F-14 had extended its wings for maximum maneuverability and even in the slower mode, it easily caught up with and began trailing the Learjet. His wingman followed into formation.

"I'm going to put some rounds across his bow," the leader said and flipped the switch in his joystick, activating the machine guns in the plane's nose. The bullets spewed out a line of tracers fifty feet in front of the fleeing Learjet.

"They're shooting at us!" the pilot screamed.

"Continue your maneuvers," Finklestein demanded.

"I'm going to take a pass," the wingman said and turned toward the Learjet. He lined up his sights and pulled the trigger but being younger and less experienced than his flight leader, misled the aircraft. His slugs fell short and hit the plane's rear, tattering the aluminum skin of the Learjet's tail control surfaces.

"I screwed the pooch on that one, Stinger Six. I didn't lead him enough and I nailed his vertical stabilizer and his tail," reported the wingman.

"It's okay, Five. Maybe he'll get the message," responded Stinger Six.

"Last warning, Learjet. Lower your flaps, turn to a heading of three five zero degrees or we will fire on you again," the flight leader said.

The Lear's pilot felt the softness and unresponsiveness of his controls the moment his tail surfaces were hit. His eyes were wild as he looked at Finklestein and shouted, "They've hit us. If we don't obey, we're going down!"

"Take it down and try to land on the water. Asam, get ready for a crash landing. Get out the raft and life vests," he yelled back to the other terrorist. "Do it!" he told the pilot, once again brandishing the weapon at the man's head.

The plane began to fall rapidly.

Strong hit the frigid water and felt as if he had been punched in the stomach and had all of his breath knocked out of him. Even in south Texas at that time of year the lakes had a shallow thermocline and were barely above freezing.

Hitting at the speed he had, he plunged deep into the lake. He struggled to free himself from the parachute and activate his "Mae West" inflatable life jacket. It blew up with a muffled pop and pulled him rapidly to the surface.

He tried to orient himself and thought he could make out the shore to the south. Only problem, he thought, was that it looked like it was ten miles away. He began to swim, slowly at first, to try to conserve his energy. The "Mae West" didn't help. It held him vertically in the water, requiring a tremendous effort to pull himself forward and allow his legs to help by kicking. Within fifteen minutes he was exhausted.

Strong knew that the most dangerous threat to him now was the possibility of hypothermia. If he stayed in this cold water for long, he could die of exposure. His body would just shut down.

He had jumped into the jet so fast that he wasn't properly outfitted for survival. *No homing beacon. No compass. No survival knife. I'm going to die out here with my dick in my hand and that's about all. Give me a break.*

Once again, he began to kick and paddle. His legs began to cramp. He tried to think of things to take his mind away. Strong remembered the old days, fifteen years ago, when he was Marine Officer Candidate in Quantico, Virginia.

He recalled the unbearable forced marches on the infamous "hill trail" that turned the biggest, strongest athletes into wheezing, glassy-eyed, gasping hikers trying to summon every bit of sinew in their character just to take the next step. Two candidates had died that summer trying to negotiate the hills to the Drill Instructor's satisfaction.

If I could last through those ordeals, I can last through this, he thought.

He kicked and pulled on his back and then on his front. He tried the sidestroke, the backstroke, anything that could spread the load on his muscles. His clothing seemed to weigh more and more and drag him down.

He stopped and floated for a minute to get his breath. He couldn't see his lower body because of the swollen life vest but he felt for his belt and undid it, kicking off his shoes and letting his trousers fall to the bottom of the lake. The chill of the cold water seemed to sting his legs even more now and he waited but a moment before resuming kicking and stroking toward the distant shore.

Strong swam like a Spartan. He ignored the pain in his limbs. He shivered as he puffed for breath but he wasn't going to quit. The shore looked closer, almost obtainable.

After an hour of constant movement Strong realized there was something seriously wrong. Although he was kicking steadily he hadn't heard the telltale splashing that accompanies a flutter kick. He struggled to look back and was for the first time truly scared when he realized his legs, contrary to what he thought, weren't moving. They dangled helplessly in the water. Strong's heart skipped when he grasped that his legs were paralyzed. It was the first sign his body was shutting down.

Strong gritted his teeth and began clawing at the water, knowing his time was running out. His muscles burned but he continued to reach and pull, reach and pull.

His arms grew heavier and his strokes shorter and more sluggish. Water splashed in his face but he couldn't seem to keep his head above the surface, the weight of his skull pushing his face into the lake with each stroke. Breath came harder and within a few moments he could see nothing and feel even less. He floated silently, his head forward, only fifty yards from the shore.

"That's a great idea but I'm not sure that I understand how we pull it off. I can see, though, why Strong would make sure he wouldn't lose you," Phillips said as he looked at her after she had whispered her idea.

"Andrew! For God's sake," she said as she put both hands on her forehead. "I've been so worried with my own problems I totally forgot about Andrew. Is he okay? I can't believe I've been so selfish."

"I don't know. His plane went down but they spotted a chute. Search and rescue is looking for him now. And I don't think you're being selfish. We're fighting one wave after another. There's not much time to do anything but keep marching." Phillips could tell Laura was disconcerted by the revelation that Strong had bailed out.

"Laura, I know this is hard, but we've got to find out what Megan knows. I've got to have your help," Phillips said.

"I know. What a hell I've gotten myself into," she replied.

"It's a hell for all of us and if we don't find out the answer to what is causing these illnesses it may be a hell for a lot more people," Phillips answered.

Laura nodded. "Here's how I think we can make Megan cooperate," she said and began to whisper into his ear.

The door flew open and Laura went stumbling through, tears streaming from her eyes and blood coming out of her nose.

"Oh, my Lord," exclaimed Megan who was sitting at the conference table in the windowless room. She jumped up from her chair and put her hands to her mouth.

"What the fuck is she doing in here?" yelled Phillips to the two men following him, one holding what looked like a stun gun and the other pushing a small makeshift surgical table with what could have been medical instruments on it.

"Get that son of a bitch out of here and put her in another room!" Phillips snapped.

"Megan, help me! They'll hurt you next! Make them stop," Laura pleaded until she was interrupted by a resounding slap across her face administered by Phillips himself. She promptly collapsed as a horror-stricken Megan was hustled out of the room.

"Don't hurt her!" Megan screamed as she was jostled down the deserted passageway.

Laura let out a bloodcurdling cry just as the door to the room slammed shut that caused Megan to sob. The man roughly shoved her into an empty room and locked the door from the outside.

Back in the conference room, Phillips quickly put a small tape recorder up to the air-conditioning vent and pushed 'Play'. Screams, pleas, muffled sobs and angry voices poured forth. He knew they were finding their way to the room that was now holding Megan captive.

Laura was sitting at the table, looking in a small mirror at the fake blood on her face and rubbing her jaw, which sported a red handprint. Phillips looked at her with a pained expression.

"I'm sorry if I was too rough," he mouthed. Laura gave him a small smile and waved him off.

Phillips began to intermittently stop the tape and after ten or fifteen minutes started it again. He repeated the procedure twice.

Laura watched and was confused. "Why are you doing it that way?" she whispered.

"Indulgence and withdrawal maximizes perception. Each time we stop it she has time to think about what has happened to you . . . what *is* happening to you and worry that she'll be next. Don't you remember when you were little and knew you were in trouble when your Dad got home? Waiting and worrying was always worse than the actual punishment. Actually, the punishment was a relief," Phillips explained softly. "By the time we're through, she'll have imagined things far worse for her than we could actually come up with. Are you ready for the next act?" he asked.

"Break a leg," she said and moved over to one of the agents in the room who applied more fake blood to her mouth, around her eyes and on her clothes. *Who said I would never use my drama classes in business?* He then placed tooth black on her beautiful teeth and even Phillips was amazed at how real it looked. Megan placed a colored contact lens in her right eye which, when surrounded by fake blood, looked exactly like a blinded cornea. The agent ripped her sleeve half off and did his best to make her look disheveled.

"This is going to hurt but if you can hold out to the end of the hall, I think it'll work."

"Whose idea was this?" Laura asked lightly, knowing full well that she was the creative power behind the plot that was about to cause her a great deal of pain.

Phillips opened the door and marched down the hall pounding his fist on the wall as he walked. He knew this would be like a ticking clock to Megan as she heard the thumps get closer and closer.

Phillips slowly inserted the key in the door's lock and twisted it. When it clicked he jerked open the door to find Megan huddling with her back to the wall in near hysteria. He walked over to her, ever so slowly, and stood just inches from her. Leaning close, knowing his hot breath was right in her trembling face, he said quietly, "Well, Megan, will you be telling me what I want to know or will you end up like your friend?"

At that point he smoothly stepped aside so she could see the burly agent drag a bloodied, toothless, bleary-eyed and blinded Laura by the hair past the door, stopping only long enough for Megan to see the metamorphosis that had occurred to this once stunningly beautiful woman.

"No, no," she sobbed. "I'll tell whatever you want."

Laura disappeared and the door was shut. Phillips produced a pocket recorder, turned it on and began to question her. After several questions he was convinced she was telling the truth. He just had to find out what she knew that would be helpful to him.

"You say that Finklestein never shared with you any of the details of what he was doing. Surely, you must have seen documents that indicated what was going on. He had to keep track of production, consolidated reports on accounting, things like that, didn't he?"

"Well, yes," she said between sobs. "He would get those reports and forward them to me to have them saved on the server."

"Did you do that?"

"Yes, I always did."

"Well, we've checked and his computer and the server have been totally erased. Every report is gone. Did you save hard copies?" Phillips asked pointedly.

"Oh, no, he wouldn't permit it," Megan said quickly.

"Listen to me and listen good. Is there *any place* we can find that information? If you know something, you had better tell us, understand?"

Phillips took a step forward. Megan tensed and Phillips moved back.

"There isn't any place," she said and then hesitated. "Except."

"Except where?" Phillips demanded.

Megan had a strange look in her eyes. Her skin was chalky and her breath short. Her mouth opened as if she wanted to speak but nothing came out except a small guttural sound. She stared at Phillips and then fell from her chair to the floor.

Phillips rushed over to her. "My God, she's having a heart attack!" He loosened the collar on her blouse and screamed to the agents outside. "Get in here! I need help."

The agent burst through the door and within minutes as Laura looked on with horror, they were loading her into an ambulance for the short trip to the hospital. With sirens screaming and a convoy of cars with flashing emergency lights she was taken to the nearest hospital, a small community facility. Phillips had made the necessary calls and the medical team was waiting at the door. They rushed her to ICU and began working to stop the heart attack.

In two hours the physician came into the waiting room and Phillips asked anxiously. "What's the prognosis?"

"I don't know. It was more of a stroke than a heart attack. I can't tell how much damage there is at this time."

"When can I talk to her?" Phillips asked.

"Only God can tell you that. She's in a coma," the doctor said and smiled sympathetically. "Do you want to see her?"

"Yes, of course," Phillips said. He and the two agents that had accompanied him were ushered down the hall and into her room. Megan lay still surrounded by monitors with tubes coming out of her.

Phillips leaned over the bed. "Megan? Can you hear me?" He got no response. She was clearly in another world.

"I know she would help me now if she could. She was ready to talk just before she had the attack. The answer is locked in her mind. If I could just get to it," Phillips said in frustration as he straightened up.

The doctor left the room and Phillips sat in a chair with a troubled look. "Damn, we were just about to make a breakthrough. I think she was getting ready to tell me that there was another place we could find the information. Now, she can't tell us anything. Damn it! Somebody's going to need to stay with her and make sure she's taken care of. Maybe, she'll come to.

"Would you mind staying here to watch Megan? Make sure she's safe and gets whatever she needs," he asked one of the agents. The man nodded agreement. "If she says anything, anything at all, let me know."

"Yes, sir," the agent replied.

"Maybe we can find the records she was talking about," the other agent offered.

"Not enough time. Not enough time," Strong muttered. "But I don't know what else to do. Let's go."

"It's a shame you're not a mind reader," the agent said.

"Yeah," Phillips said, as he moved to the hospital room door.

Phillips was the last one to the door and as he grasped the door to leave, the agent that was staying behind called to him, "Sir?" Phillips turned and paused.

"What do you bet she's been taking Zaners?"

Phillips turned shaking his head and left without answering.

In Baltimore, a twenty-six year old, overweight and frustrated reporter looked for a way to enhance her fledging career. For three years, since graduating from the University of Maryland in broadcasting, she had worked at WBAL-TV and while she wanted to be a news anchor, her boss, the News Director, refused to let her have a shot at the position. While she suspected it was because of the battle she constantly waged with her weight she couldn't prove it. There wasn't enough evidence to confront him and certainly not enough to sue the station for discrimination. At least not yet.

She had had her present assignment for two years. She was the "Health Editor," a nothing job where she spent her days chatting with doctors, nutritionists, therapists, and pharmacists. Her stories were soft news, to say the least, and only warranted being aired twice a week with reruns on weekends. She saw little future of breaking into the news slot unless she had a scoop, which was pretty unlikely on her beat.

This particular day she was visiting one of her normal stops, St. Elizabeth Hospital, where she caught up on the latest therapies for such in-vogue mental disorders as bulimia and anorexia. But today, she noticed something was different. The hospital was much busier than last week. There were more nurses on the floors and more calls over the hospital intercom system.

"Hey, what's the deal? Are you all having a special?" she asked the psychiatrist who was one of her regular sources.

"Looks like it, but actually nobody is in for exactly the same thing. Must be a full moon," he smiled, brushing off the question. He was eager to get back to the interview that might plaster his face throughout the Washington Metroplex on the 6 and 10 o'clock news.

They finished the interview and she and her cameraman went on to the next stop, Katlin Drug Company, the largest drug store chain in Baltimore. Her usual contact, the head pharmacist for the company was always on top of what was happening with the latest drugs. Plus, he could spot a medicine that was on its way out, like Rezulin, long before the Food and Drug Administration.

The reporter noticed there were six pharmacists working; two more than were normally on duty. "Got some extra help, Phil?" she asked.

Phil smiled and said, as he came from behind the pharmacy, "We do, in all our stores. Business has picked up recently. Can't say why but I'm not going to argue with it." The reporter asked her routine questions. Phil alerted her to a new drug containing shark cartilage that was supposed to be very effective in combating cancer. "Don't count on it. It's just wishful thinking," he said.

While the young woman tried to stay interested she was sensing a much bigger story that apparently no one else was picking up on. When she finished with Phil she told her cameraman, "We're going to four or five more hospitals. I want to see if they're busier than last week."

Their visits confirmed that the hospital population had, indeed, swelled. The reporter was smart and knew something was going on and was determined to find out what it was. She knew she couldn't tell her Assignment Editor her suspicions. If there were a good story, he'd just give it to the Evening Anchor. She believed was *her* story and she was going to be the one to file it. This was the one that would usher to the news anchor chair.

She went back to the station and called the Office of the Surgeon

General, the head of the National Public Health Service, and was referred to the Public Affairs Officer. After requesting an audience with the Surgeon General she was told categorically that he wasn't available. Yes, he was in town but wasn't free for an interview.

The "Health Editor" asked a few questions about the rise in the number of patients that she had seen and was told there were no reports indicating such an increase. Must just be an anomaly, she was told. That's when she came up with her plan.

The next morning she loaded up her cameraman and drove the 45 minutes to Washington and the National Health Service. Finding her way to the Surgeon General's office she announced herself to the receptionist and that she had come to speak to the Surgeon General, on camera.

The Public Affairs Officer quickly appeared and in a very angry exchange told her that she would not, under any circumstances, be allowed to see the doctor without an appointment.

She took her cameraman and settled into the most comfortable chairs they could find in the reception room. There they waited. During the next four hours the Public Affairs Officer frequently visited, at first trying to reason with her and then finally threatening to have them ejected by the building security.

"Just try it. I'm a citizen and I have a right to be here. If you want us to leave, then grant us an interview with Dr. Blasingdale. Otherwise, we have every right in the world to wait right here," she said self-righteously. The more resistance she met, the more she believed she was onto something.

At five o'clock, the receptionist said, "The office closes to the public at five. You'll have to leave."

The couple picked up their gear and went into the hall as the receptionist locked the door and left for home.

"What now?" the cameraman asked.

"Did you see Blasingdale leave? Nope, he's still in there and this is the only way out. We'll just have a seat on the floor and wait for him," his partner said.

"You're going to ambush him?" the long-haired cameraman asked. "Man, you're asking for it." The reporter had every intention of getting it, and the "it" was the story.

At half past seven she looked down the long hall and saw the Surgeon General and his personal assistant approaching. As they reached the end of the imperial-like corridor, they turned out the light, opened the tall wooden doors and stepped into the outer hall where the reporter was waiting. She was on him like a June bug. Her cameraman flipped on his high-powered strobe light and she thrust the microphone in the doctor's face.

"Doctor Blasingdale, I'm with WBAL-TV in Baltimore. Can you tell us why there's been such an alarming increase in patients in local hospitals?"

The Surgeon General was totally taken aback. He had never been the subject of such an "ambush" interview. He was discombobulated and unsure of himself and it showed. He hadn't paid much attention to the Public Affairs Officer when he reported the crew's presence today. He thought they would be gone.

"Why there's nothing to be alarmed about," he stammered. "The situation is quite under control."

"So you acknowledge that there *is* a dramatic rise in illnesses," the reporter pushed.

"I didn't say that. You took that out of context," he said defensively. The young correspondent was loving it.

"Is it true that there's an epidemic? Why haven't you announced it?" she badgered. She quickly hit him with the question that was damning on its face, "What have you got to hide?"

The Surgeon General pushed past her, muttering something about "no comment" and hurried down the stairs.

When he faded out of sight with the personal assistant glaring over her shoulder, the reporter-cameraman team smiled to themselves. *Geraldo Rivera couldn't have done better,* they thought.

"What'd you get?" she eagerly asked her cinematographer.

"A scared old man who was saying things he shouldn't," he answered with a crooked smile.

"Exactly! We're going to talk to hospitals all over Washington and Baltimore, every doctor's office, every pharmacy. Then we'll confront him again with that evidence. We already have him on tape practically admitting there's an epidemic. When we get through with him, he'll wish he'd never refused to give us an interview."

Chapter Eighteen

The arms that grabbed Strong by his "Mae West" and then went on to grasp him across the chest were muscular and experienced. He was dragged through the water to a long, dangling sling that swayed under the wash from a thumping helicopter rotor.

The diver from the Coast Guard Search and Rescue team wrapped Strong in the harness and began to ascend into the waiting aircraft. Once on board, a corpsman started administering mouth-to-mouth resuscitation. Suddenly, he felt himself coughing. He was breathing. He felt a wave of relief. He turned his head to vomit. He drank in more air. Pure air.

The flight to Corpus Christi took about thirty minutes and by the time he had landed and been checked out by the doctor at the base, he was feeling okay. Tired and sore but okay.

Dressed in a Navy flight suit and a pair of spare boots, courtesy of the dispensary, he sat down with one of the FBI agents who had seemed to become permanent fixtures at the base.

"What about the Learjet? Did it get away?" he asked.

"I don't know. They're monitoring that at the tower. My job was to make sure you got back safe and sound. I guess we just barely made it, huh?" he asked.

"As near as I can tell, I was getting ready to become one with the mighty lake," Strong answered.

"Look, you can stay here at the dispensary and rest or I can get you a flight back to Dallas. If you want, we can go to the PX and get you some clothes. The doc says you're fit, so it's whatever you want to do," the agent offered.

"Yeah, I'd like to get back to Dallas but I want to find out what's happening with the Learjet. And this flight suit is fine until I get home. I used to wear one, although it wasn't quite as snug as this one," he quipped.

"Yeah, fabric shrinks with age," the agent smiled. "Come with me to flight operations and we'll get you on a plane and try to find out what's happening on that other front."

"I don't believe this guy! Stinger Five, this is Stinger Six," said the F-14 lead pilot into his radio.

"This is Five. Go Six."

"Bandit is descending rapidly. Stay on him," ordered the lead.

The Tomcats pulled to each side of the Learjet and went down with it, foot for foot.

"Stop your decent, Learjet. You cannot escape. Level out and begin a gentle three-sixty turn," the pilot radioed. Still the Learjet fell.

"Leader, we're at twenty-five hundred and dropping fast. We're going to have to pull out," came the transmission from the wingman.

"Wait until five hundred feet. If they don't pull out then, they won't pull out at all," he responded.

Asam didn't have to be told when the battle was being lost. He had fought in too many of them. He moved to the door and began to unlock it. The plane had slowed enough and was below pressurization altitudes so he knew he could get the door open.

A deafening roar filled the cabin as the doors separated and cold air filled the inside space. He braced himself against the bulkhead and raised the M-79 Grenade Launcher to his shoulder. It was a short-range area weapon but if he could lead the F-14 on his port side enough, maybe, he could cause some damage.

Just as he got the weapon sighted, the Learjet surged abruptly to the right. Asam reached for the roof to stabilize himself but it was too late. He felt himself falling out of the plane and being slapped with a blast of winter air. As he began the fall to his death, he pointed the grenade launcher and pulled the trigger, hearing the muffled pop as it sent its round toward the pursuing F-14.

Asam never saw the flash as the grenade impacted and exploded into the Tomcat's tail section, causing a trail of smoke to stream from the plane.

"Stinger Six! I've been hit by something. I have no hydraulics and I'm on fire," yelled the wingman.

"Eject Two! Eject!" commanded the flight leader.

The wingman followed orders and punched out of his wounded aircraft watching it spiral into the Gulf of Mexico as he floated to the water, glad he got out alive.

"I can't land on the water! It's just asking for it. The controls are mushy to begin with. We need to just turn around and do what they say," the pilot pleaded.

"You do what *I* say, you infidel bastard," Finklestein barked and pushed the pistol back into the man's temple.

The pilot pulled back on the throttles and lowered the flaps thirty percent. The remaining F-14 was beside him and radioing him to turn around or be fired on. After watching his wingman go down, the Learjet pilot knew the F-14 was ready to splash him. He also knew the chances of making a successful landing on the water were slim and fully understood exactly what would happen.

First, the underside of the fuselage would hit the surface and the water would be as hard as concrete. Within seconds the wings would tear off. Fuel would begin to spew out and a simple spark could turn them into a fireball that would skim across the Gulf until it exploded. It was suicide.

He continued to descend. The F-14 pulled up and was now above him. He was at five hundred feet . . . two hundred feet . . . one hundred feet. He pulled off the power and nudged the yoke back to flare the aircraft. It responded sluggishly but the nose wiggled up and then dropped abruptly onto the choppy water.

He heard only the banging of the plane tearing apart. The last thing he saw was the evil face of Finklestein as water began to pour though the shattering windshield.

Phillips called his key people into the conference room to fill them in on the situation with Megan. "This is not a help. We were so close to learning were the copies of the records were and then," he paused and gestured by raising his hands over his head.

"But we did learn that there *are* records so now we have to find them. We've got to look everywhere. For the next two hours that's what we're going to do. Brill, take charge and organize the search, will you?" Phillips said.

Brill nodded, stepped up to a dry marking board and said, "Okay. Here's the way we'll cover the place," and began to draw. Within fifteen minutes the team had launched a massive search efforts. Every desk was ransacked and searched, every box opened and every closet scrutinized.

After an hour Brill approached Phillips and said, "Mike, everybody is coming up empty. Not everyone has reported in yet but I don't know where else I can send them to look."

Phillips nodded slightly without saying anything. Carolyn Zudi appeared and said, "From the looks on your faces, I take it no one else had any more luck than I did."

There was a heavy silence and then Phillips cell phone rang. He quickly answered and said, "You couldn't make it out? Is she still mumbling? Okay, I'll be right over."

"Megan's babbling some incoherent things. The agent couldn't understand. Brill come with me. Maybe your ear can make some sense of it if she keeps it up. Carolyn, you come too," he said and the group left the building on a run.

The sterility of the hospital room, coupled with a heavy silence, made the gathering seem even more ominous. Phillips, Brill, Carolyn Zudi and the agent loomed over the comatose figure in the bed.

"See here," the doctor said as he entered, "you can't be in here. She needs her rest."

Without ceremony, the agent pushed him into the hall, flashing his badge. "*We* are the ultimate authority in this hospital, Doctor. You don't give us orders. We give *you* orders. If you don't believe it, call your administrator." The physician stormed off.

Carolyn Zudi sat closest to the bed, actually leaning her elbows on the mattress with her head in her hands. Megan was silent.

"How long since she said anything?" Brill asked the agent.

"Since I called you," he said.

The group sat quietly for twenty minutes. Finally, Brill said, "This could go on for hours. She might not ever speak again. What do you want me to do?"

Phillips felt his heart drop. "I need you back at the Finklestein and Mark building. You better come with me. The agent can call us, I guess, if she starts again."

The group got up to leave except for Carolyn. "Wait a minute," she said staring intently at Megan. "You're right, Mike, I think she is trying to tell us something.

Carolyn Zudi kept her elbows on the bed and raised her hands to her temples. "There's a blue box. That's not much, I know but it's real clear."

The others looked at each other and stepped closer to her.

"Is that all? Can you see where it is?" Brill asked.

She sat back and let out a breath. "No. Let me have a brief rest and I'll try again. I think she's trying to help, actually. I'm just not picking up enough to make any sense. Just meaningless images. Sometimes it's like that."

The group sat silently for fifteen minutes. Phillips kept looking at the clock in the room. He knew that each minute was precious. Any second the President could give it up and the secret and panic would be on the streets. The terrorists would have won. He was basing everything on a psychic's ability to decipher thoughts. *Oh, my aching back,* he thought.

"Let's try again," Carolyn said softly and resumed her almost prayer-like position at Megan's bed. For some time she sat quietly without saying a word.

"She kept things in a blue box. I can see it. I can see it. It has writing on it. It says . . . sip . . . no . . . zip. Zip. That's it."

She looked up wide-eyed. "Does that mean anything? It was very clear. She had a little compartment in her desk. About once a week she would copy everything and put in the blue box."

"Zip? Zip drive! There's another drive we don't know about! Where is it? We didn't find it," Phillips said, excited. "Where's the disk?"

"It's hidden in her desk in a candy box," Carolyn said.

"They tore that damn desk apart," Brill said as Phillips jerked out his phone. He contacted Brown and quickly explained the situation. "It's in a special compartment in the desk. Find it and have the contents ready for me in ten minutes," he said.

The group was in the car and on their way back to Finklestein and Mark. Phillips negotiated the late afternoon traffic. Even on a Saturday it was heavy. He began to think out loud, "She was obviously afraid that if she lost something Finklestein would blame her and she didn't think she could get a job like that anywhere else.

"So, she bought one of those blue Zip drives. You know, the ones that have big storage capacity on one disk? Then she'd secretly save the things that she saved to the server. It was just in case something happened to the material."

"This is like finding the Nixon tapes," Brill said.

They arrived at the building and went straight to Megan's desk. Brown was already there printing out the index of the Zip drive.

"Tell Mr. McWaters I want a meeting in thirty minutes with the chemists to decide which files to print out first," Phillips said.

"Yes, sir," Brown answered grasping the disk in both hands before he quickly left the room.

"Come on," he said, "I've got to call my boss."

They went into Finklestein's office where Laura was waiting and Phillips pulled out his secure cellular phone but before he could dial, it began to ring.

"Phillips," he said punching the *Send* button. "Yes. Good job! Tell him good job as well. Talk to McWaters and have someone pick him up at NAS Grand Prairie.

"No survivors? Well, continue to search and make sure the Coast Guard knows if they do find any of them, they're dangerous bastards. See if we can get some kind of confirmation, bodies if possible . . . thanks."

He flipped his phone shut and looked at Laura with a smile. "Andrew Strong is okay. He was picked up and is on his way here. Finklestein and Asam, or Al-Lamri as you know him, are missing. Their plane went down and apparently no one made it out," Phillips continued.

Laura's relief with the news of Andrew's safety was promptly overshadowed by the realization that with both the terrorists gone the only chance of discovering the cure for the Zaners lay with Megan's disk.

"How long before we know what's on the disk?" Brill asked.

"Twenty minutes," Phillips said, anticipating his question.

☆

On the southern tip of Cuba nestled in the Isle of Pines, a sleek and powerful cigarette boat prodded its engines to life. A deep-throated roar tumbled from the boat's exhausts and its crew pointed the craft toward a spot midway between the coast of Texas and the large Cuban island.

Their superiors had been tracking the terrorist plane's progress and had suddenly lost it on the radar. They were expecting the arrival of their allies in the fight against America and wanted to make sure they hadn't run into trouble.

The boat began to accelerate and planed over the waves, quickly reaching its cruising speed of over 100 knots. It would be at its destination in less than two hours.

"Just a moment, Mike. I think the President will want to be in on this," said FBI Director Nall. The connection beeped and whined and soon the familiar voice of the President was on the line.

"Yes, Director. What news do you have?" the President said.

"Mr. President, I have Michael Phillips on the line from Dallas. Go ahead, Mike."

"Sirs, we have found some data that may give us what we need to counter the Zaner threat. We'll know something in the next few hours. The two terrorists' plane has crashed with apparently no survivors, so our greatest hope is the information we've uncovered."

"What information is that?" the President asked.

"We believe we're on the verge of deciphering the element that has been added to the vitamins that may be causing the illnesses. Once we have that, we can begin constructing the antidote."

The President and the Director asked a few more questions.

"Very well, keep me informed," the President said and hung up the phone.

"Mike, you don't have much time before the President goes public. I hope you can come through. I don't believe we'll be well served by revealing this vulnerability."

"Yes, sir, I know and I concur. We're doing everything possible."

"Good-bye, Mike," the Director said and the line went dead.

Phillips closed the phone as a knock sounded on the door and Coy McWaters and the Chief Chemist appeared.

"Come in, please," Phillips said.

The Chief Chemist, Dr. Janet Packard, was a middle-aged woman in a white lab coat. Phillips introduced Coy McWaters and Dr. Packard to Laura.

"Laura, Dr. Packard is from the DARPA — the Defense Advanced Research Projects Agency. She's the Chief Chemist with the Unconventional Pathogens Countermeasure Program."

Phillips read Laura's expression and realized his introduction meant nothing to her. "That's a program launched in '96 that hands out millions of dollars each year to scientists for research on projects that cover a broad range of techniques to counter infectious agents. This situation we're facing is what they exist for."

Dr. Packard spoke up. "We may have something," she said looking at a nodding Coy McWaters.

"Tell me," said Phillips.

Coy McWaters started looking through a stack of papers he brought with him. "There are 32 documents that look like they could be formulas or have something to do with formulas. We've been breaking down current Zaners to decipher their components. If they have different elements than the ones that were produced before, we'll know the toxic agent in them. Then we can come up with a vaccine."

"It's pretty clear that this agent responds to something in each person's body that is different, hence the diverse gestation times," Dr. Packard added.

"Have that and anything else you need printed out and then let's get back together in an hour. We don't have much time," Phillips said and the meeting broke up.

For the first time since Laura had met him, they were faced with a lull in the action. She sat on the couch in Finklestein's office and Phillips stood looking at the items on the freestanding bookcase.

"So what about you, Mike? How did you end up here?" Laura asked.

Phillips turned to her and smiled. "I work in Washington for the government and when this problem came up I got picked to try to fix it.

Actually, I deal with terrorist issues all the time and this fits right in," he said trying to avoid reflecting the danger in his assignment.

"I hadn't thought of it in that light, but of course, it's clearly a terrorist attack and those people were terrorists," she said. "I guess your family gets worried when you're off on dangerous assignments, huh?"

"There's no family, really. I divorced years ago and just never found anyone after that. Thankfully, we didn't have any kids so they didn't have to go through that. Have you always been in the advertising business?" Phillips asked.

"No," she explained and then told him of her past history. Phillips perceived she was distracted and deduced she had her mother on her mind.

"Look, I know you're worried about your mother. If you want to call and check on her, I'll leave you alone," he said.

"Thank you, Mike. I would like to talk to her but please don't leave. Can I use this phone?" she asked as she pointed to the Finklestein and Mark phone.

"Sure, help yourself."

"There's really just my Mom, brother and me and so we watch each other pretty closely," she said as she waited for the hospital to answer.

Laura reached the switchboard and was transferred to Dr. Lum. Her mother's condition hadn't changed and she seemed to be resting comfortably.

"I'm glad you told me about her diabetes. We've checked her blood sugar more closely and it's extremely elevated. We're working to lower it now. I can't tell you why she had such a violent attack after the disease has been under control for so long. There's no way we can tell about the Alzheimer's at this point," Lum said. "We'll keep you advised. I have your number."

She then called her brother and left a message on his answering machine, giving him the update on their mother and promising to keep him informed.

Laura hung up the phone slowly and quietly stared at the instrument.

"No change?" Phillips asked.

Laura looked up and smiled slightly. "No, although they seem to be making some progress," she said shaking her head.

The uncomfortable silence was broken by a knock on the door. Without waiting for someone to open it, the door swung out and in stepped a slightly worn and oddly dressed Andrew Strong.

"Anybody need a beat-up old fighter pilot?" he asked.

The room welcomed him with cheers and laughter.

"Oh, Andrew, you just don't know how happy I am to see you," Laura said.

"Well, I'm pretty happy to see you guys, too!" he said.

Remembering that Phillips was standing there, Laura said, "Mike, this is the famous Andrew Strong. Andrew, meet Mike Phillips. He's in charge of everything going on here." They shook hands.

"Mike, can you tell me what's happening?" he asked. "Every time I pose the question, someone tells me it's classified. I've just flown a jet that's older than I am after a person I thought was my client, parachuted in a ripped parachute and swum across Lake Gichigoomie. After all I've been through, I think I deserve to know."

Phillips had to agree. "Go get some rest and we'll talk tomorrow," Phillips said smiling and putting his hand on Strong's shoulder. "The car is waiting for you and we have rooms for you both at the Anatole."

Wearily, they agreed and left, pledging to return early the next morning.

The cigarette boat slashed though the churning sea in route to the last known location of the downed Learjet. As it neared the designated point it throttled back and began a circular search pattern. It was dark by now and they used their powerful spotlights to pierce the darkness.

"We're at the correct coordinates but all we can find is aircraft wreckage. Seat cushions and debris. No sign of life," reported the driver to his base in Cuba.

"Continue to search," came back the answer.

The boat extended its search area. Using a night scope, the first mate scanned the surface looking for anything that might be a person.

The radio came alive. "There's a vessel on an intercept course with you. Signature indicates probable U.S. Coast Guard Cutter. Break off search and return."

"Roger," the driver said and turned the boat south toward Cuba.

"Wait a minute," the first mate said. "Go right ten degrees."

"We've got to get out of here. There's a Coast Guard Cutter coming."

"Turn right! I see a person," the first mate repeated urgently.

The captain relented and idled up to the sighting. As they neared, the first mate reached over with a grappling hook and caught the figure by his clothing and pulled it to the boat's port side. He reached over and, with the help of the captain, pulled the water-soaked victim on board.

"Is he alive?" the first mate asked as he turned the man over on his back

"I don't know but we've got to get out of here or the Yankees will be on top of us," said the captain as he jumped into the driver's seat and slammed the throttles forward. The boat lurched ahead and began its high-speed run back to Cuba and safety.

"Yes, General," the President said as he answered the phone. Surgeon General Blasingdale had insisted that he be put through to the President, telling his personal assistant that it was literally a matter of life and death. Blasingdale was a short man with a potbelly who was more important in his own mind than in anyone else's.

The President was in an informal Sunday afternoon meeting with his Chief of Staff and suspected he knew what the doctor wanted. He didn't want to talk to him but given the critical nature of the crises, couldn't avoid the call.

"Mr. President, we received data last night that indicates a new wave of people has reported into local hospitals with a variety of complaints. Thousands more people, Mr. President, continue to flood the hospitals."

The President could visualize the Surgeon General at his desk pontificating into the phone.

"We are receiving increasing inquiries from local media asking if there have been any epidemics reported or if we're predicting any such widespread illnesses. In fact, I was accosted just Friday night by a reporter. It's only a matter of time until they make the connection.

"If it looks as if we've been withholding information while people are dying, it would be devastating to the Administration. We would lose all credibility. Mr. President, we must issue a health alert at the very least. I don't believe we have the luxury of honoring another hour's delay in releasing information to the public," he said.

"Just a minute, Doctor," the President interrupted. "It will do us little good to tell the American public that they're getting sick because of a pill they took, if that is it, and offer no cure. Talk about losing credibility, how would we look if everyone quit taking the vitamins and still continued to get sick?

"I appreciate your concern and expect you to continue to carefully monitor the situation but we're going to let Director Nall's people have the time we promised them to isolate the cause and find a cure. If they don't succeed, *then* we'll look to your option," the President said firmly.

"But Mr. President," Blasingdale blustered, "I—"

"Thank you, General," the President interrupted and hung up the phone. He turned around and looked at his Chief of Staff who was sitting near the center of the room. "I left him sputtering," the President said as he walked from his desk and sat in his presidential rocking chair removing his glasses and squeezing the bridge of his nose.

"Sir, do you think he'll break ranks and go public? You know, hold a press conference and resign? *Savior of the people* type thing. Maybe accuse you of stonewalling information?" the Chief of Staff asked with a worried look. "That could get out of control very fast."

"I don't know. It's certainly possible. He's got an ego to fit the *First Doctor*. He's just one of the ticking time bombs sitting all around me right now. If he does, one thing is for sure," the President said, "I'm screwed."

There was a tap on the door.

"Yes," the President answered. His personal assistant stuck her head in the door.

"I'm sorry to intrude, Mr. President, but I thought you'd want to know. Your meeting tomorrow with Senator Verity has been cancelled."

Verity was chairman of the Senate Armed Services Committee and the President needed his support of the White House's bill on military troop strength.

"Damn, I needed to talk to him. Why is it cancelled?" he asked.

"Sir, his Administrative Assistant just called and said the senator was at home and suddenly became extremely ill. They said it happened very fast and he's been taken to the emergency room at Bethesda."

The President and the Chief of Staff just looked at each other without saying a word. Words weren't necessary.

Chapter Nineteen

Strong walked into the building and went straight to Finklestein's office to find Phillips. Phillips sat, unshaven, reading a file.

"Good morning, Mike," said Strong.

Phillips looked up and smiled. "Well, good morning Andrew. I'm glad you're here. I have a feeling I'm going to need your help so you better know it all. I see you've got a Top Secret Clearance from the Marine Corps," Phillips said, looking at the record jacket in his hands, "so I'll just review the ground rules." He handed Strong a cup of coffee.

After giving the standard warning about keeping secrecy and the penalties for non-compliance, which he administered more gently than in his first encounter with Laura, Phillips began to fill-in an astonished Strong.

"That son-of-a-bitch! That's what I get for going against my better judgment. We were just being used! He was using us to poison the country. That's just great. I spend my time in the Marine Corps because I wanted to serve my country and now I end up being a tool to destroy it!" Strong lamented when Phillips had finished

"He never intended to have two campaigns," Strong said. "And the bastard never intended to pay us, either."

Phillips was silent. Strong sat there in an ill-fitting flight suit staring at the wall. He knew what was in store for him. Finklestein and Mark would never pay the monies spent thus far. The agency would be held responsible for them and, of course, could never pay such huge sums. It would, without doubt, be the end of The Idea Group.

It would probably ruin him as well. He had personally guaranteed many of the contracts that the agency had entered into on behalf of Finklestein and Mark and he didn't have the financial strength to meet those obligations. It would mean personal bankruptcy and disgrace.

Phillips must have deduced the same thing because he remained quiet, finally uttering, "I know. I'm sorry."

Strong looked up and took a deep breath. "Look. I can rebuild the agency. I can come back from losing everything. I learned that from my divorce. Hell, it's only money. But I can't recover from letting something like this happen because I was a part of it. That I can't rebound from. We've got to do something," he said.

The Oval Office was a place that the FBI Director normally enjoyed visiting. Reflecting on the momentous decisions that had been made in the room over the years gave him a feeling of participation in the most important events of his time. Today, however, he was a part of a decision he was vehemently against.

"Mr. President, I implore you. Let Mike Phillips have the time you promised him. I believe they're close to a solution," Nall pleaded as he sat squeezed into the visitor's chair.

"I'm sorry, Director. I'm afraid this is on the verge of raging out of control. Members of Congress are now beginning to become ill. Failure to act could be interpreted by some as incompetence; in fact, as high crimes and misdemeanors. If Clinton can get impeached for lying, think what they would do to me," the President said.

"Mr. President, with all due respect, the welfare of the country outweighs any personal political considerations and I believe..."

The President's face flashed red. Nall knew he had stepped in it. "See here, Director, that is my concern, the welfare of the people. No, this must stop *now* and the American people should be told of the danger they face," he said.

"However, I won't ask you to revoke my promise to Phillips. I'll call him personally to deliver the news. Thank you, Director, for your support and valuable counsel," The President said curtly.

Director Nall rose slowly, "Of course, sir. I would hope you would reconsider," he said. "If we let this plot become public it will undermine any feeling of security our citizens have. The terrorists will have won.

"Oh, we might have stopped the dying but they'll have robbed us of the comfort of living in a secure nation. People will begin to live in fear. That's what they want, Mr. President! Death is only a vehicle to get to that objective."

"Good Day, Director," the President said flatly.

Nall, shoulders slumped, left the Oval Office.

Coy McWaters could hardly contain himself. "Mike, look at this," he said as he burst into the office with his Chief Chemist close behind.

It shocked both Strong and Phillips, each one momentarily immersed in his or her own problems.

"What is it?" Phillips asked and walked over to meet McWaters.

"We started running tests simultaneously on all of the things that looked like formulas in the files you gave us," Chief Chemist Packard said. "It really wasn't that hard to find. We would have eventually found it without the formulas," she said.

"Found what, Goddamnit?" Phillips shouted impatiently.

"The agent," McWaters said. "It was brilliant in its simplicity. The agent is an antigen only found in the rain forests of Brazil. It's a . . . a . . . multiplier, I guess is the best way to describe it. There's only a minuscule amount in the vitamins—less than 10,000 molecular weight—but it begins to accumulate in the system. Remember, they're taking these little devils every day.

"Once it's activated it causes every organ in the body to accelerate. And it will push a weak organ into complete failure. Got a little heart problem, but it's under control? Bang! Not anymore.

"Got a little diabetes but you're controlling it with diet and exercise? In your dreams. I mean, if you've got a weak link, it'll exploit it. Everything from cancer to Parkinson's. That's why there's no one illness that's resulting from it."

"My mother is diabetic!" Laura, who had just entered, quickly said.

"Exactly!" Dr. Packard injected.

"But you said once it was activated. What activates it?" Phillips asked.

"Oh, I didn't say, did I?" McWaters asked almost breaking into a laugh. "Caffeine! Once the body reaches a certain part per thousand centimeters of water, it goes pow! It's called the Potentiation Effect—one substance does not have a toxic effect but when added with another chemical it makes the latter toxic.

"And that's why we had the delayed reaction times. Everybody's different. Different absorption rates, different voiding rates; hell it even varies by days of the week and gender," Dr. Packard chimed in.

Strong gave a glance at the cup of coffee in his hand and quickly put it down on the table.

"Oh, man. Those bastards! We could have had a million dead before we knew what hit us," Phillips said rubbing his hand through his hair.

"Can we fix it? What about an antidote?" he asked, urgency in his voice.

"I think we can come up with one pretty quickly, if you can just give us some time. The chemistry isn't hard; it's just diabolical," Dr. Packard said.

Phillips was about to ask another question when his secure cell phone rang. He held up a finger signaling Packard to hold her thought.

"Phillips," he answered.

"Yes, Mr. President," he said respectfully and the group suddenly got very quiet.

"Mike, I'm sorry to do this but I'm afraid I can no longer keep this unfortunate situation a secret. I must inform the American public of the threat. I know I promised you more time but I'm afraid the decision has been made."

"Uh, Mr. President, before you pull the plug," Phillips said talking like a machine gun. "I must tell you that we've found the cure, well, the cause."

"Are you sure?"

"Yes, sir, the chemists have isolated and identified the toxin. They're starting to work on the vaccine."

"How long will that take?" the President asked, warily.

"How long to complete the vaccine?" Phillips repeated looking at Dr. Packard for a quick answer.

Packard shook her head with a frightened look. Phillips waved violently at her *come on!*

"Three days," she mouthed and held up three fingers.

"We can have it in three days, Mr. President," Phillips said quickly.

There was silence on the phone for at least ten seconds.

Finally the President spoke very slowly, "No, I'm sorry, Mike. The only way to handle this is by the procedure already set forth to deal with an epidemic. By the time we could set up a new way to get the vaccine to people, the time frame could drag on too long. We could have no telling how many casualties by then. I'm afraid I'm going to have to go public and let the chips fall where they may. We can't wait any longer to start treating these people. At least we can start treating it as an emergency and us what drugs exist now through the established channels for treatment of an epidemic."

Phillips was holding his head almost as if to force the ideas, the answers to come. He put his hand over the small phone and said to the little group of those assembled, "He doesn't think we can act fast enough."

He quickly removed his hand and tried to keep the President from hanging up before he could come up with a compelling reason for him to reverse his decision.

"Mr. President, I, uh, know, uh—" The President cut him off.

"I'm sorry Michael. I'm going to address the nation on television Tuesday night at 8 pm Eastern Standard Time. I hope you can find something that'll help but we can't wait before we alert the nation.

"Thank you for your work thus far and I look forward to hearing of your further success."

The line went dead.

☆

The White House press secretary hurried into the Chief of Staff's office with a concerned look on his normally happy face.

"We need to talk, Chief," he said shutting the door behind him. The Chief of Staff didn't welcome such intrusions but knew the press secretary wouldn't take such liberty without a gripping reason.

"What is it, Tim?" he asked quietly.

"My contact at the *Washington Post* just called and said the Surgeon General has called a press conference for tomorrow. He won't let out what it's about but has put him on background that it's a *matter of conscience*. That smells like a disagreement with the Administration. Do you know what this bastard is up to? I feel grandstanding coming on," the press man said.

"I sure do, that sorry son of a bitch. He knows the President has scheduled time for Tuesday night and he's trying to preempt him. What time is the conference?"

"It's at two. Should the President know?" the secretary asked.

"I'm not going to bother him with this. I'll handle it myself. Let me know if you hear anything else," the Chief of Staff said.

"Right!" the press secretary said and left the office. The Chief of Staff quickly picked up the phone and dialed a number from his campaign Rolodex.

"Is the Surgeon General expecting you?" asked the sour-faced receptionist.

The large man in a $2,000 dark suit and regimental striped tie handed her his card. "Oh, I think he'll see me," he said sardonically, never letting his eyes leave the woman.

Disconcerted, she looked at the card and then picked up the phone and pushed the intercom button. "There's a gentleman to see the Surgeon General," she said simply, not using his name or title.

"You can go back. The last door on the right at the end of the hall," she said and lowered her eyes, refusing to make eye contact.

The man walked purposefully to the appointed door and was greeted by the Surgeon General's personal secretary. The same fusillade of questions were asked and answered in exactly the same way. "Oh, I think he'll see me."

The personal assistant excused herself and entered Dr. Blasingdale's office. In a few moments, she appeared with a surprised look on her face.

"The General is very busy but he'll see you," she said, opened the door and watched as he entered and moved to the General's desk. She noticed the doctor wasn't standing, as one would expect someone to do when greeting a friend. She shut the door wondering who was this imposing stranger?

"Hello, John," said the big man cheerfully. "I'll bet you didn't expect to see an old Medical School colleague, did you?"

"No, I can't say as I did. How are you, Terry?" he asked uncomfortably, not offering his pudgy hand.

"Fine, fine. Thank you for asking, John," the visitor said as he lowered himself into the leather guest chair. He didn't seem phased that Blasingdale had failed to offer to shake hands. He looked around the room for a moment, ostensibly admiring the trappings of the Surgeon General's office.

He turned back to the doctor and said, "Well, now, let me get to the point. As you may know, but probably don't since we haven't seen each other in forty years, I'm a big supporter and admirer of our President." Then added quickly, "and I know you are, too."

The Surgeon General said nothing.

"Medicine has been good to me. It's made me financially independent. So much so that I can afford to share my wealth with great people like the President. I've donated nearly $1 million to his campaigns since he first ran for office and only part of it was tax deductible," he laughed mildly. "I don't mind doing it. I think he's the greatest leader our country has had in seventy-five years. And he's been good to you, too, hasn't he, John?"

The visitor continued without waiting for an answer. "But you know, John, the word around town is that you're going to have a press conference here in the next day or two and try to damage the President. I know that sounds silly. How could anyone that is beholden to the President for his very job be that ungrateful and two-faced? I know you wouldn't do that," the man smiled.

"Even so," the Surgeon General said coldly shifting in his chair, "sometimes the good of the nation can outweigh personal loyalties. In those cases a man must search his own conscience. I believe my conscience is clear."

"Good! Good for you, John," the man burst out with a strange smile. "That's very high-minded. Mine is too. So you won't be offended when you have your press conference if I follow it with one of my own? Sort of like they do with the opposing political parties."

"What do you mean?" the Surgeon General said, leaning forward in his chair.

"I mean that I'll follow your show with one of my own. I'll share with everyone in television land how you financed part of your way through med school," he said with raised eyebrows.

"What are you talking about?" Blasingdale said suspiciously.

"Did you think I didn't know? John, I was your roommate, for Christ's sake! In fact, at least three of us in the class knew you were performing illegal abortions for money," the visitor said. "The only reason we didn't turn you in is that we felt sorry for you."

"Why, that's outrageous. I never did any such thing. That's a bald-faced lie," he shouted, his face beet-red and his hands shaking.

There was a nerve-racking pause. The man reached in his inside coat pocket and pulled out a photograph of a young woman, obviously taken in the early 1950's. He looked at it and then flipped it in his fingers so it was facing the Surgeon General. "Remember her, John? She remembers you. Turns out, she ended up as one of my patients in Oskaloosa. Isn't that amazing that over that many years a woman you performed an illegal abortion for in 1955, in Boston, would end up in my office in Oskaloosa, Iowa? She certainly remembers you well. Even how much you charged her. $150. Not bad wages in those days for an illegal procedure while practicing without a license.

"John, I have others and they're all willing to stand up and tell the cameras that you were an abortionist. And you did it for money. Not even to reduce pain and suffering. Not to help unwed mothers or victims of rape or incest. Just for money. I wonder how many of those *patients* died? And if I remember correctly, you're Catholic to boot!

"What a disgrace. What a humiliation. What a sad end to such an illustrious career," the man said carefully spacing the phrases making each one more dramatic. He sat back in his chair and waited for it all to sink in with Dr. John Blasingdale.

The Surgeon General looked spent. His sixty-five-year-old frame had sunk deep into the plush chair and one wondered how he would ever get out, he looked so drained. He couldn't even summon an argument.

"Well, I know you're a busy man, John, and I won't take any more of your time. I hope you'll reconsider the subject of your press conference and choose one that won't be detrimental to the President. Then you can retire as a distinguished, and untarnished, public servant. Become a professor emeritus at Harvard Med and enjoy all the adulation befitting your station.

"It would be the way to end your career on the high road."

The old classmate stood up and walked to the door, turning as he reached for the doorknob. "So good to see you, John. Have a nice day," he said with sarcasm dripping from every word and walked out of the office.

☆

Phillips flipped the cellular phone shut and looked at Andrew Strong.

"The President is going public Tuesday night. This is not good. I don't know what we can do about it, though."

"Why?" Asked Coy McWaters. "We're so close to finding the vaccine."

"He thinks it'll take too long to get it distributed and too many people will die in the meantime. He thinks he's better off to getting them into treatment now, even if they don't have an antibody and just treat them with existing medicines. I don't know how to argue with him. I've said everything I know to convince him.

"Coy, continue your efforts to perfect an vaccine. I'm sure they'll be calling for it after the broadcast."

McWaters and Packard dejectedly left the room. Phillips sat heavily down in the chair behind the desk. "Andrew, there's no reason for you and Laura to hang around Dallas. Why don't you head back to Oklahoma City? I know you want to check on your mother, Laura," he said. "I think you've both done all you can do here. We'll notify you the moment we have the vaccine and make sure it's shipped directly to you for Laura's mother.

"Please understand how much your help has meant. But now it's out of our hands We'll be in touch."

Strong shook hands with Phillips and he and Laura quietly left the office.

As they reached the front door of Finklestein and Mark, Strong said, "Laura, you go on back. I've got some things to do here. Keep your cell phone on in case I need you, okay?"

She started to ask what was going on and then decided against it. "Okay. I'll be at the hospital or at home or the agency," she said and exited to get in the waiting FBI automobile assigned to transport her to Love Field. She stopped and turned back into the building.

She caught up with Strong. "Andrew, I've got to tell you something. I don't deserve your trust. There are things that have happened that you don't know about."

Strong looked at her and his face softened. "I'm sure it's not as bad as all that."

"It is every bit as bad as all that. Andrew, I deceived you. Finklestein offered me a $350,000 a year to work for him and not tell you. And I took it," she said with tears in her eyes.

"I knew something was up. Something had to make you cheerful about staying here." Strong said. "Laura, this whole thing has been an test of each of us. We've all had dollars thrown at us at a time when we needed them and you're not the only one who didn't pass with flying colors."

By now tears were flowing freely from Laura's eyes. "Let's don't make any hasty decisions. I need you at the agency. Don't let me down. We can work out these other problems out," Strong said.

Laura sniffed and wiped her nose. "Okay, Andrew. I'll take care of things back at the shop. I'll just wait to hear from you."

Strong reached over and gave her a hug and then turned and walked down the hall.

☆

"Mr. McWaters? Do you have a moment?" Strong asked as he opened the door to the Finklestein and Mark lab. The place was a hive of activity for a normally reserved function as chemistry.

"Certainly," McWaters answered and led Strong to a table in the corner of the room.

"When do you think you'll have the vaccine? Do you think you can do it in three days as Dr. Packard said?" Strong asked.

"Packard knows her stuff. If she says she can deliver, it's a pretty reliable prediction. We've already determined it will be an active immunizing agent. That means it can be an oral vaccine. Why?" McWaters said.

"I'm just brainstorming. We do that a lot in the ad agency business. What about mass production? Can that be done here in this facility?"

"Yes, I suspect so. The place is designed to make vitamins so everything is in place. We'd just have to make some minor adjustments."

Strong continued to question McWaters and then asked to talk to Dr. Packard.

"Dr. Packard, if the President goes public, then what will be the procedure followed by the Surgeon General?" he asked.

Packard thought for a moment and then outlined the methods that would be used to in hospitals and emergency treatment locations. She explained how hospital facilities would be utilized to serve as treatment points and how the Red Cross would serve as the probable monitoring agency. Because of the wide spread panic that would ensure once the announcement was made, every facility would be overflowing and especially with a lack of any antibody, would overload personnel, space and equipment.

Strong left the lab and found a small, unoccupied office and shut the door and locked it.

Chapter Twenty

4:30 a.m., Monday

It wasn't hard to find Phillips. Strong went to Finklestein's office and walked in to find him asleep on the couch. His motionless form was illuminated by the desk lamp that was still on. Strong suspected he had spent most of his nights on the couch since this began.

"Mike, wake up," he said as he nudged the man's shoulder.

"What is it?" he asked, sitting up on the couch looking around.

"I have to show you something. It's important," Strong said.

"I thought you went back to Oklahoma City. What are you doing here?"

"I had an idea. I decided to stay and work on it. Maybe it'll be a winner," Strong said.

Phillips got up and walked over and turned on the overhead light, rubbing his eyes.

"I've been doing some research. Look at this," Strong said as he started writing on a large pad that was on an easel in the corner of the room. He wrote and talked for nearly thirty minutes.

Phillips watched every word and listened intently. When Strong finished he said, "Well, there are a couple of variables. First, can you do what you say you can and second, have you guessed right on what the Surgeon General will do?"

"I don't know," said Strong. "But it's worth a try. The alternative is a catastrophe."

"If we can't deliver, the President will be crucified and a lot of Americans will die who might have been saved. Do you want that on your conscience?" Phillips asked.

"My conscience is full of guilt as it is. I've got to do something whether it works or not."

"Okay, Andrew, I'll back your play. It's about 6 a.m. in Washington. I'm going to call the Director and try to get him on board so he'll set up the call with the President.

"Will you get hold of Coy McWaters and ask he and Packard to be here for the call? I want them in case there are medical questions we can't answer. It could happen in as little as 30 minutes so get them down here fast. Do they know about this?" Phillips said pointing to the pages that Strong had written and taped to the wall.

"I've spoken to them but they haven't seen the plan," Strong said.

"You better get them on our side before we talk to *The Man*."

"I'll see to it," Strong said and went out to the first desk and began punching in McWaters' number.

"I'll be honest with you, Mike. I tried everything I could to convince the President to give you more time. Not only was I unsuccessful, I was quite harshly rebuked. I'm not eager to be humiliated again in such a manner," Director Nall said.

"Director Nall, I know how strongly you feel and I feel that way too. But I think we have a compelling reason for going back to the President. Andrew Strong has a plausible plan and I really believe if he can get an audience to present it, he can demonstrate why it's a superior way to reach the same objective we all want. To protect the people.

"Sir, after going through all of this, we've got to persuade the President not to go public. We can do everything he wants and still protect the secrecy of the operation," Phillips pleaded.

"Just what is this plausible plan?" the Director asked.

Phillips began to recite what Strong had just presented. As he progressed he found himself getting more and more animated and enthusiastic. He finished and was actually winded. *I must think it's a pretty good plan,* he thought.

There was a pause. "Alright but I'm not making any promises. He may not even take my call so be prepared to continue on as you were," the Director said wearily. "I'll advise you *if* and when we can get through to the White House."

☆

"Director Nall, I'm afraid the President is tied up at the moment," said the Chief of Staff. "Is this regarding the conversation you had Sunday? The President hasn't changed his mind on that issue."

"Yes, that's the reason for my call. However, there have been new developments that I think the President should know about."

"Fine, sir. If you'll relay them to me, I'll be sure and give the President the update," the Chief of Staff said.

This wasn't going to be easy, thought Nall. His first inclination was to demand to speak to the President. Tell that arrogant middle manager that he was the Director of the FBI and his business was with the President and the President alone. Then, in a flash of non-ego driven insight, he changed his mind.

He paused and let the silence hang. Then in as soft a voice as he could muster he said, "I don't know what else to do. The sum total of my career and every debt I owe the President are riding on how well we manage this crisis. If I don't provide him the best counsel . . . the best alternatives . . . the best choices, I will have let him down.

"This latest development could change the entire face of this situation. Maybe it won't work. Maybe he'll reject it. But I feel strongly enough to humble myself and beg if I have to, to get it in front of him and make sure it is presented properly."

He couldn't tell what was happening on the other end but the Chief of Staff hadn't cut him off yet.

"What I'm asking you to do, and if you can't, I understand, is to let me present this to the President so he'll at least know all his options," the Director concluded.

The Chief of Staff said nothing for a minute and then said, "I'll speak to the President and let you know within the hour."

"Thank you. I'll stand by the phone," the Director said and hung up.

☆

The air in Finklestein's office was getting stale. The four people were waiting for word on whether they had one more chance to convince the President not to throw the nation into a panic and play into Osama Bin Ladin's hands.

Strong and Packard stood at the easel making adjustments and inserting details and bullet points. Phillips was sitting at the desk leaning forward drumming his fingers on the glass top.

McWaters was busy with a calculator and pad. "When is he supposed to let us know?" he asked.

"He said within the hour, but he didn't say when we'd get to talk to the President. If we get to talk to him at all," Phillips responded. He got up and walked to the door and opened it, looking out into the cavernous reception area. He stood there for a moment and then turned back into the room, shutting the door behind him.

When the phone rang, everyone jumped. Phillips ran to the desk and picked up the receiver. "Phillips here," he said.

"Yes sir. Do you have any idea how much time we have? Yes, we'll be waiting." He hung up the phone and turned to the group. "The call will come in twenty to twenty-five minutes. Once the Director gets the call, he'll patch us in. He thinks we better make our case in the first ten minutes. If it goes beyond that, it's a good sign."

The time passed at a snail's pace. The tension continued to escalate as the minutes crept by.

"If the President doesn't buy this, he isn't as smart as I had him pegged," said Dr. Packard point-blank. "It's really an exceptional plan, Andrew, and you should be commended."

Strong was about to say something and the sharp ring of the phone preempted him.

Phillips grabbed it with his normal, "Phillips."

"Yes, sir. I'll put you on speaker phone." Everyone crowded around the instrument as Phillips pushed the speaker button and replaced the handset. "We're ready sir," he said.

"The President will be on in a moment," Nall said.

A few seconds passed and then the voice, with an edge of irritation, spoke up, "Yes, Director. What's this new development?"

"I'll let Mike Phillips tell you, sir," Nall responded.

"Mr. President, Andrew Strong, the president of the advertising agency for Finklestein and Mark, is here. He knows the company inside and out and was responsible for the advertising that sold the Zaner vitamin to two million Americans in three months.

"He's been working all night on a plan and I think it's important that you hear it so I'll just turn it over to him," Phillips said. Without waiting for permission, Strong stepped in front of the phone and began speaking.

"Mr. President, I know you're looking for the fastest way to get the vaccine into action. If you'll bear with me a minute, I may have the answer."

The line was silent but Strong wasn't deterred and pushed forward.

"If we," Strong said using the third person to put everyone on the same team, "follow the standard procedure for distribution of a vaccine as in the case of an epidemic, then it will take about fifty-five to sixty-three days to get the vaccine formulated, manufactured and distributed.

"The formula will have to be delivered to the national lab in Washington and processed under government scrutiny. The last time that had to be done was in 1952 and the actual delivery time was 72 days from start to shipping."

"How did he find that out?" Phillips softly asked McWaters.

"The Internet," McWaters whispered.

"So far, according to the secret reports the Surgeon General has distributed, we're seeing three hundred to three hundred fifty deaths a day that *may*, and I emphasize may, be a result of the Zaners. We aren't sure that it's accurate to attribute all of them to the toxin.

If we extrapolate that out and add a factor for an exponential increase, say it doubles every two weeks since more people will reach the activation threshold, then we can expect to lose 200,000 to 225,000 people.

"Plus, it'll mean panicking the entire country. People will be so afraid to take any kind of medicine we'll see a dramatic deterioration in the nation's health. That alone will probably add, conservatively, 100 deaths a day. That'll cause the health care system to be overwhelmed and will cause another 100 to 300 deaths a day as a result of inadequate or no care. All the deaths will probably be blamed on the Zaner, whether or not it's a valid charge.

"So we'll lose upwards of 3,000 people a day or over a quarter of a million Americans total, damage the country's faith in the health care system that will result in ancillary casualties and destroy the confidence in the nation's ability to protect itself against terrorists, which will, of course, encourage more attempts."

"What's your point, Mr. Strong?" the President asked impatiently.

"Just this, Mr. President. We can produce the vaccine here within 72 hours and in initial quantities necessary within 48 more hours. And we can get it into the stomachs of only those people who have been infected within seven days. This operation is already set up for that kind of performance.

"We can cut the casualties down to 3,500 to 4,000 people total. Plus we'll protect the confidence in our health care facilities and the government's ability to protect its citizens."

It had been ten minutes since Phillips had begun to talk.

The President spoke up. "How do you see that can be accomplished?" he asked.

"Mr. President we use the same vehicle that infected them. We reconstitute Zaner vitamins with the vaccine and distribute them through the same channels. Only the people who have subscribed and taken them will be impacted. The same people who are now at risk."

"If those people haven't finished their initial dose, and haven't yet reached toxic levels, by the time they get the replacement vitamins, they *will* have infected themselves," the President said carefully.

"No, sir. We'll run a very powerful advertising campaign that'll have people substituting their current vitamins for new Super Zaners. My staff is standing by to start on it right now. We've got most of the materials we need to produce the campaign and can have it underway by the time the vaccine is ready.

"We'll be offering double, even triple, new SuperZaners for every Zaner that is returned. We'll promote it heavily but only to those who have already received them. As you know, they're sold direct so we know every subscriber.

"The Surgeon General can issue a health alert to hospitals that strongly encourages, spelled *demands*, that they prescribe Super Zaners for use with all patients now hospitalized and those admitted for the next two months. It won't hurt the ones who aren't infected and will surely get to the ones who are.

"He can say that tests have confirmed that they are especially good at preventing a cold or flu and can increase resistance to infection.

"It'll work, Mr. President. We can *make* it work, I promise. We can make the vaccine faster and get it out quicker than any other alternative," Strong said.

"And how will you take care of those people who took the Zaners and decided to quit before the new Zaners—the Super Zaners as you call them—are distributed?" the President asked.

"I didn't say there wouldn't be some casualties, Mr. President. But we have a reasonable chance of dramatically reducing the number," Strong responded.

"Umm. You're quite a salesman, Mr. Strong. Do you have any other ideas?" the President asked.

"Actually, yes sir. If we could figure out a way to interrupt the flow of coffee, just for a few weeks, it could help slow down the activation process until we can get the vaccine distributed."

"Yes..." the President said in anticipation of Strong elaborating.

"What if there were a strike— by the trucking industry —say in support of Columbian laborers who harvest the coffee? If U.S. truckers refused to haul coffee until some concession were granted to them. I don't know what would be appropriate but some small concession. It would be a reason to disrupt the flow to restaurants and homes. People wouldn't stop drinking it; they'd just cut back their consumption, but that might be enough to buy us some more time."

"This Administration doesn't have a great relationship with the Unions but the previous one does. Let me talk to President Clinton and see if he'll help in talking to the trucker's union. Interesting idea. It could work.

"Get me a time schedule and the details of your plan. I'm tentatively approving it. I'll have to come up with a new reason for my appearance on television tonight but then that's what press secretaries are for.

"Bear in mind, however, if this gets leaked, all bets are off. If one word of it shows up in the media, we go to full disclosure."

"Yes, sir."

The television reporter and her cameraman left the last doctor's office on the list. Just as she suspected, full waiting rooms from open to close. They drove back to Baltimore and the traffic was relatively light. Pulling up to WBAL-TV to turn in the station sedan, she let the cameraman out and asked for the videotape as he stood in the door.

"Why?" questioned the photographer,

"First, I don't want anything to happen to it, and second, I want to watch it tonight. See if I can pick up anything in gestures or expressions from any of those folks we talked to in the last two days. That kind of thing."

The photographer reluctantly handed over the tape and started to head in to put up his gear.

"Get ready for tomorrow. We'll be there at eight, so we should leave early. When we hit Blasingdale with all the confirmations we got, he'll look like a fool. He'll have to come clean or show up as a liar on television. We'll be on the air with it by tomorrow night and I wouldn't be surprised to the see the networks pick it up," she said. He nodded, shut the car door and entered the station. The reporter got in her car and drove to her apartment.

After dinner, she watched the tape a few times and planned her attack for the next day. She went to bed at ten, excited about her chance to finally bring down one of the big guys.

Waking at six a.m. the reporter got out of bed and felt lightheaded and nauseous. She made her way into the bathroom but was so short of breath that she had to hold onto the countertop. The next thing she knew she was on her back looking at the ceiling. She crawled to the bedroom, over to the nightstand and pulled the telephone to the floor by the cord. It landed with a jangle of bells and cracking of plastic. She could barely manage to dial 911.

The ambulance arrived fifteen minutes later. After checking vital signs, the paramedics quickly put the comatose subject on the gurney and wheeled her to the vehicle.

"Take a look around and see if you can find any medication or drugs that'll help the doctors figure out what might be wrong with her," the driver said.

The other paramedic made a quick sweep of the apartment and the bathroom, and came back out. "No drugs, prescription or otherwise, at all. All she had in her medicine cabinet were some vitamins."

The team took the Health Editor to the nearest hospital where she was checked into Intensive Care.

That morning the assignment editor noticed the cameraman was loaded and ready to go, but had been sitting in the newsroom for an hour. "What are you waiting on?" he asked.

"Well, I was supposed to be picked up to go to Washington by our illustrious Health Editor but I don't know where she is," he said.

"What was she working on in Washington?" the editor asked.

"Aw, it was a piece about the Surgeon General," said the cameraman. "I'm not sure exactly where she was going with it."

"Well, we'll find out when she comes in. In the meantime, George needs some help with a story he's doing on the homeless. Can you go with him this morning?" the assignment editor said.

"Okay," said the photographer and went to Edit Bay 6 to tell the reporter he was ready to go.

☆

"Okay, now we have to get after it. He could change his mind again, so we're going to get things in motion to make that harder," Phillips said looking around the room. "Coy, you and Dr. Packard get that vaccine ready and start production so it can go into the vitamins. Fast."

"Will do," said McWaters, and he and Packard hustled out of the office.

"Andrew. A lot of what we're telling the President depends on whether or not we can convince the customers to replace their old vitamins," Phillips asked seriously.

Strong's face was solemn. "I know I can do this. The offer will be powerful, but not too strong so it doesn't make people suspicious. We'll use only direct mail and that'll confine it to the previous subscribers. New customers will automatically get the Super Zaners," he said.

"Please, get started," Phillips said.

Strong hesitated and cleared his throat. "Mike, I'm not going to be able to get my vendors to jump on this without bringing our accounts up to date. Finklestein's been riding us and I'm behind on some of our bills. I don't have the credit to borrow the money to bail me out. There will be tens of thousands just in postage. I'm going to need some help," Strong admitted.

"I'll make sure your invoices are paid tomorrow and we'll pay the ones to come in advance. Will that give you enough room?"

"Yeah, I think so. I'll get this rolling. Laura is at the agency standing by," Strong said as he turned to leave.

"Andrew, one other thing," Phillips said.

"Sure. What's up?" he stopped and smiled.

Phillips motioned to a chair and shut the door to his office. He sat down across from Strong. "I've thought about this and discussed it with Director Nall. We're both convinced there's only one way we can make this work for the long term. We may be able to react quickly enough to stop the immediate threat but we're going to have to have some lasting strategy to make sure we, and the public, are completely safe and that we maintain the secrecy that has surrounded this operation."

"Is that a problem? It was my understanding that only a handful of people know the whole story and they have pretty high clearances," Strong said.

"That's correct but it's imperative that this company runs as if nothing has ever happened. If all of a sudden it just closes down, a red flag would go up in the business community. The *Wall Street Journal* has some pretty smart reporters and we don't need that kind of scrutiny."

"The WSJ guys don't miss much. They can smell a con a mile away," Strong agreed.

"I know there will need to be some questions answered, and we can provide that cover, but the company must function as always. It has to continue to market and provide vitamins with the vaccine in them until we're sure that everyone who has been infected has been immunized. As aggressive as we're being in getting them out will certainly result in new subscribers and those people have to be accommodated."

Strong stood silently wondering where the man was going with this conversation.

"Whoever takes this over and runs it is going to have to be cleared for security at the highest level plus be one tough business person. The government doesn't have anyone with those qualifications. And there aren't fifty people in the government, period, who are cleared to know what's happened here."

Phillips stood up and walked behind the desk.

"Frankly, Andrew, I'd like you to consider taking over this company and running it," he said calmly.

Strong was shocked. "Well, Mike, I'm not sure I see how being in the advertising agency business qualifies me to run a vitamin company. I don't know anything about the vitamin business," he said.

"Wrong. You know *everything* about this business," he smiled. "You and your staff know more about the product and company than anyone else, including the people who work here. I know it would mean virtually giving up your agency. No way you would have time for any other clients and I understand this wouldn't last forever. Once we've got some time under our belt and it wouldn't be a big deal, we'd close it down. The company and everything about it would just fade away. But listen to what I have in mind," he said and began to reel off the scenario.

The government would pay The Idea Group a substantial percentage of the profits, provide all the operating capital and adopt a hands-off attitude. To the outside world it would appear that the agency-client relationship was still intact. There should be enough revenue to the agency, Phillips pointed out, that at the end of the agreed upon time period Strong should be wealthy.

"By the time the threat has passed in two or three years, you'll be a rich man and never have to work again unless you want to. And there'll be enough profits that you can properly reward your employees so they, too, can share in the revenues."

Strong was stunned. His silence encouraged Phillips to continue.

"And as I've promised, I'll make sure the first dose of the vaccine goes straight to Laura's mother. That happens, no matter what you decide. You deserve that," he said and automatically extended his hand. "Give it some thought, would you?"

"Mike that's all very impressive and tempting. But, well, with all due respect, do you have the authority to make such a deal?" Strong said.

Phillips smiled, "Please be assured that I do. I'll provide plenty of substantiation before we ask you to make any commitment."

Well, I don't know what to say. I want to help fix this mess and I'm going to do just that but if you think about it, a deal like that puts my life in the hands of the government. I'm not sure I want to be back on active duty again. I'm not sure I want to pull up stakes and move to Dallas. At best I think this is probably premature. Let's get through this, first. Okay? Then we can talk about it," Strong said.

"Fair enough," Phillips said.

Strong left the office and as soon as he shut the door had a chill overtake his body. He had just pulled off the biggest scam of his life. He had no idea if the advertising would work. He was a good adman but he knew nothing was a certainty in this business. You think the damn thing will be a success and then it bombs. He was praying that this was one that would work.

It was early Saturday morning and Strong ran into Phillips in the parking lot.

"When will the advertising campaign start?" Phillips asked as they walked into the building.

"It's primarily direct mail and it's scheduled to drop Sunday night," Strong replied. "It'll hit most homes by Wednesday and we should start getting responses that day."

"Who'll answer the calls?" Phillips asked as they walked into Finklestein's office.

"We have extra telemarketers set up to work 24 hours a day, seven days a week. Some people will respond by mail and they should start arriving here by the following Monday," Strong answered.

"So we'll know if it's working by Thursday?" Phillips asked. There was a pass-fail tone to his voice.

"Pretty much," Strong replied and walked to the window. For a moment there was silence.

"So what happens if it doesn't work?" Phillips asked.

Strong pursed his lips and turned around. "That's pretty much up to you. I don't have a lot more to offer. This is my best shot."

Phillips leaned forward in his chair and put his palms on the desk. "I have to report every day to the Director," he said, looking at his hands. "If it fails you can count on the President being on television within a matter of hours."

"And you can bet we'll have a rash of terrorist attacks over the next twelve months," Strong muttered. Neither man said anything else.

Strong was deep in thought when the phone in his office rang causing him to literally jump in his chair. He caught his breath and reached for the receiver. "Andrew Strong," he announced.

"They're gone," the voice of Laura Newcomb said.

"All of them?"

"Yes. The direct mail house took them to the post office last night. I went with them and it took an entire truck and two guys to move them. I spoke to the supervisor and he thinks they'll start hitting by Wednesday," she said.

"Good," that means the phone could start ringing in a couple of days," Strong replied. "Good job, Laura. I'll talk to you as soon as things start popping here."

Strong hung up and walked to Phillips' office and reported the news. "If we're lucky, the phone will start ringing Wednesday about noon," he said.

"Let's meet here at twelve on Wednesday to assess our position," Phillips said.

☆

On his way into the scheduled Wednesday meeting, Strong looked in the telemarketing room. The operators were idle. "Any calls?" he asked.

They looked around at him and one of them said, "Only about twelve."

Strong walked into Finklestein's office. "It really hasn't started yet. They've gotten a few calls, which tell us the mailing hit. Also, Laura reported that the agency got its *shill* copy. I really didn't expect a lot of action at this point. It'll probably be the end of the week before people open their mail and react to the offer."

Phillips looked at Strong as if he were looking over glasses. "You think so?" he asked.

"Sure, it's got to have time to work," Strong said.

"So when is your best estimate we can determine if it's successful?" Phillips asked.

There was no question about it, Strong was on the spot and he knew it. He could feel the pressure building. He was certain if the phones didn't start ringing off the hook by Thursday, the campaign probably wasn't working or going to work. But maybe if he bought a little more time. "Friday," he said confidently. "We'll have the place hopping by Friday or it's a failure."

Phillips waited for a long moment and then looked at Strong. "Andrew, if we aren't flooded by replacement orders on Friday, I've got to tell the Director to go the other route. I can't give you any more time. In fact, I'm not sure he'll wait until Friday."

"I understand," Strong said and left the office to go to his own cubicle. Once there he placed a call to Laura.

"Laura, there's not a damn thing happening here. What the hell is going on?"

"I don't know. I know the mailing went out. I was there," she said.

"Okay, I want you to put some people on the phones. Get the list from the direct mail house and start calling the recipients. Have them identify themselves as quality control people from the vitamin company. Tell them we're checking to see if they received the mailer."

"And if they got it?" Laura asked.

"Find out what their reaction to it was. Did they think it was a good deal? Are they planning on taking advantage of it? If the creative is flawed then we're screwed because there isn't time to re-do it but if there's something else, we need to know."

"Alright I'll start but it will probably be this evening before we can get any calls made."

"Let me know," Strong replied and hung up the phone.

Strong and Phillips sat by the desk in Finklestein's office. The phone rang and Phillips quickly picked it up. "Yes, sir. Only a smattering of calls so far, Director," he said.

"Actually, we did expect more by this time. However, Andrew is confident that it will pick up tomorrow and begin the surge then," he said.

Strong couldn't hear what Director Nall was saying but he didn't have to. He could tell by Phillips' face he was taking a beating. Phillips finished with a quiet, "Yes, sir," and hung up the phone. He looked directly at Strong. "Today's Thursday. If we don't have activity by tomorrow when he calls, the deal's off."

"Great," Strong said and got up and went to his office.

☆

"Laura, what have you found out?" Strong asked.

"We'll we've called about 30 people but only of couple of them have gotten the mailer that they can remember," Laura said.

"That thing was sent first class. It should have been in their hands by Wednesday," Strong said.

"Maybe we should have sent it Priority Mail," she responded.

"Yeah, maybe so," Strong said gloomily. "Keep checking and call the damn post office. Call anyone you can think of but do something."

"Okay Andrew, I'll stay on it," she said.

He hung up and walked aimlessly down the hall. He felt totally helpless and felt even more so when he glanced in the telemarketing room and saw the operators nonchalantly chatting among themselves. He didn't have to ask how many calls they had gotten. Few and none. *He was a hell of an adman*, he decided sarcastically.

Strong had been in the telemarketing room since 6 a.m. monitoring the test calls he had ordered be placed from different parts of the country to ensure there wasn't a technical reason the calls weren't coming in. Each one worked perfectly. The count was now up to 600 responses, a dismal return. Laura had reported an equally poor response to her telephone survey. People were not getting, or didn't remember receiving, the mailing. In any case, they weren't responding.

He got up after the test calls were completed and walked to Finklestein's office to talk to Phillips.

"Any luck?" Phillips asked when he entered the room.

"No. And I don't know why. I think we can fix it if we just had some time," Strong said.

"It's Friday and time is what we don't have," Phillips said. "We might as well get ready for what's going to happen. When he calls—."

At that moment Strong's cellular phone rang. Embarrassed, he quickly reached to his belt and shut it off. Phillips continued, "When he calls, we'll make a plea for more time but I know what he'll say. He's getting it straight from the President."

The two men sat for nearly thirty minutes when someone knocked at the door. Strong opened the door to find the one of the agents standing there. Almost simultaneously the phone on Phillips desk rang. Strong saw Phillips pick it up and he knew it was Director Nall.

"Mr. Strong. Your office is trying to reach you," the agent said "They say it's urgent. They're trying to call you on your cell phone."

Strong had forgotten his cell. He picked it up and dialed the agency and was quickly put through to Laura. "Andrew! I've found out the problem. The ink smudged on the postal codes. It held up the delivery. They should have hit today. Have you had any calls?" she asked breathlessly.

"I don't know. I'll check," Strong said and without further comment hung up. He raced over and quickly penciled a sign saying *Stall Them.* He held it directly in front of Phillips. Strong bolted to the door and ran as fast he could to the telemarketing room.

He heard the hum before he got to the door. Every phone light was lit and the army of telemarketers was typing orders as fast as possible. There was a buzz of voices. They turned to look at him with an unspoken question, *who turned on the faucet?*

He sprinted back to Finklestein's office. Phillips was looking wild-eyed and talking gobbledy gook to the Director.

"We've got it!" Strong screamed. "The phones are flooded with orders. It's working!"

Phillips quickly reported, "Sir, we've just gotten a report that the plan is working. Orders are streaming in as expected. I can give you a more accurate assessment in a few hours but our telemarketing center is currently being overwhelmed with orders."

"Yes, sir. It definitely is working," he repeated. After promising further news Phillips hung up.

Three months later

The President stood staring out the east windows of the Oval Office. Spring was coming to the district and he was looking forward to the return of the Cherry Blossoms. It was his favorite time of year. To the President, it signaled renewal and rebirth.

"What's Blasingdale's latest assessment?" he turned his head and asked the Chief of Staff.

"He believes that the threat has passed. Deaths that he thinks could be attributed to Zaners have ceased; in fact, they hardly caused a ripple in the overall scheme of things, and the number of illnesses reported by the hospitals and physicians is actually below the rate this time last year. The damn Super Zaners must really work. Mr. Strong reported that sales have tripled and they've added literally a million people to the list of subscribers," the Chief said. "He said the new General Manager even got a call from Upjohn the other day wanting to talk merger. He had him politely decline."

"Good grief. That's incredible. A bogus company does so well, people want to buy it. Strong has done a heck of a job selling those vitamins. I saw one of the commercials the other day and I wanted some, even with what I know about them," the President said.

"I do feel kind of bad about doubting Blasingdale, though. He turned out to be a true and loyal ally. Holding that press conference to give the administration all the credit for the decline in teen-age smoking was a real show of support. And he did it at the height of the Zaner crisis, too," the President said.

"Yes, sir," replied the Chief of Staff, unable to look at him. "The doctor's a real team-player. Director Nall retires next month. Says he's enjoyed all of this he can stand. I suspect he'll recommend Mike Phillips for a promotion."

"At least something good came from this." The President turned from the window and walked over and seated himself behind his desk.

"The Saudis have agreed to step up the pressure to capture Osama bin Ladin. We're pretty sure he was behind this. Director Nall is still upset that he didn't catch him. The bodies of Finklestein or Asam were never recovered so that's another loose end for him. I think that played heavily in his decision to retire. He's convinced that this was just one of many attempts that bin Ladin will make. 'As long as radical Islamic fundamentalists exist, low level technology will be a threat.' That's what his latest memo to you said," the Chief of Staff replied.

The President looked up from his desk. His eyes were tired and the strain of shepherding his country through what could have been the greatest tragedy in its history had left its mark.

"I'm ready to focus on something that builds the country, not something that wants to tear it down. How about you?" he said.

"Me, too sir," said the Chief of Staff as he opened another file to brief the country's chief executive.

Chapter Twenty-One

Strong reached for the phone. "Hi, Toni," he said to his Oklahoma City banker. "Thanks for calling me back."

"Sure, Andrew. It's nice to get a call. We never see you anymore since you moved to Dallas. What can I do for you?" Toni asked.

"I want you to set up an educational trust for me. I want to use it for some of the relatives of my employees. Can you get that started?"

"Sure. Your name is spoken with quiet reverence around here since you made that big deposit and paid off your note. The old Topperly boys are eating their words," she said.

Strong laughed. "You all are just as friendly as your TV commercials say you are."

"Yeah, as long as you've got compensating balances," Toni quipped.

The phone buzzed indicating he had a call on the other line.

"Let me know when it's set up, will you?" he said and hung up the phone to catch the other call. He punched down the button.

"Hello," Strong said not knowing who he would find waiting for him.

"Andrew, Phillips here," said Michael Phillips.

He hadn't heard from Phillips for a month, since they had cut the deal for him to take over Finklestein and Mark.

"Hey, Mike. How are things in crime-ridden Washington D.C.?" Strong said good-humoredly.

"If I remember correctly, Dallas is not exactly crime free," Phillips retorted.

"Well, it is now," Strong shot back and they both laughed.

"What's going on, buddy?" Strong asked.

"I hear the company is doing well and the plan is working as we expected," Phillips said.

"So far, so good. I hear you're about to get a promotion."

"Well, that's the word on the street but I'll believe it when the check clears the bank. But that's not why I called," Phillips said. "Have you read about the trouble brewing in Germany?"

"You mean the neo-Nazi movement?" Strong asked." I hear it's starting to be a problem."

"Yep. It's worse than what you read. And the problem is not what you read," Phillips said.

"Why are you telling me this?" Strong asked suspiciously.

"Cause I need some help from a patriotic but broken down Marine," Phillips said lightly. Then his voice deepened and became more ominous. "Seriously, Andrew, there's a big problem and I want to talk to you about it."

"Uh, I think I have my hands pretty well full, here, Mike," Strong said incredulously.

"Maybe. But maybe not. I know the company is making a ton of cash, I know you have more money now that you'll ever need, and I also know that regardless of how cynical you'd like to appear, you care about this country," Phillips said. "Will you come to Washington so we can talk about it? The part I need for you to play can't be done by anyone else that's available right now."

"Oh, my aching back. When do you want me to come?"

"Tonight."

"Tonight?" Strong yelled. "This is crazy. I'm trying to run a business—actually two businesses. And you want me to hop up and run to D.C. to do God knows what. Do I look stupid?"

"Don't you have a friend in Berlin?" Phillips asked softly.

Stopped in his tracks from his tirade, Strong said, "Well, yes. Hans. We've been friends for years. But hell, you knew that or you wouldn't have asked. Why?"

"He's involved and doesn't know it. He could be in big trouble," Phillips said.

There was silence. Hans Heiden and his family had opened their home to Strong many times and he had watched their children grow up. He sighed, "Yeah, I'll come. But I'll probably turn around and come right home."

"Good. Leave for the airport now. Don't worry about packing. A government plane is waiting for you at Love Field. Go to the administration office and they'll put you on board. I'll meet you at National Airport and we'll have dinner."

Damn, Strong thought as he hung up the phone and left his office to catch the plane to Washington and Michael Phillips. He knew, deep down, that his life was getting ready to take a turn that would change it, again, forever.

The End

Watch for Gean B. Atkinson's upcoming novel

"Bloodmoon at Cabin Creek"

An exciting and bizarre story of a Confederate soldier fighting with Cherokee Gen. Stand Watie's Mounted Rifles in 1864. Desperately trying to save the Confederacy in pitched battle after pitched battle he approaches the decisive clash for control of the West.

Suddenly, in the middle of the melee he is transported into the future, becomes entangled in contemporary issues and is torn between loyalties to the past and the present. He wrestles to live in two worlds and finally, literally holding the power of life and death in his hands, is forced to make a choice.

Intriguing in the view of the spiritual world of the Cherokees and breathtaking in the first hand adventures of a front line soldier, "Bloodmoon at Cabin Creek" provides an electrifying voyage into the inner struggles of a man torn between his duties as a soldier and patriot and his needs as a human being.

Printed in the United States
2696